FORESIGHT

Forgotten Space, Book One

M.R. FORBES

Chapter 1

Captain Nicholas Shepherd settled into the molded foam of the primary pilot seat on the flight deck of the experimental starship Foresight. He placed his arms on the contoured rests and remained still as the automated safety system dropped a padded three point harness over his chest. It locked between his legs, pressing lightly to hold him in place. Additional restraints folded over his forearms and wrists, helping to ensure his hands would remain in contact with the ship's control surfaces during high-G maneuvers.

Those surfaces came to life as the safety system completed its check, the light going green when it deemed him appropriately contained. The touchscreen beneath his left hand offered simple control of everything that wasn't already automated through the onboard neural network. Likewise, the custom pad beneath his right hand gave him precision command over the starship's maneuverability whenever it wasn't under AI control. The belief was that human intervention would only be required five to ten percent of the time once Foresight's neural net was fully optimized and operational. Nicholas didn't give much thought to the highly technical aspects of the programming, but he understood the network used his flight data in training itself to first match and eventually exceed his proficiency.

Having let the AI take over on the last test run and nearly being slammed into a mountainside had convinced Nicholas that Foresight had no chance to make its planned operational date. The timeline would slip at least another month if not longer. As a human pilot whose job was on the verge of being automated out of existence, a part of him felt vindicated by the struggle to make a computer think and act like an experienced aviator. The other side of him was as dismayed by the glitches as were the techs who had spent the last year feverishly working on the system, his wife among them.

His success was her failure.

A failure that could doom them all.

Nicholas tried not to linger on the consequences as he tapped on the left-hand surface to quickly bring the rest of the ship's flight control systems online. They were all doing their best to see Project Foresight to completion, finishing the technological leap before it was too late. His marriage had been purely hypothetical for the last nine months while Yasmin was holed up in the lab with her team. Even if she had been accessible, they wouldn't have had any time together. His days were equally filled, alternating between sessions in the simulator and running active intercepts outside the compound while also keeping tabs on their son, Lucius. Circumstances had forced the kid to grow up fast. Too fast.

A small progress bar appeared against the forward curve of the flight deck's hardened, egg-shaped enclosure, a stylized eagle logo wrapped around a star embla-zoned above it, United States Space Force Marines written in small all-caps lettering beneath it.

A second tone sounded when the progress bar reached twenty-five percent. Nicholas tapped on the left-hand surface again, activating the ship's comms.

"Control, this is Shepherd," Nicholas said. "Establishing comms link. Do you copy?"

"Shepherd, this is Control," a gruff male voice replied. "I copy. Comms link established."

"Roger," Nicholas replied. "Initiation is at twenty-five percent. Sequence complete. ETA: three minutes, twelve seconds."

"Copy. Network link established. Data flow incoming. Wave to the camera, Nick."

Nicholas glanced at the pinhole near the left curve of the flight deck. He couldn't wave at anything with his hands restrained. "That was funny the first few times, Duff," he said, staring into the lens. "Now it's just old and tired."

"Like you, Captain?" Duffy replied with a laugh.

"You should stick to protocol, Duff. I hear the man himself is planning to observe this one."

"Grimmel? Yeah, I heard that too. If he's coming, he's running out of time."

"Is Colonel Haines on deck?"

"Negative."

"Then she's probably escorting Grimmel up to Control right now."

"Probably," Duff agreed.

The progress bar hit forty percent, becoming translu-cent as the entire front of the flight deck- enclosure lit up, displaying an ultra-high resolution composite view of the outside world. It was stitched together from the feeds of nearly three dozen cameras positioned around the ship. Secondary screens offered additional views of the sides and rear, making it feel more like being behind the controls of a race car than a spacecraft.

The view wasn't pleasant. While the interior of the mountainside hangar was clear directly ahead of Foresight, the flanks were a reminder that Nicholas' little slice of heaven behind the stick of the experimental craft was just that. The real world beyond the tomblike interior was harsh, ugly, and bloody.

Marines and their equipment hugged the sides of the hangar, intermingled with scraped and battered APCs and the hulking robots they called Butchers. The bots were filthy and dented. Thick recharge cables snaked from their ankles through the platoons of sleeping Marines—none of which looked as though they could face another night of fighting—to the bank of rechargers along the back bulkhead. A few smaller airborne drones were visible behind Foresight, ready to launch at a moment's notice.

He had been behind the stick of one of the drones a few hours ago, during the early morning hours when odds of an attack were highest. The enemy had been more relentless than usual. They were no doubt sensing that the defenses were wearing down from the nightly assaults, and that caused them to push harder for a breakthrough.

Sometimes Nicholas wasn't sure if the survivors were lucky or cursed. These days, he leaned more heavily toward cursed.

"I heard the MPs put Lucius and his buddies into holding again last night," Duff said.

Nicholas closed his eyes and groaned. "Really? Nobody told me."

"Oh. I'm sorry, Nick. I didn't mean to break the news to you like that. I figured you already knew."

"I spend eighteen hours a day behind the stick and four hours a day sleeping," Nicholas replied. "It doesn't leave much time to keep up with my son. What did he do this time?"

"I didn't get many details on my way over to the CIC. The usual general mischief, I'm sure. He's lucky you're his father, or they would have made his visits to lockup more lengthy by now."

Nicholas opened his eyes and exhaled heavily. "Luke's a good kid, and he knows what's at stake. But losing everything the way we did, and so fast...it's been hard on him."

"You shouldn't make excuses for him, Nick," Duff replied. "This has been hard on everyone. He and his little group of friends are putting unnecessary strain on very limited resources."

"I know," Nicholas agreed. "I've talked to him about it multiple times. I don't know if he's acting out because Yasmin and I can't be there for him as much as we want or what. I have to believe that's the truth because the alternative is that he's just a spoiled, selfish little asshole. Which is the worst thing anyone can be right now."

His attention returned to the exhausted Marines on the floor of the hangar. While Luke was screwing around, causing trouble, to entertain himself, these brave men and women were giving their lives to protect him. The idea of it made him sick. He had come to his son's rescue too many times already. He wasn't sure he had the stomach to do it again.

Duff lowered his voice. "Speaking of which, Colonel Haines just arrived. Looks like you were right; Mister Grimmel is with her."

Nicholas decided he would deal with Lucius later, and not with the same kid gloves as he had up till now. Everybody around him was busting their asses to keep humankind from going extinct. It was time the kid did too.

"Captain Shepherd," Colonel Haines said over the comm, her voice crisp and professional. "What's your sitrep?"

"Sir, initiation is at forty-six percent. Comms are online. Network is linked with Control. All feeds are active and monitored. Everything is nominal. Sequence complete in two minutes, eight seconds."

"Copy, Captain. I have Mister Aaron Grimmel in the CIC with me. He'll be observing the test flight today."

"Mister Grimmel, sir," Nicholas said. "It's an honor to have you with us for the flight."

"Negative, Captain Shepherd," Grimmel replied in a smooth baritone. "The honor is mine. With your help we've come a very long way in a very short amount of time."

"Don't give me too much credit, sir," Nick said. "I'm only following orders."

"Haha! Orders or not, you're the perfect pilot for this job, and your wife has been invaluable to the development of the advanced neural network. I think I can safely speak for all of humankind when I say I'm grateful for you both."

"Thank you, sir," Nicholas said. "If you want to sit back and relax, I think you'll enjoy the show."

"Undoubtedly," Grimmel said. "Godspeed out there, Captain."

"Thank you, sir."

The progress bar reached seventy-five percent, a third tone sounding to signal the ignition of the reactor that powered the massive engines. At the same time, the klaxon beside the hangar doors began blaring intermittently, the warning light flashing yellow to alert everyone the blast doors were about to open. It brought two of the Marine platoons camped on either side of the starship to their feet. They ran to the front of the hangar and took cover behind a pair of APCs, rifles pointed at the doors. The enemy rarely attacked in daylight, but it was always best to be prepared.

The klaxon ceased its ear-splitting clamor, the light continuing to flash as the massive blast doors moved slowly on their chain-driven tracks. It gave Foresight's initiation sequence time to complete before they were spaced far enough apart for the ship to slip through. A number of systems activated in the last twenty percent of the sequence, including the onboard AI.

"Good morning, Captain Shepherd," it said to him in an uncanny male voice.

"Good morning, Frank," Nicholas replied.

"Real time monitoring is online. Learning modules are loaded. Data collection initialized. What are the mission parameters for today's flight?"

"Control, initiation is complete," Nicholas said. "The neural network is online. All systems are nominal. Please upload parameters for today's training."

"Captain Shepherd," a new voice said. One he recognized all too well. "We have an updated patch for the mission. I'm uploading it directly from the lab now."

"Copy that, Doctor Shepherd," he replied. "How's your morning so far?"

"Busy, as usual," she said. She hesitated for a moment. "Lucius…"

"I heard," Nicholas replied. "I'll take care of it when I land." An icon of the new patch upload appeared in the projected HUD at the front of his seat. "Patch received. Installing now."

"Don't be too hard on him, okay, Nick?"

Nicholas clenched his jaw. If there was one point of constant friction between him and Yasmin, it was how to handle Lucius. This wasn't the time or place to have that argument again. She shouldn't have brought it up in the first place, especially with Grimmel on the comms.

"He'll get what I think he deserves," he replied.

"Patch installed," Frank said. "Parameters accepted. Captain Shepherd, you're to disengage manual control at ten-thousand feet and remain on standby in the event of a system fault."

Nicholas raised an eyebrow. "Colonel Haines, is this right? I thought you decided the system wasn't ready for full automated control after the last flight."

"We've made some significant advances in the last few days, Captain," Yasmin said before Haines could answer.

"And the timeline has changed," Haines added. "Look around you, Shepherd. These Marines can't hold out for much longer. Our primary objective is to finalize Project Foresight. Once we're done here, we can retreat to a more defensible position and wait for airlift to a secured site. Which means we need that ship fully operational ASAP."

"With all due respect, sir, if you try to rush things too much you'll end up with a fireball instead of a successful test flight," Nicholas replied.

"It's not your call, Captain," Haines said. "You have your parameters."

"Yes, sir." Nicholas didn't care if they could see him glowering through the flight deck feed. He had the distinct sense the parameters had changed because

Grimmel was in the CIC to watch the flight, not because of any significant advances. The tech magnate didn't have the same clout now as he had before the war, but it was still his factories, his developers, and his technology that had gotten them this far. "All systems are go. Requesting permission to launch."

The massive hangar doors shuddered as they came to a stop. Daylight streamed into the hangar, blue skies, brown mountains, and a series of long, low barracks visible ahead. From here, the world looked peaceful and idyllic. A beautiful day for a test flight.

If only that were true.

"Permission granted," Duff said.

Chapter 2

In Nicholas' opinion, the control pad under his right hand was the greatest innovation to come out of the construction of Foresight. With the miniaturized combination of joystick, throttle, pointer and tactile buttons, he could easily control the ship without ever needing to take his eyes off the forward view. It had taken him only a few hours to master the system in the simulator but hours of additional flight-time to increase his aptitude and precision. As though it were an F-35, despite its size and weight, maneuvering the ship required only the slightest movement of his fingers on the pad.

Of course, such fine grain control would be impossible without the onboard neural net. Its consistent, finely-tuned judgments cancelled out any potential error from an errant muscle spasm or slip of the hand. Nicholas couldn't do anything that would accidentally crash the vessel.

Even if he wanted to.

As soon as Duff confirmed his permission to launch,

Nicholas used a finger to switch the action of the stick and throttle for liftoff. Sliding the throttle open increased power to the row of counter-gravity coils aligned along the bottom center of the fuselage beneath the matte black alloy that composed the craft's outer shell. The ship rose gently from the floor, leaving it to hover over the deck as if by magic.

Nicholas understood there was nothing magical about it, though he had no idea how the technology actually worked. It was in another range of inventions Grimmel Corporation had patented over the last fifteen years, part of an incredible explosion of advancement that Nicholas had once felt certain would completely alter the course of human civilization.

But that was before human civilization collapsed.

Before disease and then the trife came and ruined everything.

The silver lining, if there was ever going to be one, was that the advancements Nicholas thought would bring rapid global transportation, abundant green energy, and other life-altering benefits had, in aggregate, turned out to be the one thing that might give humankind a chance to survive. Just not in the way anyone had thought. Foresight. This flight. They were the final pieces of a massive puzzle that what was left of the world's governments had been fitting together at lightning speed for nearly a year. What they had already accomplished would have seemed impossible two years earlier, but they had done it.

Almost.

Foresight's control systems needed to be completed and proven out. Not just for this ship.

For every ship.

Another tap from his finger reset the throttle control for thrust. A glance at the diagnostics projected on the console in front of the control pad confirmed nominal operation. Frank would have already warned him if it were otherwise.

Satisfied, he opened the throttle, the physical stress of acceleration minimal courtesy of the computer-controlled gyroscope his seat sat on. However, the force of the main thrusters engaging still pressed him back into his seat, the ride butter-smooth and soundless for him.

Outside the craft was a different story.

The Marines, visible through the flight deck's clear surround , jerked their heads around to watch the launch. Some of them cheered as the spacecraft rocketed away, their exhaustion momentarily forgotten.

The starship cleared the hangar in seconds, exploding into the open landscape only a few feet above the road leading down the mountain and into the now-abandoned section of Fort Hood. Hundreds of dark alien shapes, the aftermath of the prior night's fighting, lay dead across the road, the ship's shadow passing quickly over them. It was a scene Nicholas had grown numb to in the two years since the creatures had fallen from the skies and started their quest to become the dominant species on the planet.

As a pilot with the United States Marines—and now the United States Space Force—he had been part of the war from the start. He was over Hoboken when President Wayne had given the order to drop nukes on American cities in a desperate attempt to slow the rising tide of the trife. He had watched the mushroom clouds billow above the city, circling back over it to survey the outcome. Hoboken had already been evacuated, the human casualties minimized. Even so, to see the once majestic skyline ripped to shreds, to gaze on the crumbled buildings and rain of ash, remained one of his worst memories of the war.

One of the worst, but not *the* worst. That came *after* the nukes. Nearly half a million trife died in the bombings, but the explosions and resulting radiation didn't even make a dent in their numbers. Worse, the radiation provided an unexpected fuel for the creatures, allowing them to multiply even more rapidly.

Not only had they failed to hurt the aliens, they had unwittingly helped them.

Since then, whenever he saw a slick of dead trife, the memory flashed through his mind. Today was no different. For all of their efforts, for all of their sacrifices, for all of the death and suffering, no one could avoid the truth that humankind would lose the war. They had been surrendering ground to the trife for months, their resources dwindling, their morale destroyed. While he had heard some pockets of survivors managed to avoid the creatures, the writing was on the wall. They could either accept their destiny as a fallen civilization, eke out an existence spent under constant threat.

Or they could escape. Leave Earth. And never look back.

The ships were nearly finished. Sixteen in total. Massive vessels that would carry forty-thousand people each to the stars. Some called them ark ships, some generation ships, the name wasn't as important as the purpose. Get humankind off Earth. Settle a new world. Multiple new worlds actually. The ships would go in different directions, to different systems, landing on planets that the best scientists on Earth, the ones still alive, believed could harbor human life. It was a risky proposition. No guarantees. But there was no shortage of volunteers. In fact, you couldn't win a ride on any of the ships. You had to be chosen.

By test piloting Foresight, Nicholas had cemented his family's ticket on one of the USSF ships. Not that Yasmin wouldn't have earned them a place anyway. She was part of Grimmel's top cabal of scientists, and he wouldn't leave the planet without them. Even so, it seemed unfair that they were guaranteed escape just because Yasmin worked for a man who was so wealthy, so powerful he couldn't be left behind. Yet, for all his status, Grimmel had been reduced to fighting for his life, just like everyone else.

It helped Nicholas sleep better at night, knowing he and Yasmin had at least a hands-on part in making this life-saving endeavor happen. As far as Nicholas was concerned, Grimmel wasn't much more than a money man.

Surplus baggage.

Foresight shot across the landscape, covering ground in a hurry. Nicholas kept to a low flight path, skirting five thousand feet as he crossed the terrain. Small towns came in and out of view, all of them deserted. Cars had been left in the middle of streets. Doors left open. Businesses unlocked. Windows shattered. The bodies of both people and trife had mostly been picked at by carrion, leaving behind an eerie scene he would never forget.

"Mission parameters require climbing to ten-thousand feet," Frank said without a hint of emotion. The AI wasn't the kind popular in books and movies, with a programmed personality that made it seem not only human, but a hell of a lot more entertaining than any human he had ever met. Frank remained a machine. Not even that. It was a software-based neural network running on off-the-shelf hardware. The marvel was that Yasmin's team had managed to get something so advanced stuffed into so little random access memory.

"The mission parameters didn't outline when I had to climb to ten-thousand feet," Nicholas replied, fully aware that Control could hear everything he said. "If this is going to be my last flight, I want to enjoy it for as long as I can."

Frank didn't reply.

Nicholas continued guiding Foresight south. He only needed a couple of minutes to come into view of Houston, or rather what was left of it. While the densest part of downtown had mostly been spared bombardment, the rest of the city lay in ruins, the buildings crumbling, the streets strewn with rubble, cars, garbage, and other debris. That included the remains of a number of USSF Butchers, APCs, and even a few tanks, their treads shredded to ribbons by the sharp claws of the alien trife.

What every military on Earth had learned was that it didn't matter how superior your firepower was. When the bullets ran out, when the gas tanks ran dry, when the batteries died, the most powerful fighting force on Earth was reduced to flesh-and-blood hand-to-hand combat.. And the trife outnumbered humans by a factor of at least a hundred to one.

Nicholas wasn't sure why he wanted to see Houston again. Maybe because he had been in the skies overhead the day it had fallen, watching helplessly as a slick of trife a quarter-million strong had descended on the city. Maybe because he had been born there. Maybe because he wanted to be reminded of what this flight was about. He had indirectly asked Colonel Haines for a few minutes, and she had granted them in her silence.

Closure. That's why he guided Foresight over Houston. He needed closure. He knew Haines well enough to believe she wanted some too. After holding the compound for nine months against constant trife assaults, their time here nearly done, he wanted to make a statement.

Chapter 3

"Colonel," he said, using his thumb to make a quick right turn, orienting Foresight toward San Antonio. Toward the Interenergy solar array. "I noticed weapons testing isn't part of today's mission parameters."

"That's correct, Captain," Haines replied.

"I was thinking that since Mister Grimmel joined us for the occasion, it might make sense to add to the parameters. It's been a while since we activated the spines."

"The power draw is significant," Yasmin said, still linked to the comms from the lab. "Besides, the parameters are already uploaded. They can't be altered."

"I can pull the charge for the spines from the batteries instead of the reactors. We can recharge the system with the compound's power supply. If everything goes according to plan we won't need the base tokamak for much longer," he said, referring to the base reactor. "And as long as I stay under the threshold ceiling Frank can't take over."

"I wish you wouldn't keep calling it Frank," Yasmin said. "It's a machine. It doesn't have a name."

"Frank is a lot easier to say than Foresight Automated Flight Control, love," Nicholas said. "And FAFC isn't much better. I'm sure Mister Grimmel would agree."

"Standby," Colonel Haines said.

Nicholas remained on course toward the array, occupying himself by guiding Foresight through a series of maneuvers that put high-G stress on both the airframe and his body, even wearing a G-suit. He had flown fighter jets long enough to know his limits, and he pushed Foresight to its edge as well, careful to remain below the angels ten ceiling that would force him to relinquish control.

He rolled the starship in a tight corkscrew before throwing it into a turn just hard enough to marginally overstress his G-suit. His ingrained response was automatic, his stomach muscles tightening to prevent enough blood from rushing to his lower body to leave him lightheaded.

Haines' voice broke through the comm just before Nicholas put Foresight into a hard descent. "Captain, when you're done doing loop-de-loops, parameters are updated to include a complete test of the spines. Mister Grimmel is very interested in seeing them in action."

"Yes, sir," Nicholas replied slightly breathlessly, quickly flattening Foresight's flight path. "I already have a target in mind."

Haines laughed. "I assumed you did, Shepherd. From the flight pattern, it looks like you're heading for the Interenergy nesting ground."

"I know it's a futile effort, but it'll make me feel better," Nicholas said.

"It'll make me feel better too, Captain," Haines replied.

"Then I guess it's decided."

Two buttons on the control pad activated the spinal array, something Nicholas couldn't see from inside the flight deck surround, but he could picture it in his head. Made from the special metal alloy invented at Grimmel Corporation, nearly one hundred of the long, whisker-like barbs spread out from the fuselage when they received an electrical charge. Each one was an individual weapon that fired a focused blast of energy, but they could also be used to concentrate energy onto a single spot to devastating effect.

That same energy could also be used defensively, by forming a shield around the craft. According to Yasmin, the defensive posture was the true purpose of the spines, but granting the same technology an offensive capability had been "relatively trivial."

After twenty-six years of marriage, he remained amused by what his wife found trivial.

The Interenergy solar array, a field of thousands of mirrors, was already in view. A good portion of the mirrors were in ruin, leaving the outline of the reflective surface jagged and uneven. The generating tower was dark, its entire two-hundred-meter height coated in the rough black material that soaked up the intense heat generated by the mirrors. It was heat the broken internal mechanism of the tower couldn't use.

The ground beneath the mirrors appeared equally as dark as the tower, as if someone had laid fresh asphalt across the dirt before installing the reflectors. Nicholas knew that wasn't the case.

The darkness under the array undulated and writhed like a black sea, occasionally broken by a yellow crest. It appeared to have taken on a life of its own.

Because it had. It was alive with trife.

No one had ever taken an exact count of the trife

that occupied the array. There was no point. What they could see from the air was only the tip of the iceberg. More of the creatures lived inside the tower and below ground, including their queen. Looking at the massive slick, Nicholas guessed somewhere around one million of the demons were down there, soaking up life-giving radiation in preparation for another night of hunting.

"Spines activated," Nicholas said, pulling back on the throttle to slow Foresight for the approach. "Charge at eighty percent."

The Interenergy array wasn't where the trife that attacked the base nightly came from. This nest was too far away. They had learned that the alien queens tended to be more competitive than cooperative, though there were documented occasions when multiple queens had joined forces against hardened human defenses. It had created a strange dynamic during different stages of the war, where a battle between a slick of trife and a company of Marines suddenly became a three-sided affair that devolved into total chaos.

"Ninety percent," Nicholas said. Even if the array wasn't part of their immediate problem, it was just too juicy a target to ignore, especially if destroying it and the trife with it meant putting on a good show for Grimmel. Of course, even if they were able to destroy the entire array and kill over a million trife with one shot, it wouldn't make any difference in the outcome of a war that was already lost.

But it would make him feel better. For a little while, at least.

Nicholas tapped the control surface beneath his left hand, activating the fire control HUD. The spines could fire at multiple bogeys at once, selected by looking at the display and blinking to confirm when a box appeared over the intended target, his eye movements precision-tracked by Frank. Within a literal few blinks he had assigned the spines to six locations among the mirrors with half of his firepower. He directed the other half at the base of the tower.

"Targets locked," he announced. "Spines fully charged. Firing."

Nicholas pressed the third button on his control pad to trigger the spines. He imagined the blue balls of energy forming at the tips of the spines, and a split-second later, the ion beams launched from the spines, creating a blue glow through the camera feeds.

The beams cut through the piles of trife under the mirrors and dug into the ground, creating a ripple of energy that tossed the creatures in every direction. Some disintegrated into fine dust amidst the plasma toroids and balled lightning as it whipped out from the contact points.

The same force struck the tower. The beam slid along its length, slicing through the aliens clinging to its exterior and burning clear through to the other side. The tower shook, putting unsustainable stress on the structure and shedding trife like a dog shaking off water. The dead and dying landed amidst the aliens sleeping below, waking them to rage at Foresight as the starship shot overhead. From the flight deck, Nicholas imagined the unnatural sound of their unified scream.

He banked Foresight hard, using his left-hand controls to switch camera feeds so he could continue watching the destruction behind them. The tower groaned and shifted, more trife falling off, while the aliens on the ground did their best to untangle from one another and flee before it collapsed.

They weren't fast enough.

The base of the tower snapped, and then the whole thing toppled, thousands of trife crushed when it smashed to the ground. It didn't end there. The weight and force was enough to weaken the structure beneath the dirt. The ground opened up, swallowing the collapsing lower half of the tower, killing even more trife.

Nicholas smiled, elated by the death and chaos he had wrought and equally amazed by Foresight's weapons system. At the same time, knowing the ship was a prototype and that all of the onboard tech was intended for the ark ships, he hoped they would never need to use it.

"Spine test successful, Colonel," he announced over the comm. "What do you think, Mister Grimmel?"

It took a moment for the businessman to get back on the comm. "Perfection."

"Okay, Shepherd," Haines said. "You've had your fun, and Mister Grimmel got his show. Head to ten thousand feet and let the AI take over."

"Copy that, sir," Nicholas replied, guiding Foresight into a lazy ascent. "Frank, you're up."

Chapter 4

"Control, manual flight ceiling has been reached," Nicholas said. "I'm passing navigation to Frank."

"Copy, Captain," Duff said.

A brief tone signaled the handover, and Nicholas lifted his hand from the controls. At first, Foresight remained on the same gently ascending course, headed south toward the equator. The Texas coastline sat just up ahead. Hundreds of boats of all sizes bobbed in the glistening blue water—a reminder that humankind might be down, but they weren't giving up. The trife couldn't swim or fly, leaving the world's oceans as the only true refuge from the creatures.

It wasn't enough to survive. They would never thrive out there. And they still had to send parties ashore to search for potable water if nothing else.

"I have control," Frank announced. "Setting coordinates. Captain Shepherd, prepare for rapid acceleration to escape velocity."

"What?" Nicholas replied, confused by the statement. He tapped on the left pad, bringing up a display of the mission execution list. His role once the neural network had full control of Foresight was mainly to ensure the AI followed that list down to the last decimal.

Yasmin and Colonel Haines had briefed him yesterday and they hadn't mentioned anything about an exo-atmospheric test. But it *was* in the outline, along with checkboxes for full thruster burn and something called a slip test. He already knew some of the parameters had changed.

Now, it seemed all of them had.

"Frank, standby," Nicholas said. "Colonel, the mission parameters don't match what we covered in the briefing at all."

"Initiating acceleration in thirty seconds," Frank announced.

"I said standby," Nicholas replied.

"Interrupting network control this early into automated flight will result in mission abortion. Shall I confirm the cancellation?"

Yasmin's voice cut in before Nicholas could answer. "The patch I uploaded contained the new parameters."

"Frank hasn't even completed a single autonomous flight, and now you want him to take the ship into orbit and run through zero-G testing? I understand we're running out of time for this project, but this is suicide."

"Fifteen seconds to acceleration," Frank announced. "Shall I confirm the cancellation?"

"I told you, Nick," Yasmin replied. "We've made some significant progress since the last flight. I know it seems like we're skipping ahead and I completely understand your concern. You have to believe I wouldn't send you out there to pin your life on software I don't trust. It'll be okay. I promise."

Nicholas exhaled sharply. He trusted Yasmin, but at

the same time he couldn't dodge the feeling that his wife and her team were rushing things. Not for the benefit of the exhausted Marines fighting to hold the base against the trife hordes, but because she wanted to look good in front of Grimmel. He didn't want to think she was capable of doing something that calculating. Of risking his life to make herself look good. But there it was.

They were still together, but it wasn't as if their marriage had always been smooth sailing. Yasmin had never chosen him over her career. And while he was grateful they were able to spend their last days on Earth together, it was circumstance that had brought them back into one another's orbit, not devotion.

He didn't want to pin all of the blame on her, though. They had both made sacrifices since the trife rained down on Earth that had taken a toll on their marriage, and maybe that was the issue with Lucius. His parents were so busy they didn't have time for each other, let alone him. They both knew how badly humankind needed a win, and in the process of throwing themselves into their work, they had overlooked how badly Lucius needed them.

"Five seconds to acceleration. Shall I confirm the cancellation?"

"Okay, love," Nicholas said. "I trust you. Negative, Frank. Proceed with assigned parameters."

"Mission continuance confirmed," Frank said. "Accelerating to escape velocity."

Nicholas shifted his right hand to the end of the armrest, holding on for the ride as Frank opened the throttle, the thrusters creating a barely registrable hum and shudder through the airframe. The spacecraft burst forward, at first continuing on the shallow ascent and then increasing both speed and altitude. Nicholas watched the counters on the HUD, monitoring the G-forces and altitude. He'd been forced to abort earlier missions because Frank hadn't honored safe human thresholds. That wasn't the case today.

Frank adjusted the vector, maintaining a smooth, steady climb toward space. Nicholas continued tracking the starship's course. Everything seemed smooth so far. Better than he had experienced in any of the earlier flights. There was no wobbling, no over-adjustment or inconsistent burn. Yasmin had said they'd made progress, and it showed.

The sky continued to darken as they ascended, his heart pounding harder with each second that passed. Not with fear, but excitement. While he had piloted Foresight to orbit multiple times before, both in and out of the simulator, the goal had always been for Frank to handle the duties. After the last test flight he had assumed that day was still months away.

"Entering thermosphere," Frank announced. "All systems nominal. Flight control steady."

The view from the feeds gained a reddish hue as Foresight pushed through the thermosphere, heading into the black expanse of space. The minimal G-forces on the flight deck lessened but didn't fully subside, the constant acceleration still keeping Nicholas pressed more comfortably into his seat than during the initial burn.

Then, just like that, it was over. Frank cut the main thrusters, using only the smaller vectoring nozzles to make finer adjustments to their course. Nicholas stared at Earth in the display. His view of the still predominantly blue and white ball had been shrunk to fit the screen, but he could still see the entire northern hemisphere.

He had seen pictures of Earth captured from space

before the trife arrived. While it remained incredible, he knew how beautiful the view had once been, before the permanent scars of war in the form of dark splotches marred the surface. The remnants of the first rounds of bombing that had turned out to be utterly futile.

"Exo-atmospheric launch complete," Frank said, interrupting his thoughts.

Nicholas used the control pad to confirm the success before relaying it back to the ground. "Control, this is Shepherd; we've reached orbit. So far, so good. Nice work, Yasmin. Whatever you did to Frank, he's looking a lot more capable." He heard guarded cheering in the background of the comms, Yasmin's team likely listening in from the lab. The launch was a success, but it was also only the first part of their primary objectives. Until the AI completed them all, the mission, and their work, wasn't complete.

"Thank you, Nick," Yasmin replied. "It's good to see our efforts paying off."

Nicholas glanced at the updated parameters. The second sequence consisted of Frank executing a full thruster burn, guiding the spacecraft around the moon and then decelerating back into geosynchronous orbit above Texas. It was the kind of advanced navigation control the generation ships would need to evade potential obstacles while crossing the expanse and to land the huge craft once they reached their destinations.

"Frank, initiate mission sequence two," Nicholas said.

"Confirmed. Initiating sequence two. Setting coordinates and executing burn."

Foresight rotated just enough for the bow to come into a direct line with the moon. As soon as the forward display stabilized, the large ion thrusters at the rear of the ship ignited, spewing plasma and once again shoving

Nicholas back in his seat.The ship picked up forward velocity, launching itself toward the Earth's one natural satellite, the numbers speeding by on the HUD until Nicholas found himself tightening his stomach and focusing on his breathing as the Gs increased beyond comfortable.

"Frank, you're burning too hard," Nicholas said, his eyes narrowing as the fingers of his right hand dug into the soft faux leather of the armrest.

"The spine test delayed exo-atmospheric entry," Frank explained. "A harder burn is necessary to meet the mission parameters."

"Our velocity will be too high. You won't be able to slow down enough to stay within the Moon's gravity well."

"Incorrect. Observe the projected pattern."

A second path appeared on the HUD. It still met the general goals of the second sequence, but deviated significantly from the planned approach, bringing them closer to the Moon's surface than he expected and then using the additional gravity to help slow them as they maneuvered around the rock. The path itself was simple, the advanced mathematical calculations to derive it pure genius. It was a testament to how much progress Yasmin and her team had made on the neural network in only a handful of days.

There was only one problem.

The slightest variation, the smallest error in vector or velocity, and Foresight would either faceplant on the Moon's surface or be flung out into deep space. Nicholas could deal with the latter. It would take more time to get back to base, but the craft's reactors had more than enough power to handle the error.

The former? He had an issue with that.

After everything he had already survived, he didn't really want to die on the Moon.

In other words, the plan was perfect. Too perfect. Without any margin for error, any unforeseen circumstance—like a wayward unmarked piece of space debris hitting the hull—could have a catastrophic effect.

"Yasmin, are you receiving Frank's updated approach vector?" Nicholas asked, his voice taut, strained. He was pretty sure his take on Frank's proposed path was right, but he needed verification.

"I am," she replied. "It's a perfect reflection of adaptation and improvisation, exactly the type of response we were hoping for with your latest updates."

"But the margin of error is pretty damn tight. A bit too tight, don't you think?"

"The network isn't capable of making errors," Yasmin replied. "What you see is what you'll get."

"You're certain?" Nicholas asked.

"Yes. I told you to trust me."

"That would be easier to do if this wasn't the first test flight where Frank didn't flunk the first complex sequence."

"It'll be fine, Nick. All you have to do is sit back and enjoy the ride."

"Copy that," he replied, saving the rest of his arguments for later. If there was a later.

It was easy for her to tell him to enjoy the ride. She wasn't the one who would be pulling a constant five to eight Gs for the next twenty minutes. Granted, it wasn't a major problem for him. His G-suit and experience would allow him to withstand the constant stress, though not very comfortably. An ark ship full of inexperienced, unsuited passengers couldn't do the same. If Foresight was really supposed to be a proxy for the full-scale craft while they trained the AI, the neural network would still need tweaking to dial back the tolerances.

Knowing Control was listening in on all of the comms, he opened his mouth to raise the new objection with Yasmin when Grimmel's voice streamed onto the flight deck.

"Captain Shepherd, abort the mission," he said. "Resume manual control and return to base."

The request took him by surprise. He had jurisdiction to make that decision for himself based on his experience and judgement, but he couldn't take orders from a civilian even if he wanted to. Even Grimmel's. "Colonel Haines, can you confirm?"

"Mister Grimmel, sir," Yasmin said, cutting in. "There's no reason to abort. The system is operating as designed."

"Then it's designed wrong," Grimmel snapped. "Doctor Shepherd, I appreciate the extreme amount of effort you and everyone on the team have put into this project, and you should congratulate yourself on both the successful exo-atmospheric launch and the rapid and correct calculation the network derived. Those are both impressive steps forward, and perfectly suitable for a demonstration of the onboard AI's increasing intellect. However, it's one thing to risk a single human test pilot to such precision over a short time horizon. Quite another to risk over forty thousand lives and the potential survival of the human race during a journey that can take as long as three hundred years. It's clear from this exercise that the system requires a much higher degree of range tolerance. There's no sense risking both Captain Shepherd's life and more importantly Foresight on an already failed experiment."

"Y...yes, sir," Yasmin said. "We'll get to work on making the changes immediately."

Nicholas cringed at her response. He knew her well enough to sense how Grimmel's comments had just crushed her, even if he did agree with the perspective.

"Thank you, Doctor Shepherd," Grimmel replied. "I have every faith in the capabilities of you and your team."

"Yes, sir. Thank you, sir."

"Captain Shepherd," Colonel Haines said. "Mission abort confirmed. Retake the stick and come on home.

Chapter 5

Nicholas guided Foresight to a hover a few feet off the hangar deck before slowly spinning the starship on its axis to face the closing blast doors. Unlike during the launch, the Marines on either side of the cavernous bay didn't pay the landing any mind. They remained focused on their individual tasks, catching a few minutes of sleep, playing cards, eating, cleaning their rifles, or just sitting together and talking. Whatever worked to pass the time. Nicholas knew as well as they did that the trife would come again tonight. They would come every night until there were no more humans left in the compound.

The thought made Frank's failure harder for Nicholas to take. It didn't matter that the responsibility for the AI's programming fell to Yasmin and her team. They were all in this together, which meant he was part of their team too.

"Control, mission complete," he said as he sat the starship gently down on the deck on its extended landing skids.

"Copy, Captain," Duff replied. "Nice work out there."

"Was it?" Nicholas snapped, immediately angry with himself for the attitude. "Sorry. I'm a little frustrated." He tapped on the left-hand controls, initiating the ship's shut-down sequence.

"It's not a problem, Shep," Duff said. "I get it. I feel the same way. We'll get it next time."

"Yeah, next time," Nicholas agreed as the automated safety system released him from his restraints. "Shepherd out."

He unstrapped and lifted the helmet from his head, tempted to throw it across the flight deck in evidence of his frustration. He sighed instead, getting up and placing the helmet on the seat. The external feeds to the seat went dark.

Nicholas tapped the control on the back of the seat to open the small door at the rear of the flight deck. Stepping through brought him into a short passageway. Immediately to his right, the airlock was just big enough for a person to move through to whatever Foresight might dock with at any given time. Straight ahead, a common area occupied the center of the ship, a round holotable and projection system in the middle of the compartment. Six seats ringed the table, bolted into the perforated metal flooring and mounted so they could swivel to the stations along the perimeter. A railed ladder in the corner led to an upper deck with berthing for six, a head, and small kitchen. A second ladder, diagonal from the first, dropped to the lower deck, which was reserved for storage while a door in the rear allowed access to the reactor and engines for maintenance.

As he understood it, perfecting the neural network

was the first stage of Foresight spacecraft's existence as a technological testbed. After the automated flight testing, he and the starship would go to the launch site in Nevada, where a sea of engineers and technicians were putting the finishing touches on the arkship Pilgrim. He didn't know how the USSF would use Frank once it got there, but he assumed there was a reasonable explanation for the small ship's ability to support a full crew.

Whatever the brass had planned for the ship, that knowledge was beyond his pay grade. He was just the test pilot, and he knew better than to ask too many questions.

Descending the ladder to the lower deck brought him to a narrow passageway lined with a series of storage lockers, all of which were empty. The hatch leading out of the craft had been oddly positioned beneath the flight deck, at the base of the rounded slope. With the ramp fully extended, the profile view gave the impression the ship was sticking out its tongue. The smooth surface and sleek shape of the ship only served to magnify the effect.

He hit the control to open the hatch. Some of his frustration dissolved as he watched the hatch opened and the ramp extended. The hint of an amused smile appeared on his face, his mind's eye painting the tongue pink. He didn't wait for full extension before starting down, riding the ramp like a surfboard until the end of it touched the floor.

One of Yasmin's fellow scientists waited nearby, and he hurried over as Nicholas stepped off the ramp.

"Hey, Greg," Nicholas said. "Here to download Frank's logs?"

"Yup," the younger man replied. "No sleep for us tonight. Not after what happened out there. I really thought we had it this time." He paused, his expression suggesting he had more he wanted to say before he thought better of it and changed the subject. "Nice flying out there, Captain Shepherd. As always. It's too bad we can't just make a copy of your brain. That would solve all of our problems."

"I thought the learning module was supposed to be like a copy of my brain?"

Greg laughed. "More like a merge of your brain with your wife's," he said, correcting himself. "With all of the tech Mister Grimmel's people loaded on this baby, it's embarrassing that we're struggling so much with the AI."

"From what Yasmin tells me, you're asking it to do a lot of heavy lifting on processors that weren't designed for the task. You should be proud of what you've accomplished."

"I'll be proud of it when it works. I should hurry up, Yasmin wants to start reviewing the logs right away."

"Say hi to my wife for me, will you?"

Greg nodded. "You should come down to the lab some time and say hello yourself."

"And distract her from her work? I'd rather wrestle a trife."

"See you later, Captain Shepherd."

"Take care of yourself, Greg."

The engineer vanished up the ramp of Foresight. Nicholas headed beneath the rear of the craft, toward the primary blast door leading out of the hangar. He ran his hand along the starship's hull as he walked, fingers slipping along the matte-black, slick-as-ice alloy. Nicholas knew absolutely nothing about the metal, except that there was nothing else like it in the world. It was so rare Grimmel had used all that was available to cover Foresight's frame.

The blast door slid open ahead of Nicholas as he

reached it. He immediately pulled to a stop and came to attention as Colonel Haines stepped through the door, her silver-haired bob framing her heart-shaped face. Was she wearing makeup?

Indeed she was, obviously for the man with her.

Nicholas had seen plenty of pictures of Aaron Grimmel splattered all across the Internet from the time he had been old enough to care about world news. He had always thought Grimmel bore a strong resemblance to Abraham Lincoln, and seeing him in person only cemented that view. Tall and lanky, with a long, narrow face framed by a neatly trimmed beard. A sharp nose between hawkish eyes, with a smile that was either overly friendly or subtly malevolent.

Nicholas' heart raced in response to the unexpected presence of the world's most powerful man.

"Captain Shepherd. It's an honor to meet you," Grimmel said, putting out his hand toward Nicholas in greeting.

"At ease, Captain," Haines said, smiling at him as he shook Grimmel's hand.

"It's a real honor to meet *you*, sir," Nicholas said, smiling as he endured the magnate's iron vise grip. "I'm just a pilot. You're—"

"What? Amazing?" Grimmel supplied. "Rich? Handsome? Powerful? Haha!" His smile expanded. "You're the one risking your life flying my spaceship, Captain. You've been out there fighting the trife. It's easy to sit behind a desk and pay the bills. You do the hard work. You and your wife."

"We both do our best, sir." He drew his hand back as Grimmel released it, resisting the urge to flex and shake it to get the blood back.

"Yes, well, you've both been working too hard, don't you think?"

Nick's eyebrows rose in surprise. "No sir. We'll keep at it as long as it takes."

"I know you will, but everyone needs to take a little time to recharge once in a while. Even if it's only for an hour or two. That's why I came down here. To catch you before you disappeared and invite you to my quarters for dinner this evening. You and your wife. And your son. Lucius, isn't it?"

"That's right."

"Colonel Haines will join us as well. Nothing fancy. Only the best of what's left. Haha!"

"I appreciate the offer, Mister Grimmel. But I might be needed to handle one of the drones during tonight's attack."

"You'll be on call as usual, Captain," Haines said. "Mister Grimmel's quarters aren't that much further from the hangar than yours. And offers like this don't come along every day."

"I *would* like a chance to have dinner with my wife and son. It's been awhile," Nicholas said. "Even if it means having to eat with probably the most interesting man on the planet." He grinned. "What time?"

"Haha! I like your sense of humor," Grimmel replied. "Seven o'clock sharp. Three hours."

"I'll be there," Nicholas said. "Speaking of Lucius, Colonel, if you don't mind, I need to go see him."

Haines nodded knowingly. "Of course, Captain. We'll see you at seven."

"It was a real pleasure to meet you, sir," Nicholas said to Grimmel again. "Colonel." He nodded at her before slipping past them both and into the compound.

Human civilization was on the verge of collapse, the

base's defenses were getting weaker by the day, their best hope for survival just failed a major test run, and the most powerful man in the world had just invited him to a formal dinner?

Whatever Grimmel was up to, Nicholas had a feeling it involved more than breaking bread.

Chapter 6

Luke Shepherd leaned against the back wall of the holding cell, casually tossing a rubber ball against the opposite wall and catching it as it bounced off the floor on its way back to him.

Three hours. His father should have been here by now. What was taking him so long?

"Luke, seriously," Briar said from her place on the bench that jutted out from the wall. "You've been tossing that ball for over an hour now. Aren't you tired of it yet?"

"I can do this all day," Luke replied. "It beats sitting there twiddling my thumbs."

"Breaking into the simulator room was your idea," Scott said. He sat on the far side of the bench, feet up on the minimal cushioning and back against the adjacent wall, arms folded over his knees. "The least you can do is try not to be annoying for the entire day."

Luke tossed the ball again, catching it cleanly as it returned. "You know I can't stop being annoying," he replied. "It's in my DNA. I get bored easily."

"And that's not boring?" Briar asked.

Luke shrugged. The act itself was boring. But getting a rise out of his friends provided a measure of entertainment for all of them. Otherwise, they would be sitting around the cell in mopey silence worrying about how much trouble they were going to be in with their parents.

"My father will be here eventually," he said. "He'll talk to the MPs like he always does, and get us out of here like he always does."

"One of these days he isn't going to come bail us out," Briar said. "He's going to get sick of your shit."

"My shit? You went along with the idea."

"Because you swore we wouldn't get caught." She lowered her voice, mimicking his. "The simulator room has basic security and no cameras. I used my dad's datapad to make sure nobody's scheduled for training. We can set the simulators into combat mode and dogfight one another. It'll be awesome." She exhaled sharply, shaking her head. "Except one: you're the only one who knows how to work the simulators. And two: we got caught."

"You were starting to get the hang of it," Luke countered, bouncing the ball off the wall again. "You managed to get off the ground at least, unlike monkey-boy here." He looked over at Scott. "Big muscles. No finesse."

"Keep it up and me and my big muscles will come over there and shut you up," Scott shot back, turning his frown on Briar. "What are you so worried about anyway, B?" He smirked at her. "Captain Shepherd will clear things up."

"With the MPs maybe," Briar said. "I still have to deal with my parents. They told me last time that the next time I get in trouble they would confine me to quarters." She grunted in frustration. "The rules here are ridiculous. I'm almost eighteen. They shouldn't be able to ground me."

"Just be glad you aren't eighteen," Luke said. "Regs are regs. Once you're no longer a minor the MPs can lock you up for good. Or more likely, you'll be conscripted into the USSF Marine Corps, where it's pretty much assured that you won't see nineteen. Besides, you only have to spend a couple of days in your suite watching old movies until your folks forget they were mad at you. I can think of worse punishments."

"A girl can only watch Star Wars so many times before it gets old."

"Blasphemy," Scott said.

Briar raised an eyebrow toward him. "It's really not that great."

"Guards!" Scott shouted. "Get me out of here. I can't share a cell with a Star Wars hater."

"I can't share a cell with a Star Wars fanboy," Briar countered. "The original movie is what? Seventy-five years old?"

"And it still holds up."

"No, it doesn't."

"Guards!" Scott shouted again.

Luke bounced the ball off the wall again. Before he could catch the return, a second hand swept in front of him, snatching the ball away.

"Enough already," Jennifer said, quiet until now, obviously stewing in her own juices. She tucked the ball into the pocket of her jeans. "You're giving all of us a headache."

"I can still get that back," Luke said, reaching toward her pants pocket.

"Not if you want to keep your hand," she replied,

grabbing his wrist and twisting him into an arm drag, until she was behind him with one hand under his left arm, the other across his chest, her forearm digging into his neck.

"Owned," Scott crowed as Luke struggled, unable to break free.

"Okay, okay," Luke said, laughing. "You got me this time."

"I get you *every* time," Jennifer said, letting him go. "I've offered to teach you, but you only like to do things you're better at than us."

"That isn't true," Luke said. "I like to do things that are fun. We'll be headed off to the arkship any day now. I won't need to know Marine restraint holds once we're on board."

"You won't need to know how to fly an experimental starship either," Briar countered. "That didn't stop you from learning."

"You're just jealous because I have a cool dad. Not a pair of nerdy scientists for parents."

"Your cool dad would die down here with everyone else if not for my nerdy parents," Briar said.

"My mother can kick your father's ass," Jennifer said.

"Please," Scott said. "You all sound like you're five. At least you still have parents."

The comment silenced the banter instantly.

"I'm sorry, Scott," Luke said, the wind sucked out of his sails.

His friend's mother had died from the original sickness that had fallen to Earth with the trife. His father was slaughtered by the aliens during their escape from Baton Rouge. Unlike the majority of the civilians here, he hadn't been airlifted from a hot spot and brought in as a VIP or relative of a VIP set to work on Project Foresight.

He had crossed the wastelands on his own, surviving weeks outside alone with the trife. Luke knew Scott had seen horrible things out there, things he refused to talk about. Not only violence between human and trife, but between human and human. It had taken weeks for Luke to get Scott to warm up to him and his group of friends. The trauma was real. But the fun they had together provided good therapy for the other teenager and helped him forget about his ordeal...most of the time.

Of course, they all had stories they could tell. They had all lost at least one person they had known or cared about to the sickness or the trife. Luke had lost both sets of grandparents. Briar, her brother and sister. Jennifer, her father and three brothers. Nobody had gotten through this unscathed.

That's why they had to stick together. That's why they had to depend on one another.

And never waste a single second of life, because every one they had was a gift.

"Me too," Jennifer said.

"We're your family now, bro," Briar added. "Even if you do like Star Wars."

Scott laughed. "Thanks, B."

The security door to the holding area opened. One of the MPs stepped up to their cell door.

"See," Luke said to the others. "I told you he would come."

The MP used his fingerprint to unlock the door, pulling it open. "Let's go, Shepherd."

"What about my friends?" Luke asked.

The MPs' eyes shifted to the group. Briar and Jennifer offered hopeful expressions, while Scott continued brooding. "Just you this time, kid," he said to Luke.

Briar groaned. Luke winced. Normally, the MP let them all walk and his father chewed him out once they got back to their quarters.

He didn't think any of them would be so lucky this time.

Chapter 7

Nicholas remained seated as the door to the small interview room opened and the MP ushered Luke in.

"Dad," Luke said, offering a sheepish smile Nicholas had seen hundreds of times over his son's lifetime. When Luke was younger, the smile had successfully disarmed the worst of his anger or frustration over the boy's care-free mindset and reckless choices. Even as soon as a few weeks ago, he might have let the small dimples on Luke's cheeks and the wrinkling around his eyes dissuade him from making a big deal out of the latest transgression.

But needing to retrieve the kid from holding so he could get him ready for a dinner with Aaron Grimmel had sent a wave of embarrassed anger rocketing through him, and he wasn't quite ready to forgive.

Luke's smile faded when Nicholas didn't budge from his seat at a small, empty table, instead maintaining his rigid posture, a stern expression on his face.

"Sit," he ordered, glaring at Luke as he pointed to the metal chair on the other side of the table.

Any hint of relief or thought of another rescue

vanishing from his face, Luke walked over, pulled out the chair and sat down as instructed. He folded his hands in his lap and waited for the hammer to fall.

Nicholas glanced at the MP. "Thank you, Justin."

"Any time, Captain Shepherd."

"Well, I'm going to make sure this is the last time."

"Yes, sir." The MP left the room, closing the door behind him.

"Dad," Luke started. "I know you're mad at me, but—"

"Shut up," Nicholas hissed.

'But Dad, I promised last time I wouldn't do anything to get in trouble before Project Foresight wrapped up. And—"

"Just. Stop. Talking."

Luke fell silent, jaw tight. Those three words spoken softly were more menacing than had his dad shouted them.

Nicholas stared at him, letting him squirm, if not physically, then mentally, for a few heartbeats before he pressed his forearms to the table and leaned forward. "Do you want to join the Marines, Luke?" he asked sharply. "Is that why you're so completely incapable of going two weeks without doing something stupid?"

"What? No, Dad. I—"

"Shut. Up." Nicholas growled, silencing him again. "I'll tell you when I want you to speak."

"Yes, sir."

Nicholas fell silent again too, returning to his cold stare. He didn't want to have the same conversation with Luke that he'd already had a dozen times before. He needed a new tactic. Something that might sink in.

"Do you know how I heard you were locked up?" he asked, pleased when Luke didn't say anything. "Corporal

Duffy told me while I was strapped into the pilot's seat of Foresight. Right before takeoff of the most important mission I've ever flown, and only seconds before Aaron Grimmel walked into the CIC. Do you know who Aaron Grimmel is, Luke?"

Luke opened his mouth, reconsidered, and settled for a nod.

"I don't need to tell you again how hard your mother and I are working, and why. I'm sorry we can't be there for you the way you want or might need. At your age, I would have thought you would understand the trouble we're in and realize how lucky you are just to be alive."

"I do, Dad," Luke said, jumping in. "That's exactly the point. I—"

A fresh glare shut him down. But Nicholas had to hand it to him; he didn't shrink back. He didn't even look down at the table. He continued to meet him, eye-to-eye.

"I wish I could teach you to respect the people out there fighting to keep us alive here night after night. Maybe we've been safe here so long that you think they'll be able to hold out forever. Every last Marine out there…" He pointed at the door. "…believes that too, but only because they have to believe it if they want to stay sane. In the back of their minds, they know that sooner or later the trife will overpower our defenses. Or a shipment of fresh ammunition won't come through. Or maybe the depot itself will fall and we'll lose our supply lines. Every single one of them knows that odds are they're going to die. Those odds are greater than ninety percent, I would say. Do you think they want to spend every night fighting to protect a bunch of scientists and their kids? Especially when those kids think this base is their own personal frigging playground!" Nicholas shouted, Luke finally flinching.

This wasn't the way Nicholas had intended for his talk to go, but he couldn't keep his anger under wraps anymore.

"I've had it Luke! I've had it with your immature bullshit. The acting out. The need to be the center of attention. I've had it with you putting a strain on our resources, with your disrespect and disregard for the rules, and I've most of all had it with your assumption that I'll always come and smooth things over. I've tried that a bunch of times now, and do you know what I've gotten in return?" He paused, glaring at Luke. "Go ahead, answer me."

"I don't know," Luke said softly. "Nothing...I guess."

Nicholas smiled sardonically. "Nothing would actually be a net positive at this point. Not only do your antics make me look bad to my superiors, Sergeant Bruce whom I highly respect, and all the other MPs, you made your mom and me look bad in front of Aaron Grimmel. And that's not even the worst of it. I've been down here six times in the last year. I've never seen anyone besides you and your friends in the holding cells. Not one other person. You seem to be the only misfits in this entire compound that can't look past yourselves to see there's something bigger than you going on here. And I can't even begin to describe how furious that makes me."

Nicholas was certain his body language helped that description. His face pounded from the increased blood flow of his anger, his one hand balled into a fist on the table, his other forefinger jabbing at the air in front of Luke's face.

"I just wanted to fly Foresight," Luke said. "I know

the Marines are putting their lives on the line for us. I know they're making a huge sacrifice. But try living in here sometime, Dad. Too old to be in school. Too young to be part of the solution. Waiting to start a new life on an arkship. We're stuck in Purgatory, spending every day with nothing to do and every night waiting for the trife to break through and kill us in our sleep. At least you and Mom have a purpose. A role here. Something to keep you occupied so you aren't constantly trying to find any distraction you can to forget we have to leave Earth, the only home we've ever known, before the trife kill us. To forget that so many people you cared about are dead."

The statement drained the anger out of Nicholas. His raised arm dropped to the tabletop, his glare changing from fury to surprise. Damn Luke for finding another way to disarm him.

"I didn't think there was any harm in helping my friends enjoy their last days on Earth instead of spending them doing too much thinking about what's going on out there. And being scared all the time. Honestly, I didn't think anyone would know we were in there. We're all just trying to find a way to survive, Dad. To make it through from one day to the next."

Luke had tears in his eyes as he spoke, which nearly caused Nicholas to tear up too. He hated being a hard-ass when it came to the kid, but whether he could relate to what Luke had said or not, he couldn't just let him off the hook. Not this time.

"I get it, Luke. Believe it or not. But that doesn't give you the right to spit in the face of the men and women who are busting their asses day and night to keep you safe. You could have come to me first and asked me about the sims. I'm sure I would have been able to arrange something. I've got some clout around here, you know."

Nicholas nodded. "Yeah. You're right. I know. It was spur of the moment, and I didn't think. Scott lost his whole family out there, and Briar's been really down lately. Jen's a harder read, but I could tell she was getting stir crazy too."

"You're a good friend. Kind. Compassionate. A natural leader. But you need to stop leading your people in the wrong direction." He paused to think. "You said you need something useful to do?"

Luke's face tightened. "Yeah," he replied hesitantly.

Nicholas sat back in his chair, the tension leaving his shoulders "I have an idea."

Chapter 8

Nicholas used his best drill-sergeant face as he entered the holding area, his eyes squaring on Luke's friends. He had met all of them before, of course. He had already bailed them out of holding several times for different acts of mischief. In retrospect, he realized he should have tried harder to solve their problem before it had come to this, but it wasn't as if he'd had a lot of free time to give consideration to his son's personal life.

And that was a sad revelation.

Nicholas sighed heavily.

Not only had it been a mistake, it didn't reflect well on him as a parent. Or on the USSF. Luke and his friends were caught in that limbo area between teenagers and adults. Without guidance, they had found their own ways to meet their needs. To cope.

Luke had opened up to him in a way he hadn't before, fighting harder to help him understand the root cause of their insubordination rather than simply apologizing and telling him it wouldn't happen again. Maybe because they both knew that promise wouldn't stick if something didn't change. Nicholas was thankful for the chance to try to fix things for Luke, and maybe for his friends too. Like he had told his son, he had some clout within the facility.

"Captain Shepherd, sir," Jennifer said, always the first to speak after Luke. She didn't quite stand at attention, but she took a more respectful posture behind the bars of the cell, making eye contact with him when he looked at her.

Briar jumped up from the bench after Jennifer spoke, joining her at the bars to the cell. Scott remained on the bench, looking across at him from there, his expression still flat.

"Captain Shepherd, is Luke okay?" Briar asked.

"Why wouldn't he be okay?" Scott said from where he remained sitting on a bench. "His father isn't going to kill him."

"Luke's waiting for you outside," Nicholas said, keeping his face tight. "He's only outside instead of in here because we made a deal. The same deal I'm going to offer you."

"I don't like the sound of that," Briar said.

"You aren't bailing us out this time?" Scott asked.

"Without strings? No. Not this time."

Scott nodded, barely affected by the statement. Nicholas understood why. The cell was still a thousand times better than being out in the wilds with the trife.

"What do we need to do, sir?" Jennifer asked.

"Luke told me you're bored. Like you're just stuck here waiting to be delivered to the arkship with no way to make a positive contribution. Is that true?"

The three teens looked at one another, unsure how they should answer. Of course, Jennifer spoke up first.

"Yes, sir," she said. "I think that's true."

"It's partially our fault," Nicholas admitted. "The USSF, I mean. We didn't make accommodation for people in your age bracket, leaving you to your own devices. But there's no reason we can't change that."

"What's the deal?" Scott asked, finally seeming interested.

"There are two companies of Marines living in the hangar," Nicholas said. "They're already exhausted from fighting the trife every night. Morale is low. They need to be fed, hydrated. Whatever you can do to make their lives a little easier. There are also a number of Butcher robots that require maintenance every morning. Recharging, cleaning, simple stuff anyone can do. And their techs could probably use someone to hand them tools. The point being, there's plenty of opportunity for you to pitch in. I can take you down there and introduce you to Lieutenant Carter. He's the air boss; that means he's in charge of the hangar. He can help set you up with some basic tasks." He pulled back the sleeve of his shirt to check the time. Six o'clock. An hour until he had to be at Grimmel's for dinner. "You've got thirty seconds to decide."

"I don't need thirty seconds," Jennifer said. "I'm in."

"If Luke and Jen are in, then I'm in," Briar said.

"Scott?" Jennifer said when he didn't respond right away.

Scott shrugged. "I guess so. It's probably better than sitting here."

Nicholas dropped his stern face, letting it relax into a smile. "I'm glad you all agree. I'll have Sergeant Bruce open the cell for you. Meet you outside."

"Thank you, Captain Shepherd," Jennifer said.

"Don't thank me," Nicholas replied. "Just do your best and stay out of trouble from here on out. I'm putting my seal on this, so if you look bad, then I look worse."

"Yes, sir."

Nicholas left the holding area for the small MPs office. Four simple metal desks occupied the room, only one of them occupied.

"Well?" Sergeant Bruce said, looking up from his computer. 'How did it go?"

"You can let them out. I'll assume responsibility for them."

"Yes, sir," the sergeant replied. He got up from his seat and crossed to the holding area. "Are you sure this is a good idea?"

"I need to have faith in Luke to do the right thing," Nicholas replied. "If he blows this one, he won't get another chance."

Bruce nodded and disappeared through the door, returning a minute later with Luke's friends in tow. "They're all yours, Captain."

"Thank you, Justin," Nicholas said, looking the trio over again.

Jennifer always had the neatest appearance. Auburn hair pulled back into a ponytail, black t-shirt tucked into high-waisted khaki pants, a navy blazer over the shirt. Briar was less composed in an oversized cable-knit sweater and baggy blue jeans, while Scott wore a pair of slightly faded surplus USSF Marine utilities, issued to him when he had come to the base with only the clothes on his back. Nicholas knew the outsider wanted to join the Marines and had tried to convince Colonel Haines he was old enough. Maybe he was, there was no easy way to be sure. But given the time they planned to remain on Earth and the question of his age, Haines had decided against it.

They were a motley group, to be sure. But they were all good kids at heart.

"Follow me," he said, leading them out of the MP station and into the corridor beyond. Luke was already there, but he didn't greet them. Instead, he fell in with them, all of them, walking behind Nicholas.

Like the Pied Piper, he led them through the corridors of the compound taking them from the MP station near the CIC forward into the hangar. The scene there hadn't changed much since Nicholas had been there a couple of hours earlier. The Marines still flanked the cavernous space with the butchers and armored vehicles, though their posture had changed somewhat. More of them were in the process of cleaning their rifles and preparing for the nightly attack, their weariness replaced by alertness.

Techs surrounded the butchers, using brushes to fill the scrapes in their armor with epoxy that would offer a little extra protection from the demons' sharp claws.

"When do the trife usually come?" Briar asked, her voice shaky in response to the scene in the hangar. The fact that she didn't know proved to Nicholas how insulated the non-combatants were against the nightly fighting. Maybe they understood the Marines were out here keeping them safe, and by now they had to know what the trife were like. Even so, without seeing it first-hand he imagined it still seemed to them like it was all happening somewhere miles away, not meters away.

"Any time after sundown," Nicholas replied. "Closer to early morning most of the time, but there's no guarantee. That's why we have spotters out there twenty-four seven."

"What about the Reaper drones?" Scott asked.

"We're down to our last two, and they're combat

craft, not recon. They can only stay up for an hour or two at a time. Plus, combat equals limited ammunition. We save them until things start getting dicey. But take a look at the Marines. Take a look at the bots. They're worn down. This stalemate won't last forever, which is why we need to finish testing Foresight."

"Captain Shepherd, sir," Jennifer said. "I don't understand why we need to do the testing here, instead of at a safer location."

"This facility was designed for military research and development," Nicholas replied. "The labs are the most advanced in the world. The progress we've made here in a month would have taken a year somewhere else. Believe me, I wish we could do the work somewhere else too, but we just don't have the time."

He stopped walking long enough to locate Lieutenant Carter standing near the edge of the Marine camp on the left side of the hangar, speaking with Sergeant Jones and Corporal Patel. The Lieutenant looked tired, her drawn back blonde hair fraying, her blue eyes drooped. Nicholas knew Samantha well enough to know she hadn't gotten a decent night's sleep in weeks, and it showed.

The three Marines stopped talking, turning to face Nicholas and standing at attention when Patel noticed her headed their way.

"Captain Shepherd, sir," Carter said.

"At ease," Nicholas said. "Lieutenant, if I could have a word with you."

"Of course, sir," she replied.

Nicholas pulled her away from the other Marines to where Luke and his friends waited. "Lieutenant Carter, I think you already know my son, Luke."

"Yes, how are you today, Luke?"

Luke smiled. "I'm not sure yet, ma'am."

Lieutenant Carter smiled. "Uh-oh."

"Lieutenant, these three are friends of Luke's. That's Jennifer, Scott, and Briar."

"Nice to meet you all," Carter said. "Briar. That's an interesting name. I like it"

"Thank you. My parents named me after Sleeping Beauty," Briar said. "Do you know that fairy tale? The original title from the Brothers Grimm is the Briar Rose. Because the castle she's in is surrounded by thorns."

"I didn't know that," Luke said.

"Because you never asked," Briar replied.

"I'm sorry, Captain," Carter said. "Not to be rude, but why are these civilians in my hangar?"

"That's exactly what I wanted to talk to you about. I just picked these four out of the holding cell at the MP station. They decided to break into the simulation room to play X-wing versus Tie Fighter."

"See, Star Wars," Scott said.

Nicholas ignored him. "They got caught. Luke brought it to my attention that they would be less inclined to break the law if they had something more useful to do than just hanging around. So I brought them down here to see if you could put them to work."

Carter smiled. "I see." She looked them over again. "We could always use a few more hands on deck. I didn't realize we had some extras floating around or I would have requisitioned them already."

"They're technically underage, so they can't do anything that might get them hurt or have their parents screaming at me."

"Fair enough. I have filler that needs applying to the bots. I have magazines that need loading with rounds. I have canteens that need filling. And some other tasks that should keep them occupied for a few hours."

"Then I'll leave them in your capable hands, Lieutenant," Nicholas said before turning to Luke. "I'm having dinner with your mother and Mister Grimmel. I'll check in on you afterward," he said, deciding to leave Luke out of the dinner to work alongside his friends. He shifted his attention to the others. "Jen, Briar, I'll let your parents know where you are."

"And why we're here?" Briar asked hesitantly.

"Not this time," Nicholas replied.

She smiled. "Thank you, Captain Shepherd."

"Don't make me regret this," he said.

"No, sir. We won't."

Nicholas nodded at the kids before answering the lieutenant's salute and heading for the hangar exit, his thoughts automatically shifting from Luke to Yasmin. They hadn't spent more than a few minutes together at one time in weeks.

He couldn't wait to see her.

Chapter 9

Nicholas returned to the quarters he shared with Yasmin and Luke, located a few floors below the military barracks in the civilian section of the base. He would have preferred to be closer to the hangar or the drone cockpits off the CIC, but none of the quarters topside were large enough to accommodate them all. As it was, their current living situation would have felt uncomfortably cramped if he, Yasmin, and Luke ever occupied the small two-bedroom apartment at the same time.

A worn brown leather sofa dominated the central living space, a lamp on one side and a narrow table on the other. A computer rested on a desk in the corner. A television hung from the wall beside the door. A kitchenette occupied one half of the apartment's rear. The bathroom filled the other. A pair of doors flanked the living room, each leading to a bedroom.

A single framed photograph on the left-hand wall provided the only decoration in the quarters, the only personal item they had managed to salvage from the wreckage of their home. To Nicholas, it felt like a lifetime since they had lived in the yellow three-bedroom in San Diego. It felt like a lifetime since they had spent entire days together, all three of them as one family. In the photo, Luke was twelve years old, posing with Yasmin in front of the polar bear exhibit at the zoo. They both looked so happy.

He couldn't remember the last time anyone on the planet was that happy.

It only took a dozen steps to cross the living area to his and Yasmin's bedroom, itself little more than a stacked twin bunk and small closet. Even in the rare instances they were here at the same time to sleep, they couldn't share a mattress. Nicholas opened the closet, crouching to reach his clothes on the bottom, everything neatly folded. He retrieved the components of his dress uniform and left the room, crossing to the bathroom. A quick shower and a shave left him feeling somewhat refreshed.

He had just stepped out of the bathroom and crossed to the closet beside the door to retrieve his jacket when the door opened, nearly hitting him in the process. He sidestepped out of the way before lunging forward and wrapping his arms around Yasmin as she entered the quarters.

She shrieked in surprise, throwing her elbow into Nicholas' stomach with enough force to knock the air from his lungs. He let go, coughing and laughing at the same time.

"Damn it, Nick," she said, whirling around, her brown eyes sparkling in amusement. "Are you okay?"

"I'll be fine," he replied breathlessly.

"Why were you standing behind the door?"

"I was just getting my jacket. I didn't want to waste

the opportunity to surprise you. I wasn't expecting the elbow."

"You scared me. Next time, I'm going for the groin."

Nicholas laughed as best he could, the air returning to his lungs. Yasmin looked like she had achieved a level of exhaustion that dwarfed Lieutenant Carter's. Large bags occupied the space between her eyes and her high cheekbones, while her full lips were dry and cracked. And she smelled sterile like her lab.

He leaned in to kiss her. She allowed him a quick peck but nothing more, stepping back from him before he could put his arms around her. "I need to hurry or we're going to be late," she said.

"You really need to get some rest, Yaz," Nicholas said. "You're beautiful exhausted, but you're exquisite when fresh." Yasmin responded to the praise with a token smile. He didn't need a flashing red warning sign to tell she was upset. "What's wrong?"

"Not now," she replied, disappearing into the bedroom. She emerged a few seconds later, underwear in hand. "My only decent dress is in the closet with your jacket. Can you grab it for me and bring it into the bathroom?"

"Sure," Nicholas said.

He returned to the closet while Yasmin entered the bathroom, finishing off his dress uniform with jacket and shoes before picking out the white floral dress.

Yasmin was already in the shower when he arrived, her clothes piled on the floor at his feet. He hung the dress from a hook on the wall and picked up her blouse, buttoning and folding it neatly. The base couldn't spare the water to wash every garment after every wear.

"How's the lab?" he asked, putting out a feeler to confirm her mood.

"How do you think?" she replied, a hint of venom in her tone. "The mission was a failure. Again."

"Partial failure," Nicholas countered. "The exo-atmospheric nav was perfect. The ride was as smooth as it's ever been."

"Great. At least we can get the arkship population to space before we kill them."

She turned off the water and violently pulled the small curtain aside. Nicholas couldn't help staring. He hadn't seen his wife naked in months. She was still as beautiful as the day he met her, almost twenty years ago now. Slender, athletic, with a slightly olive-toned complexion, the product of a mixed Iranian and Indian heritage. She had told him multiple times she could see her body aging. Maybe her breasts weren't as perky as they used to be, maybe her rear hung slightly lower or she had a bit more cellulite around her thighs. To him, she was as sexy as she had ever been.

"Stop looking at me like that and hand me my towel," she said, breaking him out of his trance.

"You're beautiful, Yaz," he replied, passing her the cloth.

"Try that again when I'm not so angry with you."

"Okay, I knew you were angry. But why with me?"

She ran the towel over her face before pausing to answer his question. "I asked you to trust me, Nick. The system's route was well within your tolerance levels. Why did you have to question it?"

Nick raised an eyebrow, surprised by what she was angry about. "Yazz, any variation at all could have sent the ship crashing into the moon at a ridiculously high velocity, or spinning out into space at a ridiculously high velocity. I know you're disappointed with the outcome, but you can't ignore the facts. Especially since Grimmel aborted the mission because of those facts."

She finished drying off her body and started dressing. "He wouldn't have even paid attention to the data points if you hadn't pulled them to the forefront by asking for confirmation. None of the calculations put you in the red zone and Frank would have completed the maneuvers perfectly."

Nicholas noticed that she referred to the neural network as Frank, but he didn't point it out. "You don't know that. Besides, even if the maneuver was perfect the Gs were too high for the arkship thresholds. They're building entire cities inside the hulls. Nobody in them will be strapped in. Neither will the structures."

"But the arkships will have counter-inertial systems that'll limit the effects. The tech's too large to put on a ship the size of Foresight. Calculating the difference, it would have fallen into safe limits. That's part of my point. If you had trusted me and just done the maneuver, I could have explained that to Grimmel after mission success. Instead, we aborted. Now our evac is delayed and he thinks I'm reckless with people's lives. Your life."

"I don't think you were reckless with my life."

She glared at him. "Then why the hell didn't you just do the maneuver and keep your mouth shut?"

Nicholas didn't answer right away. The response angered him, but he didn't want to blow up at her and escalate the argument. He knew she was exhausted and stressed. They both were.

"Are you going to say anything?" she snapped as she pulled on her dress.

"You look incredible in that dress," Nicholas replied.

"Don't sidestep the question, Captain Shepherd. You

had the calculations, you say you trusted me. Why not just let Frank run the gauntlet?"

"Because that's not how it's done. I've survived this long by flying by the book whenever possible. I had a concern, I requested clarification. It had nothing to do with trust. It could have been Aaron Grimmel urging me to continue and I would have done the same thing."

Yasmin bit her lower lip. "We could have been out of here, Nick. Tonight. Before the next attack. Damn it, I want Luke away from this place."

"Me too," he replied, offering her his embrace. She took it this time, falling into him. "I want you out of here with him."

She looked up at him, tears in her eyes. "You should have listened to me. You should have kept going."

Nicholas nodded. "Maybe you're right. There's nothing we can do about it now. You can update Frank. You can fix the tolerances. I know you can. We'll do another flight tomorrow, and I'll be more lenient in voicing my concerns. Okay?"

Yasmin pursed her lips in consideration, and then nodded. "I'm going to be in the lab all night because of you."

"I'll bring you coffee."

She smiled as she wiped her eyes. "Pathetic apology, but I'll take it."

Nicholas laughed. "Don't think I didn't notice that you called the neural network by its name."

"Only to you, Nick. And only because Frank is admittedly easier to say."

"I'm going to tell Grimmel you called it Frank."

"You wouldn't."

He shrugged. "Maybe. Maybe not."

"Give me a few minutes to dry my hair and put on some lipstick, and I'll be ready to go."

"Sure thing, boss. Still mad at me?"

"Yeah, a little."

"Fair enough. I love you, Yazz."

"I love you too, Nick."

Chapter 10

Nicholas and Yasmin nearly collided with Colonel Haines as they each approached the corridor leading to Grimmel's temporary quarters, reaching the same intersection in the passageway at the same time.

Pulling to a sudden stop, Nicholas came to attention, while Yasmin jumped back to avoid colliding with the other woman. "Colonel Haines, ma'am." He did a double-take, his eyes dropping from his commanding officer's very made-up face to the navy blue dress she had chosen instead of her Marine dress uniform. It fit snugly to her body, with a low neckline revealing a bit of cleavage, her hem just above her knees. He stared but couldn't find a response he considered both respectful and complementary before his time ran out.

"At ease, Captain," Haines said, allowing Nicholas to relax his posture. "What, you've never seen a woman in a dress before?"

The comment elicited a laugh from Yasmin. "Good evening, Colonel Haines," she said. "I think he's just not sure how to balance respect for your position and the fact that you look incredible in that dress."

"Something like that," Nicholas said.

"We don't get many opportunities to impress a man," Haines replied. "I don't know if you're aware, but Aaron Grimmel is unattached."

"And you're hoping to change that?" Yasmin asked.

Haines shrugged. "It wouldn't be the worst thing that could happen to me. Once we board the arkship I'll be converted to a civilian role in the initial onboard government. It's just good tactics to make my case to the most revered man on the ship before competition increases."

"It doesn't hurt that he's handsome," Yasmin said.

Haines smiled. "Not at all."

"No offense, Colonel, but I prefer you barking orders at me over discussing Grimmel's sex appeal with my wife."

Both women laughed. "There's time for both, Captain," Haines said. "Especially since we're reaching the endgame. I'm confident both you and your beautiful, intelligent, hard-working spouse will make us all proud very soon."

"We're close," Yasmin admitted. She glanced at Nicholas. "We could have been closer, but we'll get there."

He sensed the lingering venom and anger in her statement and resisted the urge to sigh in chagrin. Maybe she had mostly forgiven him, but the outcome had left a burn that would take a little more time to heal.

"Anyway," he said, segueing away from the topic. "I didn't realize Aaron Grimmel had his own living space down here. Last I heard, he spent all his time holed up in his ivory tower."

"You can do that when you have your own personal military the size of a small country's," Haines replied.

"You should be glad for it, Nick," Yasmin added. "I spent six months holed up there with his team. The facilities are top notch, and we made a lot of progress on a lot of tech in very little time. Including everything you see in Foresight. We don't get off Earth without Aaron Grimmel. But I understand why you would be jealous."

"I'm not jealous," Nicholas countered.

"Mmm-hmm. I believe that."

"It's true. What does all the money or power in the world mean now? Just a better seat on the first arkship out of Dodge. That's about it."

"You'll probably think differently when he's the Governor of Metro and you're a Deputy Sheriff."

"I'll still have you, and he won't." Nicholas glanced at Haines. "No offense, ma'am. I think Grimmel would be an idiot not to give you a shot."

Haines laughed. "Thank you, Captain."

The trio made their way down the corridor, passing other quarters on the way. Grimmel had taken up residence in the research area of the compound, in the single master suite reserved for the head of the lab. From what Duffy had told him, Nicholas knew Doctor Rashburne hadn't been happy about relinquishing the poshest apartment inside the bunker, but he also couldn't argue with the temporary accommodations considering who had taken his place.

Besides, they would all be out of here soon enough.

Nicholas deferred to Colonel Haines, letting her take the lead in knocking on the simple aluminum door to the quarters. Grimmel surprised him by answering the door himself, pulling it open and offering a wide smile to his guests.

"Colonel Haines," he said, his eyes flicking over her dress. "What an unexpected delight to see you in a dress. You look fabulous. Haha!"

"Thank you, Mister Grimmel," she replied, face flushing. It felt strange to Nicholas to see his CO react like a regular woman.

"Please, call me Aaron," he continued. "That goes for you as well, Captain Shepherd, and Yasmin. But only when we aren't in the lab, my dear."

"Of course, sir," Yasmin said.

Grimmel cupped his ear and leaned toward her. "What was that?"

"Of course, Aaron," she repeated, slightly uncomfortable to use his name.

"Better."

"You should definitely call me Avril then, Aaron," Haines said. She glanced at Nicholas. "You can continue using Colonel Haines."

They all laughed.

"Come in, come in," Grimmel said, stepping aside so they could enter. Even though his quarters were the largest in the compound, they weren't any more poshly decorated than any of the other apartments. A worn orange sofa joined an end table, television, and a pair of smaller chairs in the living room, while a hallway to the left led to two bedrooms and a larger bathroom.

Nicholas stopped and inhaled deeply. "What is that wonderful smell?" he asked.

"I went down to the kitchen after meeting with you in the hangar," Grimmel replied. "I cooked up a little something. It's nothing too fancy, the kitchens don't have a lot of my favorite herbs and spices and I didn't have time to fly back to HQ. But I believe you'll enjoy it."

"You cook?" Nicholas asked.

"I wasn't always the man I am today, Nicholas. And when you think about it, cooking is a science of its own. Chemical reactions, genetic composition, and all of that. Understanding those things is an excellent building block to more advanced pursuits." His gaze shifted past them, back to the still-open door. "Where's Luke?"

"He couldn't make it," Nicholas said. "He's sort of grounded."

"Sort-of? Elaborate."

"He broke some rules. The MPs caught him. Now he's doing community service, helping Lieutenant Carter out in the hangar."

Grimmel's face darkened slightly, just enough that Nicholas noticed before it brightened again. "I see. Well, hopefully I'll get to meet him once we're transferred to the Pilgrim. Which I'm absolutely certain will be any day now."

"About that, si... Aaron," Yasmin said. "I'm—"

"If you were planning to apologize, you can stop right there," Grimmel said. "No apologies needed. And no need to be cross with your husband for raising his concerns. He did the right thing, Yasmin."

"But the counter-inertial systems on the—"

"Yes, I'm aware," Grimmel said, cutting her off again. "I studied the systems before approving the prototypes."

"Then why did you recommend aborting the mission?"

He looked thoughtful for a moment. "Wine?" he asked, heading over to a combination dining and conference table that sat in an open area to the right. Grimmel had laid out a spread on it, with a seating for six. Roast vegetables, chicken, gravy, rice pilaf, and even an apple pie along with two bottles of wine.

He picked up one of the bottles. "Two years ago, these bottles sold for over ten thousand dollars each. I'm not saying that to brag. Do you know what they're worth now?"

"Nothing," Nicholas said.

"Exactly," Grimmel replied. "If I were one of the unfortunates stuck out in the wilds, I'd be lucky to trade one of these bottles for a can of sardines. I wish we could help those people. I wish we could help everyone. But even a man like me has limitations. And these things are worthless if we forget what truly matters." He paused and smiled. "Go ahead, ask me what that is."

"What matters?" Haines said, taking the bait.

"People," Grimmel replied. "The survival of the human race. Our exodus to the stars. We can't save everyone, but we can save hundreds of thousands. All the faith and trust in the world isn't enough to put that at risk."

"Excuse me, sir," Yasmin said. "Doesn't that statement imply a lack of faith and trust?"

"Hmmm," Grimmel said, rubbing at his beard. "I can see how you might arrive at that conclusion, and from a purely logical perspective that argument is solvent." He picked up a glass and poured some wine into it. "But that's only because you don't have all of the inputs."

"Are you going to fill me in?"

"Only if you stop calling me sir." Grimmel smiled and handed Yasmin the first glass before turning back to the table to pour another.

"Okay, Aaron," Nicholas said. "I'm game. If you have trust and faith that Foresight would have passed its tests, why did you recommend the abort?"

Grimmel handed Nicholas the next glass. "That's

why I invited you here, Nicholas. I have to admit, this isn't purely a social call. We have very important matters to discuss. Matters that could have an incalculable impact on the arkship program, and Project Foresight." He poured two more glasses, handing one to Colonel Haines before raising his glass up. "A toast. To the future."

"To the future," the others said, clinking their glasses.

"We can talk while we eat," Grimmel said. "Haha!"

Chapter 11

"Excuse me," Luke said, approaching five Marines grouped together near the hangar blast doors. They were busy with rags and lubricant, cleaning their rifles to ensure weapons that were put to the test of life and death every night remained in good working order. A tired-looking older woman with a bandage on her cheek looked up and met his eyes. Luke knew better than to look away if he wanted any measure of respect from her.

"Who are you?" she asked.

"Lucius Shepherd, ma'am," he replied. "I'm volunteering up here with my friends. We're just trying to help support you in any way we can."

The woman's hard expression softened to a smile. "Shepherd. You're the Captain's son?"

"Yes, ma'am."

"Your father's going to get us out of this shit, ain't that right?" one of the other Marines asked. He had light-colored peach fuzz on his face and sleeves rolled up to his elbows, exposing a large dragon tattoo on one forearm. "Every time I watch that bird of his take off my heart pounds like I'm with my girl for the first time all over again."

"What the hell are you talking about?" a third Marine said. She looked at Luke. "Don't pay Gills any mind. He thinks he's Don Juan or something."

"Don who?" Gills asked. "Never heard of him. Alls I'm saying is that I'm damn excited to get out of this place already. Auntie took a claw to the cheek last night." He nodded at the older woman. "Bastard missed taking her out by this much." He spread his thumb and forefinger, and then pulled them closer together. "That ugly ship there is our ticket to survival."

"Ugly?" the fourth Marine in the group said. A Black man who looked ready to take on the next wave of trife single-handed. "I think it's sleek."

"You got that right, Rocky," Auntie agreed, smiling at Luke. "I wish your father could take us joyriding in it. I bet it's a blast."

"That would be so cool. Like Auntie said, I'm Rocky."

"Nice to meet you, sir," Luke replied, reaching out to shake his hand.

Rocky laughed. "So polite. We're simple jarheads, man, not officers. That's Gills, Mackey, and of course, Auntie. Or sometimes we call her Sarge. And the quiet guy there is Toast."

Toast looked over at Luke, the reason for his nick-name immediately obvious. The entire left side of his face was badly scarred. "Childhood accident," he said, his voice slightly raspy. "I always thought that would be the worst thing that could ever happen to me." He laughed.

"Great to meet all of you," Luke said. "Like I said,

I'm volunteering to help out. Is there anything I can do for you?"

"Got any Budweiser?" Gills asked.

Grinning, Luke shook his head. "I've already raided the food supply a few times. I never found any beer."

"Damn shame," Rocky said.

"Do you know how to clean a rifle?" Auntie asked.

"No, ma'am."

"Do you want to learn?"

"Sure, but I'm supposed to help you, not the other way around."

"Letting us teach you something is helping," Rocky said. "Anything that gets the mind off the routine for a little while does that for us."

"Besides," Mackey said. "Once you know how to do it, you can clean all our rifles every night while we sit here like big shots and watch."

The Marines laughed. Luke laughed with them. "Okay, sure. Just tell me what to do?"

"We should probably start from scratch," Auntie said. "Let me put my MK back together and then I'll—"

Auntie stopped speaking immediately as the klaxon beside the blast doors suddenly sounded in one long, steady blare, the light flashing orange. Seconds later, the loud peal died out with a long whine, followed by Lieutenant Carter's voice over the loudspeaker.

"Attention all Marines. Attention all Marines. Spotters have eyes on a slick coming in from the east. Form up. This is not a drill. You know what to do."

"Shit," Rocky said, grabbing the pieces of his rifle he had laid out on a rag as they all quickly began reassembling their guns. "Bastards are early today."

Activity in the hangar increased as Marines jumped up and ran for their assigned positions. Groups of combatants hurried to the APCs while techs bounced from one Butcher to the next, pulling their charging cables and setting them in motion.

"Should I be worried?" Luke asked.

"Naw, nothing to worry about," Mackey said. "This is SOP. Standard operating procedure."

"Trife come every night," Gills said. "Screw the trife, man."

"There's a nest somewhere to the east of the compound," Auntie said. "We think it's underground because we haven't been able to find it. Every night they pour in from that direction and give us hell. The spotters catch sight of them about ten klicks out. Forward defenses will head out to harass them from there all the way back through four different choke points. Units take turns alternating positions so everyone has a fair shot at being on the front line. That's where we were last night, which is why I have this nice souvenir." She pointed to her cheek. "On a bad night, they'll get to the second choke point."

"What if they get through all four?" Luke asked.

"Never happen," Toast replied.

"Toast's right," Auntie said. "As long as we have enough ammunition and some Butchers left standing, they won't get through."

"But what if they do?"

"They'd still have to make it through the blast doors to get into the hangar. And then they'd have to get through the base defenses. Since we were front line last night, we get the easy job tonight, babysitting Foresight."

"The boring job, you mean," Gills said. "Might as well not even bother putting this MK back together. Not gonna need it."

"Your father wouldn't have let you anywhere near

the hangar if he thought you'd be in danger," Auntie said. "Although the trife *are* a couple of hours early today. It happens sometimes."

The blast doors slid open, stopping after leaving enough space for the APCs to get out. A few of the butchers climbed onto special racks on the back of the vehicles, hitching a ride as they pulled out of the hangar and down the slope to the abandoned part of the base.

Auntie finished putting her rifle back together before removing a hardened computerized tablet from a pocket on the leg of her fatigues. She tapped on the interface a few times, until a video feed appeared.

"This is a live feed from the lead APC," Auntie said. "We can watch the main event unfold from here."

"Hey, Luke," Jennifer said, approaching the Marines. "The base is under attack. We should get clear."

Briar and Scott followed close behind her.

"Just let me borrow a rifle," Scott said. "I can help out."

"Auntie," Luke said. "These are my friends. Jennifer, Briar, and Scott." He pointed to each of them.

"Nothing to worry about here, folks," Gills said. "We've essentially got the night off. Been here almost a year, trife have never breached the third choke point. Not once."

"It's fine here," Luke said. He motioned to Auntie's tablet. "I want to watch."

"Are you sure, bro?" Scott asked. "It can get pretty ugly, believe me."

"I may not have been on my own out there, but I've seen plenty of ugly too," Luke replied.

"We all have," Briar agreed.

"Besides, it might be cathartic to watch the Marines decimate those bastards."

"In that case, who has the popcorn?" Scott asked.

"And the beer," Rocky agreed.

"All right, that's enough chatter," Auntie said. "We're still on the clock. Luke, you're welcome to stay and watch for now, but if I give the order, you'll need to get clear at a run."

"Yes, ma'am," Luke said.

Auntie leaned over, using her pack to prop up the tablet. Luke took a moment to look around the hangar. Nearly all of the Marines were already gone, leaving only their bedrolls, discarded MRE wrappers, and personal effects behind. A pair of ragged Butchers remained in the hangar as well, the single red eye at the center of their large square heads active.

The tablet showed the scene from the front of the APC marked in the top left corner as A1. The vehicle had already cleared the eastern side of the base, passing through the open center of a half-collapsed fence and moving onto a road along flat terrain. The final choke point before the base quickly became visible ahead in the form of a man-made barrier across the road. Extending nearly a half-mile in either direction, it was composed of abandoned cars, old construction vehicles, sandbags, and other found debris. It created a twenty-foot high barrier with a single lane down the center. Metal bars had been welded to the vehicles, and wood planks ran across the detritus, forming walkways for the Marines to move safely about on should the trife break through the other choke points.

"Why don't the trife just go around?" Briar asked, noting the width of the choke point.

"Because they dumb," Gills said.

"They aren't dumb," Scott replied. "They exist to kill

humans. Marines are humans. Why would they go around? The base isn't the target. We are. All of us."

"Exactly," Auntie agreed, glancing at Scott. "Are you eighteen yet? You have the look of a Marine."

"Not yet," Scott replied. "Another year and a half. I don't think we'll still be Earthbound by then."

"Let's hope not," Rocky said.

"I spent almost a year alone out there," Scott said. "I'm pretty good at killing trife with arrows, knives, and bare hands. They're pretty brittle, actually."

"Yeah, they're built like birds," Rocky agreed. "Some big brain downstairs claimed it's because they grow so fast. Bones don't really have time to harden or some shit."

"Maybe if there weren't a metric ass ton of them, we would have stood a chance," Gills said. "I think I must have killed ten thousand of the bastards already. I don't want to have to off ten thousand more."

A1 passed through the center of the chokepoint to the next one two miles down the road, similar to the first. The third and fourth also had the same base materials, though the last barrier was considerably larger than the first.

The driver kept the APC back from the center of the area. As soon as it came to a stop, the camera shuddered as Marines jumped out and ran past it, rushing from the vehicles and scaling the makeshift walls. The butchers pounded past too, taking up positions in the center of the open lane.

Auntie picked up the tablet and switched the feed to one marked B1. From the view and height, it was obvious to Luke they were looking through one of the Butcher's eyes.

"This should be more exciting," she said.

"Not so far," Gills replied. "Booooorrrinnnggg."

"Look!" Briar said, pointing past Luke at the tablet.

An incline in the road reached its apex about five hundred feet or so from the Marine's barrier. A single trife appeared over the crest, its long, lean humanoid body bent slightly, its demonic head tilted upward toward the Marines on the wall. It opened its mouth to hiss, revealing rows of long, sharp teeth.

A single round hit the creature in the head, knocking it down.

"That was easy," Briar said.

"Wait for it," Rocky replied.

Another trife appeared, quickly taken down. Then another. And another. The first dozen or so succumbed immediately to a single round each.

Then, as if someone had their hand on an invisible spigot, the floodgates opened. Dozens more trife crested the hill at once, hissing as they frog-hopped agilely forward on both hands and feet, rushing the choke point.

"Here we go," Gills said.

Chapter 12

"Initial rush is the easiest to manage," Gills said as the Marines opened fire for real on the advancing aliens. The constant gunfire came through the feed as a rain-like patter, but dozens of the demons succumbed to Marine fire within the first few seconds.

"And they don't believe in tactics," Rocky said. "They just rush themselves right into our rifle fire and die by the hundreds."

"You don't need tactics when you can reproduce an army of ten thousand inside of a week," Auntie said. "That's what the researchers estimate a small nest can produce. I heard there's a nest in the Everglades that puts out nearly a hundred thousand a week, thanks to the abundant solar radiation."

"Why didn't we blast that nest?" Luke asked, mentally answering his own question. "It would have to be out in the open, wouldn't it?"

"It is, but we've given up on hunting nests. We're in full evac mode. Have you ever heard of the Vultures?"

"No. Should I?"

"I'm sure your father has. Led by Sergeant Caleb Card."

"Legend," Gills said.

"He's got a reputation," Auntie agreed. "Him and his whole team. If you need someone important pulled out of a real shitstorm, you send in the Vultures."

"I wouldn't be surprised if they came for Grimmel, in the event we somehow got pinned down here," Rocky said. "Oh, they noticed the Butchers. This should be fun."

Luke watched the trife continue pouring across the road and the shoulders on either side. They rushed head-long into the Marine crossfire, collapsing like waves against a seashore. A bunch of the demons spotted the butchers, and they seemed more angered by the robots than they did the Marines. They changed direction at the walls, rushing the metal men, mouths open in silent hisses.

"They kill humans like we swat bugs, without a thought," Gills said. "But they freaking *hate* Butchers. Gang up on them every time like flies on shit."

Through the Butcher's feed, they saw the head of its axe-bladed arm come up in preparation for the trife charge. Some of the trife collapsed, hit by rounds from either side of the barrier. The first trife to leap at the Butcher was met with a hard swing that sliced off its head, leaving the body to smack harmlessly into the robot's metal shell. More trife lunged at the machine, slashing at it with their claws. It crushed their throats and tossed them aside with one hand, the other swinging the axe to slice others in half, sever their limbs, or decapitate them.

Ten trife fell to the Butcher within seconds, but the demons continued to intensify their effort, still more of them joining in to bring the robot down. Even laid out on the ground, the Butcher didn't stop slashing and hacking, tireless for as long as its battery lasted. Meanwhile, the Marines continued blasting the trife from the wall, killing hundreds. More and more replaced them.

"This is crazy," Briar said, watching the assault as dozens of trife reached the Butcher. It slashed and choked and kicked as they scratched and grabbed at it, eager to put it out of action. One of the trife wound up directly in front of the camera, giving them all a close-up view of its large teeth and demonic eyes. The Butcher ripped it away and tossed it to the ground, heel-stomping it until it died.

"Wow!" Jennifer said, impressed by the robot.

The fighting continued for nearly another minute as the trife pressed the attack on the Butcher, so many demons clinging to its hard shell—scratching, clawing, and biting at the metal and the filler epoxy—it limited the machine's effectiveness. The Marines moved around it, falling back from the wall as the slick grew too thick to manage.

Rounds cut into the trife, the Marines helping free the robot as they retreated, enabling the robot to throw the dead bodies off and get back up. The Marines positioned themselves behind it, using it for cover and shooting past it as it stepped backward, swinging its axe, in retreat.

So far, the heavy machine guns mounted to the tops of the APCs had been silent, but they blazed to life now, their thunderous roar a muffled crackle through the feed. Large, heavy rounds tore through the demons, mowing them down like blades of grass. The sudden barrage gave the Marines the time they needed to get back to the vehicles, quickly loading up and making U-turns to head back toward the base. They only stopped long enough for the Butchers to climb on board before accelerating away, leaving the trife slick to advance on them at a faster pace.

"They breached the first choke point," Mackey said.

"Is that bad?" Briar asked.

"They do seem a bit more aggressive today, but it's still nothing to worry about. Even if they make it to the third choke point that leaves plenty of space between us and them. You're fine."

"Okay. Good."

Auntie leaned forward, switching the feed to B6. Another Butcher, this one waiting at the second choke point. The APCs from the first became visible through its feed a moment later, well ahead of the oncoming slick.

"How many do you suppose they killed?" Luke asked.

"At least a thousand," Rocky replied. "Not their best effort, to be honest. Sergeant Isaiah didn't even let them get close enough to use bayonets before calling the retreat."

"Pansy-ass," Gills said.

"A thousand irreplaceable rounds," Auntie said, voicing the downside of the trife death toll. "And they'll make up for their losses within a day or two."

"The Butchers from the first position will drop off to bolster the second choke point," Mackey explained. "The Marines will fall back to the third choke point and regroup. They'll see how many Marines they have bullets to support and send the rest back here to reload and join the hangar defense."

The APCs went around B6, vanishing from sight. A moment later, B1 entered B6's peripheral vision, easily identifiable by the claw marks in its hard shell.

"How long do these attacks usually last?" Luke asked.

"Depends," Rocky replied. "Sometimes only a few hours. Sometimes all night. We'll see what they throw at us next. Whatever it is, we'll turn the tide on them pretty damn quick."

The Marines at the second choke point were already on the walls, and they started shooting sporadically, taking out targets of opportunity from a distance. The pattern continued for a few more minutes before the pace of gunfire slowly increased. The oncoming mass of trife were visible through the Butcher's feed by the time the barrage had reached a nearly constant rhythm.

B6 didn't wait for the trife to spot it. It launched its attack, running forward to meet them. The feed shook as it lumbered toward the writhing black blob.

"Yeah, you get 'em Butch!" Gills said.

The scene played out similarly to the attack on the first choke point, though it seemed to Luke that the extra Butchers served as an additional distraction to the trife, drawing them from the Marines and enabling them to riddle the thick swells of bodies going after the robots.They didn't care they were dying by the hundreds. And why should they? Fear was nothing to them. They were hard-wired to obey their queen, who could produce them in the thousands in virtually the blink of an eye. So what did she care how many she lost in battle? They were nothing to her. Expendable.

"There sure are a lot of them today," Toast said, looking past the immediate mass of trife to the huge slick moving in behind them..

"Yeah," Mackey agreed.

The mood in the unit of Marines seemed to shift, from comfortable observation to a tense alertness. The situation wasn't developing the way it normally did. The way it should.

Something had changed.

"We'll hold them back at choke point three," Rocky said, trying to sound optimistic. "I'll take bets on that."

B6 fought hard, fighting through the trife that approached it like a swarm of gigantic locusts. The Sergeant in charge of the choke point must have called a retreat, because the Marines on the walls started coming down, the demons close enough to lunge at them as they fled. Luke flinched when he saw one of the Marines go down under a pile of four trife. A second Marine tried to help him, only to be overwhelmed himself. A moment later, B6's feed was blotted out by dark alien flesh, the trife finally gathering around it in great enough numbers to pull it down.

"Come on Butch," Gills said. "Get back up."

Auntie tapped the screen to switch the feed.

Her head jerked up as the entire hangar began to shake.

Chapter 13

"I never would have taken you for such an incredible cook," Nicholas said after swallowing his first bite of the Chicken Adobo Grimmel had prepared. Moist, juicy, and flavorful despite the man's lamenting the lack of spices in the kitchen. "At least something positive came from another planet."

Grimmel coughed, choking a little on his own bite. "What do you mean?"

"The gravy," Nicholas said. "It's too good to be from this solar system."

"Ah. Figure of speech. Right. Haha! Thank you for the compliment, Nicholas. I try my best to be a good host."

"This *is* fantastic," Yasmin agreed. "I haven't had anything like this in ages."

"And you probably won't ever have something like it again," Haines said. "Once we're on the ark ship, we won't have access to chicken anymore."

"That's not completely true," Grimmel said. "The ship has culture farms on board. Meats will be grown on scaffolding instead of blood and bone, but it should be a decent substitute."

"Surely not enough for forty-thousand people," Nicholas said. "The resources for that would be immense."

"An astute observation. You're right. Foods we enjoyed as simple staples here will become a luxury out there, but I do believe the trade will be worth it."

"How could it not?" Colonel Haines said.

"Speaking of which," Nicholas said. "You mentioned that you had business to discuss."

"Nick, have a little more wine and cool it," Yasmin said. "We have all night to talk business, and this is too good to let anything detract from it."

"Sorry, Yazz. I don't want to spoil the mood or the fine taste of the meal, but I think it will all digest better if we get this conversation out of the way."

Yasmin glowered at his pushback, which only added to her general annoyance with him. "Not for me, it won't."

"Nicholas has a point," Grimmel agreed. "If there's one thing I've learned over the years, it's that there's no time like the present." He smiled before taking another bite of his meal, talking as he chewed. "Have you heard anything about the plans for Foresight once the systems testing is completed?"

"I haven't," Nicholas replied. "To be honest, I was just wondering about that earlier today. Once we're on the Pilgrim, what's going to happen to the prototype?"

"The perfect question," Grimmel said. "And I already have a potential answer, but it all comes down to you, Nicholas."

"Me?" Nicholas said. "What do I have to do with it?"

Grimmel took a sip of wine. Placing the glass back

on the table, his gaze shifted between the three guests. "I'm going to let you in on a little secret. Actually, it's a pretty big secret, since my lead developer doesn't even know about it yet. Haha!" He paused as though he was trying to decide on how to broach the subject. "The ark ships are supposed to each go in a separate direction, toward systems within one hundred light years of us where we *think* there are inhabitable planets. Seventeen ships. Seventeen directions. Seventeen worlds. That's nothing you don't already know. But I think we can all agree the process is inefficient, with a high probability of leaving a minimum of five to seven of the ark ships stranded, floating in deep space or orbiting an otherwise toxic environment. Not a pleasant future at all."

"You're talking about recon," Nicholas said. "A scouting mission."

Grimmel smiled. "I knew I wouldn't have to feed you very many crumbs. Yes, that's my consideration."

"But there's no way to survey a planet a hundred light years away from here, is there? And no way to go there in person."

Grimmel lowered his head. "Yes, you're right, of course. No way to get there. I should have thought of that." He fell silent for a moment before picking his head up. "Unless there *is* a way to get there."

"That's not possible," Yasmin said.

"Define not possible," Grimmel challenged.

"Sir, I've been with your company for five years. I admit, I've already seen so many things I never thought possible that I shouldn't question this. But you're talking about faster than light travel. To hit seventeen planets within the next two months, you're talking about *a lot* faster than light travel. I don't know everything, but I've never encountered any scientific theories that would make something like that work. And even if you figured it out, why would you keep it secret? We could use the same technology for the ark ships. We could shuttle back and forth to pick up everyone. I–"

"I appreciate your thought process," Grimmel said, putting up his hand to interrupt her. "And your passion for the idea. Obviously, if it was possible to do more than I'm aiming to do, I would have done it already."

"So what are you aiming to do?" Nicholas asked. "I know this has to do with Foresight. And it doesn't take a genius to guess it's related to the ship's ability to carry a small crew."

Grimmel shrugged. "I think the goal is self-explanatory based on the information I've already provided."

"A little more description would be helpful," Haines said.

"And also, what this has to do with us," Nicholas added.

Grimmel didn't hurry to explain. He took another bite of his chicken. Another sip of his wine. Nicholas didn't touch his food, growing antsy with the suspense. He liked things as direct as possible. Up front and blunt.

"Well?" he said after nearly a minute passed.

"Where was I?" Grimmel asked.

"Elaboration," Nicholas replied.

"You can start with how you plan to get Foresight to seventeen different planets before the ark ships take off," Yasmin said. "Pioneer is scheduled for launch in forty-three days. Pilgrim in sixty-one. Deliverance, ninety-four. She's the last ship out."

"Haha! Yes. Let's start there. I'm sure you both noticed the slip test in the mission parameters?"

"I noticed," Nicholas said. "But I didn't know what it

meant. We didn't cover it in the briefing because it was added in the patch."

"From what I understood, it was supposed to be a simulated test of automated evasive maneuvers," Yasmin said. "A progression of navigational and control challenges."

"Technically, that's correct, Yasmin," Grimmel said. "The slip test is related to navigation, but not precisely in the way you were thinking. I intentionally obscured the true purpose of the test, primarily because it's a risky maneuver without proper neural network contribution. The tolerances are tighter than racing around the Moon. Which, consequently, is the primary reason I called for the test run to be aborted. I didn't want you to enter the slip test based on the performance of the AI."

"I see," Yasmin said. Nicholas sensed her annoyance shift from him to her boss. "I wish you had said that in the first place, sir."

"It wasn't possible at the time, but that was the catalyst for my bringing you here, now. I decided the final tests would be smoother if I let you in on my secret. But understand, this can't go any further than this room, and the four of us."

"Why not?" Haines asked. "We should report this to General Nguyen."

Grimmel shook his head. "No, Avril. The military's plans are set. Giving them anything that could lead to adjusting tactics might prove costly all the way around. The best approach is to act first and report later." He locked eyes with Haines. "To achieve the fullness of my plan does require your complicity."

"You mean outside the chain of command," Haines guessed.

Grimmel nodded. "An offense worthy of a court-martial, if such a thing would even be possible these days. You'll be on board the Pilgrim and relegated to civilian status long before that could occur. But, there are some potential personal benefits." His smile shifted, from friendly to disarming. Nicholas almost laughed at the way his CO melted under the wealthy man's gaze.

"What do you need me to do?" she asked.

"Foresight has berthing for six," Grimmel replied. "A pilot and a unit of your best Marines. I wanted Caleb Card and his Vultures, but there was no way for me to get them here without revealing the nature of my request."

"I see," Haines replied. "I think I can make that happen without risking a court-martial, or revealing the nature of your plan. After all, Marines are dying out on the field every day. But you need to make a strong case for why I should."

"I thought I already did," Grimmel replied. "Five to seven ships stranded at a minimum. That's two hundred thousand lives. I'm only asking for five Marines."

"And a pilot," Nicholas said, glancing over at Yasmin. "There's only one pilot qualified to fly Foresight, and he'd need to leave his family behind to do it."

"Yes," Grimmel said. "That's why we needed to have this conversation."

"And the wine is to help me agree?"

Grimmel laughed. "Not at all. But you deserve whatever compensation I can offer for considering the request."

"What's to consider?" Yasmin asked. "Two hundred thousand lives could be saved because of you, Nick."

Nicholas nodded. He wasn't surprised Yasmin didn't hesitate to push him. She was so career oriented. He needed to at least consider his family first. "That's not lost on me. I'm thinking about Luke."

"Luke is almost an adult. He needs to take responsibility for himself. Besides, this whole plan is pointless if you aren't supposed to make it back before the ships leave." Yasmin looked at Grimmel. "Unless you've solved real-time interstellar communications, too?"

Grimmel shook his head. "Not yet."

"So what's the real risk?"

"I assume the plan is to crew a unit of Marines for a reason," Nicholas said. "Instead of scientists who can make judgments about the quality of the planets we visit."

"The habitable quality of the worlds will be self-evident," Grimmel replied. "Considering we have aliens knocking at our door nightly, my assumption is that you may encounter other hostiles. While I hope you won't need to disembark during your mission, the possibility does exist. In that situation, it's better to be prepared."

"Traveling faster than light, exploring new worlds. It sounds pretty exciting to me, Shepherd," Haines said.

"Project Foresight," Nicholas said. "This is what it meant all along, isn't it? The rest of the stuff was all smokescreen."

"Not smokescreen," Grimmel countered. "Fringe benefits on the path to scouting the potential new worlds ahead of time. The ark ships need the AI under development."

"Okay, but explain that to me then. You're saying we can zip across the universe, but we can't develop a neural network that can do some standard navigation?"

"What?" Yasmin said, taking offense at the statement. "There's nothing standard about what we're doing. I thought you understood that."

Nicholas winced, already wishing he could retract his choice of words. He would need to extract his foot from his mouth for that to happen. "I do. I didn't mean it that way. It's just… I don't know. Maybe it's because I don't understand the tech, but there seems to be a Grand Canyon sized gap between those two things, in terms of technological advancement."

"No technology develops in a straight line," Yasmin argued. "Sometimes different concepts leapfrog one another. Take the pyramids in Egypt for example. They were built thousands of years ago, and we still don't know how they did it. Even so, I'm as interested as anything in how you did it, sir."

"I'm sure you are," Grimmel said. "But if I don't have a pilot, there's no sense moving forward. The neural network's operations are satisfactory for the ark ships."

All eyes turned back to Nicholas. He looked at each of them. Grimmel, Colonel Haines, Yasmin. His mind rotated to his conversation with Luke. The fact that his son had so readily accepted volunteering in the hangar was a good sign of his growing maturity.

"You have a pilot," he said.

"Haha!" Grimmel replied, raising his wine glass. "Cheers to you, Captain Shepherd."

"Now tell us more about how this goes down."

"Of course. I…" Grimmel trailed off, his expression going flat, his eyes fixed into the distance.

"Aaron, are you okay?" Haines asked when he remained that way for more than a few seconds.

"No," he replied, his mood suddenly dour. "None of us are."

An unexpected knock on the door caused Nicholas to

flinch. When Grimmel didn't move to answer it, he hurried to the door and pulled it open.

"Captain Shepherd," Second Lieutenant Ames said, his face flushed. "Is Colonel Haines with you?"

"I'm here, Ames. What's going on?" Haines said, getting to her feet and approaching the door. Ames' eyes stuck to her dress for a moment before he looked her in the eye and came to stiff attention.

"Colonel Haines. The base is under attack."

Chapter 14

"W...What's going on?" Briar asked, her voice quivering.

"I don't know," Luke replied. "But I don't like it."

"Attention all Marines," Lieutenant Carter said over the loudspeaker. "This is a red alert. I repeat, this is a red alert. A second slick of trife are on the mountain. Spotters have confirmed a queen. Assume defensive posture. Brace for incoming."

"Shit," Auntie hissed, grabbing the tablet as she stood up. "Luke, you and your friends need to get out of here, now." She tucked the tablet back in its pocket and picked up her helmet, dropping it on her head. The other Marines did the same.

"A queen?" Jennifer said. "I don't understand."

"Bad news," Scott replied. "If a queen is coming our way, she's looking for a new place to make a nest and she's decided on the facility."

"Why now?" Briar asked.

"I don't know. Bad luck, I guess. Auntie, get me a rifle. I can fight."

Auntie turned to Scott. "You're too young. You need to get into the bunker with the others."

"I'm sorry, ma'am, but we both know the bunker isn't going to save us from a queen. Our only chance is to fight."

Auntie froze. Then she nodded. The hangar continued to shake, which seemed impossible to Luke. How could there be so many trife on the mountain they could make this huge cement and steel structure tremble like Jell-O?

"All units are falling back," Auntie said, listening to the comms. "They'll regroup with us here in the hangar. Rocky, help set up the M2s while I get these kids armed."

"I don't know how to use a gun," Briar said.

"Point the muzzle at the enemy and hold down the trigger until the gun clicks empty," Auntie replied. "There will be too many of them for you to miss."

"What? No, we need to evacuate."

"Normally, I'd agree with you. But our bolt hole is up there." She pointed toward the top of the mountain. "Which is also where the trife are."

Briar panicked. "We're going to die, aren't we? After everything, it's all going to end just like that."

"We might die," Auntie said. "But we'll die fighting and that's better than hiding without taking any of them with us. Follow me."

Auntie ran toward the rear of the hangar while Rocky and the other Marines in her unit made for the front, taking positions closer to the hangar door. Luke ran after her, grabbing Briar's arm when she didn't move.

"Briar, come on," he said. "We can do this."

"No, I can't."

"They need us, B. We can make a difference."

She looked up at him with terrified eyes, but nodded and followed him, chasing after Auntie.

"Sergeant Ramos," Lieutenant Carter said, emerging from the rear doors to the compound already outfitted with a helmet and hardened vest. "What are you doing?"

"Sir, I'm getting them rifles."

"They need to go to the bunker."

"Yeah, she told us that already," Luke said. "And we told her that we're not stupid, and we know the score. We want to go down fighting, if we're going to go down."

Like Auntie, Carter considered it for a moment before acquiescing. "Fine. I can't argue with that. But we're going to need runners to bring fresh magazines to the defense. You'll be more useful that way."

"I think I'll be more useful with a gun," Scott said.

"Fine. We don't have time to argue. Ramos, get back to your unit. I'll show them what to do."

"Yes, sir," Auntie said. She turned to them again. "Good luck."

"You too," Luke said. "Give 'em hell."

Auntie nodded and hurried off. Carter grabbed a rifle off the nearby rack and tossed it to Scott. He caught the weapon, checked the magazine, and released the safety.

"Not my first rodeo," he said.

Carter wasn't impressed. "You three, the magazine crates are back there." She pointed to a stack of boxes in the corner. A pair of dollies rested nearby. "Two kinds. MK ammo. M2 ammo. They're labeled. Load an even number of each, bring them to the front line. No more than one pair per platoon at a time. If they need to fall back, we don't want them tripping over boxes and losing all of that valuable ammo."

"Fall back to where?" Jennifer asked.

Carter glared at her. "Just do it."

Jennifer nodded.

"Luke, your father never taught you to shoot?"

"I know how to shoot, Lieutenant," Luke replied.

"Good. Grab a rifle. You and Scott will run cover for these two. Anything tries to take them out, you need to take them out first."

"Yes, sir. Does my father know what's happening?"

"If he doesn't yet, he will soon enough. He needs to pilot the Reaper."

Carter lowered her voice to speak into her comms. A moment later, the hangar doors began slowly sliding open.

"What are you doing?" Briar asked. "Letting them in?"

"Letting our people back in," Luke said, going to the rack and taking one of the rifles. He had never fired anything larger than an M18, but he had a vague idea what to expect. "Let's get back to the ammo and prep the dollys."

The group left Carter behind, hurrying to the ammo carts.

"Am I the only one that noticed the two men have the guns, and the two women are pushing the carts?" Jennifer said.

"I'll trade you," Luke said. "You have to know how to use a gun; your mother was a Marine."

"Give me the rifle," Jennifer said. "You're stronger, which means you can load the crates faster. Plus, it's equal opportunity."

Luke handed her the MK and joined Briar at the crates. "Help me lift them onto the dolly." He took one side, she took the other, and they heaved one onto a rolling cart.

"Here they come," Scott said, getting Luke's attention. "The Marines, I mean."

Luke looked past the open hangar doors. A line of APCs zoomed up the slope toward the hangar, their heavy machine guns firing at something positioned over the top of the entrance. That something appeared a heartbeat later as the first of the trife slick began dropping from overhead, landing between the incoming Marines and their next line of defense.

Immediately, the two units of Marines already inside the hangar opened fire, letting loose with a pair of large machine guns that had been hastily bolted into the ground. Metal barriers quickly went up in front of them, the heavy slugs tearing into the trife, ripping them apart before they could recover from their drop off the mountainside.

"Let's go!" Luke said, grabbing the next crate and dropping it onto the dolly. "Briar, two more, then we split up."

He helped her load her dolly as more of the trife dropped down off the mountain, the Marines catching them in a crossfire. Between the M2s and the APCs, they didn't last long enough to block the entrance to the hangar.

"Come on," he said. "Take the closer side. I've got the other." He pushed his cart, Jennifer sticking close as they ran toward the two fixed defensive positions. Luke's heart pounded, but his head remained clear. Everything had happened too fast to stop to think about the danger.

Right now, he had a job to do.

He sprinted across the hangar with the cart, ducking to pass beneath Foresight to reach the other side. The shooting stopped suddenly as the APCs reached the hangar doors, colliding with trife as they charged through, each of them splitting left or right to clear the line of fire for the M2s. The break in the chaos only lasted a few seconds before the crackling thunks of gunfire returned, trife continuing to fall at a rapid pace.

Luke skidded to a stop as one of the APCs came to a rest in front of him. The door opened and Marines jumped out, the first through hurrying to him. "We need fresh mags!"

Luke grabbed one of the crates and tugged it off the cart before unlatching it and throwing it open. The Marines approached it hungrily, snapping up the magazines inside, one for each of the rifles, two more for their belts. Luke didn't wait before moving on, bringing the M2 rounds to the fixed guns.

The gunfire intensified as the Marines in the APCs joined the defense. The final choke point was too much for the trife to handle and they fell in bunches, their corpses quickly clogging up the entrance.

Careful to stay away from the Marines' fire lanes, Luke circled the APCs to the fixed machine gun battery. One of the Marines noticed him, smiling when he saw the ammo crate.

"Good man!" he shouted over the shooting, lowering his rifle and helping Luke with the crate. "Grab as many as you can for the APCs, next trip, unless it's over by then."

"Yes, sir," Luke replied.

The klaxon on the hangar doors sounded again, flashing yellow as the doors started their slow trudge toward closing up tight.

Luke ran back for more ammo, his heart pounding. Watching the Marines work and the lines of trife collapse at the hangar entrance, he felt certain the defenses would hold long enough for the doors to close. So far, very few of the demons had managed to cross the threshold alive, none of them making it more than a step before a Marine gunned them down.

Once the doors were shut, they would be safe. The trife wouldn't linger outside after they were cut off. That wasn't their style. They would go back to their nest and wait to try again the next night.

Luke froze as an inhuman scream so loud it rose above the sound of the klaxon, so loud and blood-curdling it sent a chill down his spine. He winced at the pain in his ears as he turned his head back toward the hangar doors. His confidence in the Marines' victory flagged in a heartbeat when he saw the trife queen.

She appeared at the outside edge of the right blast door. Easily eighteen feet tall, she reached up with a claw and smashed the klaxon off the bulkhead, silencing the blaring noise. The light continued to flash, but she ignored it.

With a massive head and gigantic teeth, her limbs were thicker, stronger than the others, and she had a hide that appeared to be made of thick rubber. Luke could swear her small eyes looked right at him where he stood in the back of the hangar, making contact that kept his feet riveted to the spot.

The queen opened her mouth and screamed again before bursting forward, hitting the corner of the blast door with such force that it shuddered and cracked. It stopped moving, bent on its tracks.

It would never close again.

The Marines turned their guns on her, but she moved out of the line of fire, vanishing back behind the blast door while more of her offspring surged through the entrance.

Luke finally managed to pry his feet off the deck. Making it to the crates, he lifted them on his own, adrenaline helping him manage the heavy loads. He had just finished stacking three of them when Briar returned with her own empty dolly.

"Jen, keep us covered," Scott shouted, putting his rifle on the floor to help her load her cart. They piled the crates up quickly, not speaking as Luke and Briar broke back toward their respective sides to re-equip the Marines, Jennifer with Briar, giving her cover. Scott picked up his rifle and resumed shooting as he jogged along beside Luke.

The trife queen screamed again. A moment later, she appeared in the open space between the hangar doors. Bullets smacked her body, but she shrugged them off as she exploded into the hangar, reaching one of the M2 placements in one quick lunge to swat the gunner and the Marines with him aside before turning on the other gun.

"Shit," Scott said. "This is where we die."

Chapter 15

"Spell it out, Corporal," Colonel Haines said. "We come under attack every night. Why are you here?"

Ames' voice quivered as he spoke. "Sir, a second slick of trife is coming over the mountain. It's at least five times larger than the eastern slick, and the spotters say they ID'ed a queen."

"What?" Haines hissed, her head turning toward Nicholas.

"Luke is in the hangar," Nicholas said, sudden panic racing through him. He had only seen a trife queen a couple of times before from the air. He knew what kind of damage the larger, stronger, more vicious trife could do. "I need to get the Reaper in the air." With the drone, he could better help the Marines.

He started for the door without waiting for Haines' approval or dismissal. In the moment, he forgot about everything except Luke.

"Nicholas, wait," Grimmel said behind him, his voice so commanding it brought him to a full stop.

He whipped his head back to the scion. "My son."

"I know," Grimmel replied, rising from his seat and crossing to the apartment's bedroom. "Give me ten seconds."

Tension rushed into Nicholas' legs as Grimmel disappeared. He didn't want to wait even one more second, but something about Grimmel's tone suggested he would be better off if he did.

Yasmin came over to him and wrapped his hand in hers. "Nick, what does this mean?"

He met her gaze. "It means we're out of time. The best we can hope to do is get as many people out of the base as possible before the trife overwhelm us. It's over, Yazz."

The words were sour coming out of his mouth and bitter as Yasmin received them. "Over? It can't be over. Not now. Not when we're so close."

"There's nothing we can do," Nicholas replied. "We have enough to hold against one small slick. Not one small and one large, and especially not a large one with a queen at its head. It's impossible."

"Didn't we just have a whole conversation about the impossible?" Yasmin asked, trying hard to stay positive. Nicholas knew she was worried about Luke too.

Grimmel returned from his bedroom with a metal box in his arms. He dropped it onto the floor next to Nicholas and knelt to open the lid, revealing a small armory of guns and ammunition.

"Like I said before," Grimmel explained. "It's always best to be prepared." He handed an M18 handgun to Nicholas, along with a pair of magazines. "Colonel Haines." He passed her one of the MK rifles when she looked, keeping a second for himself.

"What about me?" Yasmin asked.

Grimmel smiled, handing her a second M18 and extra rounds. "I didn't know you could shoot."

"I don't need this," Nicholas said in response to the weapon. "I just need to get to the drone control room."

"Forget the drone," Grimmel said. "It won't help. The base is already lost. Only the bravest will admit it and adjust their plans accordingly." He looked directly at Colonel Haines, who nodded.

"I need to call the evacuation," she said. "Corporal, with me. Captain Shepherd, do whatever you can to get to safety."

"Yes, ma'am," Nicholas replied, but she was already out the door, running in her heels to get to the CIC. "This night turned to shit in a hurry," he added.

"You have no idea," Grimmel replied, straightening up after emptying the crate.

"What's your play, Aaron?"

"Our play, Nicholas. Luke is our top priority. We need to get him to safety."

"At least we agree. He's got to be out of the hangar by now if the base is under attack. We'll intercept him on his way back to our quarters."

"Lead the way, Captain."

Nicholas nodded. In the moment, he was too worried about Luke to think about how calm Grimmel remained despite the fearful urgency of the situation. It was a little odd that a man like Aaron Grimmel owned Marine-level firepower and seemed to know how to use it, but the last two years had taught a lot of people skills they never imagined they'd need before the trife arrived.

He ran out of the apartment, sprinting through the corridors back to the emergency stairwell leading out of the civilian area. MPs were already in the hallways, knocking on doors and ordering the scientists to prepare for evacuation. Colonel Haines would surely make an announcement too once she reached the CIC.

Nicholas entered the stairwell, taking the steps two at a time as he raced to the top floor of the compound. Grimmel easily kept pace with him, not even breathing hard as they charged up the steps. Yasmin fell further behind, but Nicholas didn't consider slowing for her. She wouldn't want him to stop for anything before they knew Luke was safe.

The emergency lights on the walls of the stairwell ceased flashing orange and began to flash red. Haines' voice echoed in the enclosed space, spilling out of the loudspeakers connected to the warning lights.

"Attention. Attention. This is Colonel Avril Haines. All personnel are ordered to head to their nearest evacuation zone for escort out of the facility. I repeat, all personnel are ordered to head to their nearest evacuation zone for escort out of the facility. This is not a drill. This is not a drill."

Nicholas grunted, pushing himself harder to get up the damn steps. He needed to be out before the rest of the people in the base clogged up the corridors.

Throwing himself through the door at the top of the steps, Nicholas' heart leaped to his throat when he immediately heard the sound of gunfire, much too close to be coming from the hangar. He spun to his right, spotting a pair of trife at the end of the corridor, moving through the base unopposed. They hissed when they saw him, immediately rushing his way.

Two cracks from Grimmel's rifle and both trife went down.

"They're already in the base?" Yasmin said breathlessly as she caught up to Nicholas and saw the trife.

"They must have found the escape hatch," Grimmel said. "They're entering the facility from both ends."

"If we can't get out..." Yasmin said, her voice trailing off as another group of trife came around the corner. They reacted the same way as the first pair, and suffered the same fate as Grimmel cut them down, one bullet for each demon. His aim was impeccable.

"Where'd you learn to shoot?" Nicholas asked.

"I'm a man of many talents," Grimmel replied. "Let that be a reminder never to underestimate anyone."

"We're going to die down here," Yasmin said. "We're trapped."

"There's another way out for you," Grimmel said. "We need to find Luke and get him out of here."

"Why do you want us to save Luke so badly?" Nicholas asked. "Not that I disagree with the idea, but what's in it for you?"

"Family is important to me," Grimmel replied. "More important than you realize."

"Then stay behind Yasmin. Don't let them get to her from the rear."

"Affirmative, Captain." Grimmel backed up a step, shooting another trife as it cleared the corner. "We should hurry."

Nicholas took off at a run, fighting the urge to sprint as fast as he could so he wouldn't leave Yasmin behind. The chaos inside the facility increased as he crossed through the corridors, the MPs he passed rushing back toward the escape hatch, heavily armed and ready to fight. It should have been Marines heading back that way, but they were no doubt busy enough in the hangar.

Where he had left Luke.

Where he should have been safe.

The only thing that kept him from blaming himself

for his son's predicament was the fact that with the escape hatch located and breached, Luke wasn't safe anywhere. Maybe that would help him feel better later, once he knew Luke was alive. His mind refused to process any other thoughts before that.

Gunfire echoed in the corridors behind them as the MPs engaged the trife. More military personnel turned the corner ahead, running in their direction. Comms specialists, techs, and other USSF enlisted non-combatants, they had hastily grabbed rifles from the armory to join the defense.

"Captain Shepherd," Duffy said, spotting him as he entered the next passageway. The older, slightly overweight Control Operator carried a rifle and an ammo belt cinched around his waist. He paused in front of Nicholas.

"Duff, I'm looking for Luke," Nicholas said, stopping to speak to him. "Have you seen him?"

"No. I'm sorry. But word is the hangar is about to be overrun. Haines directed everyone who can fight to the escape hatch to try to clear a path out while the Marines hold off the main group. You should go that way too, Shep."

"Not without Luke," Nicholas replied. "Good luck, Duff."

"You too," Duffy said before continuing on.

Nicholas, Yasmin, and Grimmel did the same, making it to Nicholas' quarters.

"Luke!" Nicholas shouted as he shoved the door open. "Luke, are you in here? Luke!"

No response. Nicholas ran to his room, checking it and the bathroom before hurrying back to the front door where Grimmel and Yasmin waited. Yasmin's expression had paled again as she realized Luke wasn't there.

"We'll find him," Nicholas said. "We aren't far from the hangar."

He whirled toward a hiss coming from down the corridor, handgun coming up as a group of trife turned the corner, coming from the direction of the hangar. He beat Grimmel to the punch this time, taking out the lead pair of demons before the other man smoothly dispatched the rest.

"They've overrun the hangar," Yasmin said, tearing up again. "He's lost, Nick."

"Don't you give up on me, Yazz," Nicholas said, voice hard. "I won't accept he's gone until I see for myself."

"A small group could have broken through, it doesn't mean the fighting is over," Grimmel said. "And it doesn't mean Luke was anywhere near the hangar."

"Where else would he be?" Yasmin asked.

"He could have gone anywhere," Nicholas replied. "Maybe the MP station. Maybe the CIC. We start at the hangar and go from there."

He grabbed Yasmin's hand and started running.

Chapter 16

Luke went deathly still, stunned by fear as the trife queen turned on the other M2 position, her high decibel scream so loud it reverberated through the hangar, nearly drowning out the sound of gunfire. The M2's large shells tore into the queen, penetrating her thick hide and drawing blood.

He thought for a moment she might go down, but she gathered herself and leaped at the gunner, who had no time to duck. Her razor-sharp claw sliced backbone-deep across his belly, tearing him wide open. She grabbed him as he clutched at his entrails, tossing him aside like a rag doll trailing its stuffing.

Her tail wrapped around the M2 and tore it from its mooring. As if the heavy gun weighed virtually nothing, she threw it at one of the APCs, pushing the armored vehicle back into the Marines taking cover behind it. Some managed to flee, but most went down under the vehicle's crushing weight. The pause in Marine gunfire allowed her offspring to swarm the vehicle and come down on the surviving Marines before they could get their guns up to fire.

"Luke!" Jennifer shouted behind him, pulling on his arm. He looked over at her, his mind stuck in neutral from indecision. "Snap out of it! We need to get out of here."

"Where are we going to go?" Briar asked, tears streaming down her face as she cowered behind Jennifer, looking frantically around for a way out.

"There's a bolt hole in the rear of the base," Scott said. "That's the way out. You three should go. I'm staying here with the Marines."

"But Scott—" Briar started to argue.

"Not your decision," he replied, shouldering his rifle and shooting at a group of trife headed straight for them. His aim was spot on, the trife collapsing under his burst of rapid fire. He looked back at his friends. "Now get out of here. I can take care of myself."

"Luke, come on," Briar said, motioning toward the hangar door. "If he wants to stay here and die, that's his choice. I want to live."

Luke glanced at Scott, at Briar, and then at the scene near the blast doors. The queen's arrival had changed everything, her assault on the M2s reducing the defenses enough to allow the regular trife access to the hangar. More and more of them survived entry, getting through the Marine's sporadic crossfire and attacking them head-on. Each fallen Marine meant more trife got through, in a cascading domino effect that wouldn't end well for any of the humans in the hangar.

And once the trife were past the hangar, there would be no chance to stop them. No way to keep them from killing everyone inside the base, even if the escape route remained clear. They would come up on the scientists and civilians and their families from behind and kill every adult male and woman of childbearing age, leaving only children and elderly alive.

"No," Luke said. "If I can slow them for one second, help one more person escape, then I'm staying." He eyed the racks of rifles nearby. "I want my father to be proud of me, and running isn't going to do that."

He broke for the guns, Scott right behind him. Jennifer hesitated a moment before making the same decision, leaving Briar to stand there alone.

At the front of the hangar, the queen slammed into another of the APCs with her shoulder, sending it skidding into more Marines.. She hissed loudly and a huge swarm of trife poured over the APC, falling onto the stricken Marines before they could recover.

"Retreat! Retreat!" Lieutenant Carter's voice shouted through the loudspeakers, overcoming the gunfire. the hissing and screams of the trife queen. "Fall back!"

Luke grabbed one of the MKs and spare magazines, joining Scott in shooting at a pack of trife. There were so many it was impossible to miss. They dropped the creatures one after another, their sudden defense intensifying as Jennifer joined them.

"There," Scott said, motioning to a group of Marines fighting their way through the trife. Two Butchers fought beside them, helping keep the demons back. "Give them cover, we can help them get back to the main doors."

"Look!" Briar said, having decided to join the group. She pointed to one of the other doors on the side of the hangar. A group of trife had just finished tearing it open and were escaping the hangar and entering the base.

"Shit," Luke said. "They're already inside."

"Should we go after them?" Jennifer asked.

"No, stay with the Marines. We need them."

They concentrated their firepower on the trife chasing the Marines, helping them thin the masses as they retreated toward the group. Luke recognized them as they got closer.

"Auntie, this way!" he shouted, waving his free hand and hoping she would hear him over the noise or see him gesturing.

She did, and the entire group broke toward them, staying low so Luke and the others could shoot over their heads. Behind them, the trife queen finished wrecking another APC before attacking one of the Butchers. The robot tried to slash the queen with its axe-hand, only to have the queen grab the arm and tear it clean from the machine. It did the same to the other arm before knocking the Butcher down and removing its legs, taking it out of the fight.

"Luke," Auntie said, reaching the group. "You shouldn't be here."

"The trife went through the side door," Luke replied. "They're in the base."

"Damn it," Auntie said. "I don't know what we can do. Colonel Haines ordered a full evac, but the escape route is blocked off too. All of our personnel are grabbing guns and heading there to fight, but if too many of these bastards get through it won't matter."

"We can't hold them off here," Rocky said, coming up beside her. His left arm hung limp at his side, blood staining his uniform. "We can choke them in the passageways, and queen bitch won't fit."

"She'll dig her way in," Scott said. "It'll take a while, but if she plans to nest here she's got time."

"Anything that slows her down is good with me," Auntie said. "Come on."

She started for the main doors out of the hangar and into the base, Rocky, Toast, and Gills joining her. Luke's heart dropped seeing that Mackey hadn't made it. He turned his rifle on the trife again, helping lay down cover fire as they retreated toward the door.

The fighting in the hangar had calmed considerably. The number of Marines still shooting had dwindled to less than a few handfuls, most of them having managed to get into decent defensive positions near the corners. It was a brave, futile effort. They would run out of ammunition soon enough, and then they would all die.

Luke respected them for their sacrifice to save others inside the base. He hoped it would be worth it.

The group reached the main blast doors. Auntie paused to tap in the code to open them, stopping there and turning back to the hangar. A second unit of Marines broke for the cleared exit, one of them with an injured squadmate in his arms. The trife continued spilling into the hangar from outside, a slick nearly a thousand strong already in the space and thousands more waiting to enter. They rushed at the fleeing Marines, right on their heels as they desperately ran for the open blast doors.

Luke swung his rifle toward one of the trife as it lunged at the rearmost Marine, squeezing off a burst that sent it sprawling to the floor. Another trife tried to tackle the same Marine. Jennifer unleashed a volley and brought it down.

"Fire in the hole!" Rocky shouted, tossing a grenade over the heads of the fleeing Marines. It landed somewhere amidst the trife and exploded, sending dozens of them sprawling. The second Marine unit reached the door, practically falling through in their exhaustion.

There was no time to input the code to close the

doors. It wouldn't have mattered anyway. The queen would have barrelled through them like a freight train.

"Move it!" Auntie cried, turning back to unleash a barrage of bullets at the queen as she scuttled into the doorway. The bullets stopped her there, but Auntie had no chance against her. She went down fighting, crushed beneath the queen's clawed feet, but not before she and Rocky distracted the witch long enough for Gills and Toast to leap through the blast doors just ahead of her slashing claws. Hissing, spittle flew from her gaping mouth as she screamed and slashed at Rocky, decapitating him.

The queen threw her head back and screamed even louder. Luke barely noticed. The queen had cut them off from the hangar's exit, leaving them trapped inside with her and a thousand of her minions.

"I told you we were going to die," Scott said, so calmly it sent a chill down Luke's spine.

The queen turned toward them. The rest of the trife stayed back, not wanting to interfere with kills she wanted for herself.

"Oh my gosh," Briar said, her voice a whisper.

Luke glanced at her out of the corner of his eye. Jennifer and Scott too looked terrified of the queen. His attention shifted back to the open blast door. With the trife minions standing back and allowing the queen to have her fun, he could take her on and buy them a few seconds to escape with Gills and Toast.

His father had told him earlier that he believed in him. That he knew he had a good heart, was a good friend and a real leader.

It was time to prove him right.

"Hey!" he shouted, sidestepping away from the others, waving his free hand to get the queen's attention.

She turned toward him, her small eyes locking on him and sending a wave of panic down his back. What the hell was he doing? "You want some? Come on!" He fired his rifle, putting a few rounds into the queen's chest.

She barely noticed the damage, but it was enough to put her focus more squarely on him.

"Luke, what are you doing?" Jennifer screamed at him.

"When she comes for me, break for the door," Luke replied.

"We're not leaving you."

"You have a chance. Take it. Come on, bitch!" He shouted to the queen. He took another shot at her, still moving away from the others, positioning himself closer to the hundreds of trife in the hangar.

The queen opened her mouth, hissing softly. Luke shuddered, her attention giving him the impression she recognized him. But that was ridiculous. Wasn't it?

"Luke!" Scott shouted, his fear battling his desire to stay and help Luke.

"We don't all have to die here!" Luke yelled back. "When she comes for me, you go! Get B and Jen out of here! Don't let me die for nothing!"

He had barely gotten the words out when the queen lunged at him. He moved, running perpendicular to her, the trife backing up to give him space. The queen came down where he had been a moment earlier, rotating to slash at him. Luke felt the breeze of her claws at his back as he neared one of the APCs, hoping to use it as cover. He didn't need to last long out here. Just long enough for his friends to get out of the hangar.

The queen's tail swept in front of him, taking his legs out from under him with enough force to flip him end-over-end until he landed hard on his back. The blow pushed the air from his lungs, but he didn't stay down. Rolling to his knees, he faced the queen and raised his rifle, sighting down the barrel.

"Luke!" his mother screamed.

Luke looked past the huge trife, to where his parents stood in the entrance of the hangar—Scott, Jennifer, and Briar there with them—all of them with horrified expressions on their faces.

"Nooooo!" his father shouted as the queen's claws sank into Luke's chest, her hand so large they dug in from his chest to his abdomen.

Luke convulsed, suddenly unable to breathe as pain exploded throughout his body. He turned his attention back to the queen, who lifted him up toward her face, holding him there dangling from her claws and staring at him.

"I'm not afraid of you," Luke forced out, his vision dimming.

She hissed softly back at him before tossing him aside.

He died before he hit the deck.

Chapter 17

"Luuukkee!" Yasmin wailed as she dropped to her knees.

Beside her, Nicholas poured his grief into anger, howling with rage as he brought up his gun to blast the trife queen in the back. To do as much damage to the alien bitch as he could for killing his son.

The grief of watching the queen toss Luke aside as though he were a slab of spoiled meat, watching his body contort lifelessly in the air before landing on the deck made his hand shake. He drew his other hand up to steady his aim, only to have Grimmel grab the pistol from his hands, stealing his thunder.

"What are you doing?" He rounded on the man, ready to fight him for the gun, his pain and anger stealing every ounce of sanity he possessed.

He went for Grimmel, but the man jammed a hand against his shoulder, stopping him at arm's length. "You can't hurt her with that," he said. "You'll only get us all killed."

The trife queen screamed again, the hideous shriek

piercing Nicholas' heart. He dropped his head, almost in tears, his legs threatening to give under him.

Grimmel almost imperceptibly shook his head, his consoling hand squeezing Nicholas' shoulder. "This wasn't supposed to happen. He needed to survive." He paused, a thoughtful look passing over his features before he looked away from Nicholas. "We can fix this."

"What are you talking about?" Nicholas growled, looking up at him in confusion. "You're not making any sense."

Grimmel turned away from Nicholas to the two Marines and Scott's friends just inside the door. "All of you," he said, lifting his hand in appeal. "Captain Shepherd needs to escape in Foresight. If you want any hope for survival, you'll help him get there."

Nicholas couldn't contain his grief and rage. He grabbed Grimmel, turning him around and shoving him back against the bulkhead. "What the hell do you mean?" he shouted in his face.

"Captain Shepherd," Grimmel replied calmly. "In the next few seconds that queen is going to send thousands of trife into this base. You're lucky she's giving us a sporting chance, as meager as it is. Your son wasn't supposed to die here. None of this was supposed to happen. Something's changed, and I don't know how or why or what, but it's absolutely critical you get that starship out of here."

"Something's changed?" Nicholas said, confused by the statement. "What do you know?" He pushed harder against Grimmel. "What do you know!"

"Haha! Probably too much. The universe is much bigger than you understand, Captain Shepherd. You need to get out of here so you can learn." Grimmel shoved him back easily with one hand. "I'll do my best to keep the queen away from you. Now go!" He jerked his head at Foresight.

"Wait," Nicholas said, off-balance from Grimmel's words and still reeling from watching the trife queen kill his son. "What are we supposed to do?"

"Find your way back here before it's too late," Grimmel replied.

"It's already too late."

Grimmel shook his head. "No. You don't understand yet, but you will." He looked at the others. "Now, go! All of you!"

Then the wealthiest, most powerful man on the planet turned away from the group, stepping out into the open between them and the queen. "I know you know me," he shouted at her as if she could understand him. He dropped his rifle on the deck, leaving himself unarmed. "Let's dance."

"He's crazy," Briar said.

"Who gives a shit?" Gills said. "You heard the man. That bird's our ticket out of this mess. Let's move, people!"

"He's right. Let's go." Nicholas couldn't begin to make sense of what was happening, so he didn't try. "Yazz, come on," he said, grabbing her around the waist and hauling her up off the deck. She fought him, trying to shove him away. He gave up trying to persuade her and hauled her up over his shoulder.

"Let me go!" she shouted, pounding his back with her fists. "Please, Nick," she sobbed when all he did was run faster. She braced her palms against his back and pushed herself up to look back at Luke as if just keeping her eyes on him could somehow bring him back to life. "Please," she begged. "I need to be with him. Put me down, damn you!"

He ignored her, carrying her as she flailed, the two Marines leading them back into the hangar. Luke's friends brought up the rear.

"Look at me!" Grimmel shouted at the trife queen when she turned her head in their direction. She swiveled her head back to him, his voice unnaturally loud in the hangar.

The other trife were done waiting. They broke from behind the queen as though she had fired a starting gun, hissing and lurching forward toward the seven fleeing people.

"Shit," Gills said, rifle spewing rounds. Toast joined him a split-second later, Luke's friends immediately after that. Dozens of rounds crossed the hangar, cutting down the lead vanguard, the next few creatures behind them tripping over their bodies and falling. It caused a minor domino effect. But that was all. Those behind them skirted the pile and rushed toward their prey.

The ramp leading into Foresight waited less than fifty feet away. To Nicholas, it seemed like fifty miles. There was no way they would make it. Not with over a thousand trife bearing down on them.

Luke was dead. He couldn't imagine how he could change that if he flew Foresight out of here. He didn't know what Grimmel meant by that. It was crazy as all hell, but if by some miracle it changed things...if it could somehow turn back time or whatever and bring Luke back, he was damned well going to make it to the ship and take off.

Not even thousands of trife were going to stop him.

"Pick up the pace, Marines," he growled before looking over his shoulder. "They're going to come at us from both sides. Jennifer, take the left flank. Briar, the right. Scott, cover our asses."

"Copy that, Captain Shepherd," Scott said. He didn't need to shoot behind them yet, so he continued targeting trife on their flank, running out of ammo and quickly switching magazines.

Gills and Toast ran faster, the trife only a dozen feet behind them. Gills let out a loud howl, blasting the incoming demons while reaching to his belt for a grenade and pulling the pin. He tossed it into the lead mass of creatures, blowing enough of them away to put a little more distance between them and ultimate death.

Nicholas gritted his teeth, sticking close to the two Marines in front of him, Luke's friends hugging his heels. He didn't look back to see what Grimmel was doing, but the trife queen hadn't come for them yet, so he had to believe that whatever the man was doing, he might just save their asses.

They made it to within twenty feet of Foresight before the trife were close enough to begin launching themselves at Nicholas. He turned and cracked one of them in the head with his elbow, knocking it away as Jennifer put a bullet through its head. Gills fired point-blank into the rest, each round killing multiple trife. Toast and Scott did the same, blasting trife after trife until their guns clicked empty.

"I'm out!" Scott shouted, turning the rifle in his hands and using it like a club.

"Me too, damn it," Gills said.

They were still fifteen feet away and out of steam. Sensing their weakness, the mass of trife surged toward them.

A loud scream echoed in the hangar. The trife queen came out of nowhere, but not as a threat. She hit the deck and slid into the trife horde, scattering hundreds of them like bowling pins, her hands and feet scrambling to find purchase so she could pull herself upright. The disturbance allowed them to sprint under Foresight for the ramp, only a handful of feet away now.

The queen hissed and charged back at Grimmel. Confused, Nicholas risked a glance back, finding the man still standing near the inner blast doors, his sleeves rolled up, his hands obscured by dark black gloves. Grimmel noticed Nicholas and winked at the same time bolts of blue energy exploded from the gloves, striking the queen.

Nicholas turned his head forward again and skidded to a stop, his heart jumping into his throat. A group of trife had moved into the path between them and the ramp, blocking their escape. They were so damn close. They had to get through or around them. Somehow.

Scott and Toast raised their rifles and went into mirrored batting stances, just as a dark blur charged down the ramp and plunged into the trife. One moment the demons surrounding it were all upright, the next their flailing torsos littered the deck like dolls with their legs torn off. A small black humanoid robot stood in the midst of them, a dark blade extending from each wrist. They watched as it stormed after more trife in a blur of spinning, whirling blades.

"What the hell?" Gills said from in front of Nicholas, his mouth hanging open as he watched the bot go to work on more trife closing in behind them.

"Who cares; get up the ramp!" Nicholas shouted back.

The two Marines scaled the ramp into the ship, Nicholas right behind them. He paused at the bottom, turning to urge the others up, Yasmin had gone limp over his shoulder. She had either calmed to the point of mental exhaustion or she had passed out, making it easier to carry her.

"Come on, come on, come on!" he yelled, waving them up into the ship. The trife tried to close in on them, wary of the robot despite its diminutive size as it brought up the rear. Nicholas didn't wait for it. He cast one last look back at Grimmel—the businessman had his back against the wall, desperately trying to avoid the queen's claws—before scaling the ramp into the ship.

Nicholas entered the ship, hitting the control pad to bring up the ramp. The black robot was there in a flash, riding it up as it retracted, the outer door sliding closed behind it.

"Scott, take Yasmin," Nicholas said.

"Is she all right?" Scott asked as Nicholas shifted her onto his shoulder.

"She's still breathing. Listen, take her up to the crew level and strap her and yourself in. Jen, Briar, which one of you did better in the simulator?"

"Definitely Jen," Briar said.

"Okay, Jen, follow me to the cockpit. You can back me up, just in case."

"Me?" Jennifer said. "In case of what?"

"In case something happens to me. Let's go."

The thought evaporated as the ship shook slightly, the trife no doubt climbing onto it and trying to dig their claws in. Nicholas knew the alloy could take the beating from them, but he wasn't so sure if they could take off if the queen got involved, especially if she was smart enough to jam up the atmospheric flight surfaces.

He hurried to the ladder, climbing to the next level with Jennifer right behind him. They crossed to the cockpit.

"Sit there, put on the helmet. The safety system will activate automatically."

"Yes, sir. Captain Shepherd, about Luke..." She sounded close to tears.

"Not now," Nicholas said, grabbing the flight helmet from the first seat and dropping into it. He quickly tapped the control pad to activate the ship, starting the initialization process. He pulled the helmet on before the safety system secured him.

Foresight shook harder, the number of trife crawling around and on top of the ship likely growing. The camera feeds came online, but it took Nicholas a moment to realize they were showing him the view from outside because they remained dark. So many trife blocked the cameras it was impossible to see anything but them.

"Good evening, Captain Shepherd," Frank said.

"Good evening, Frank," Nicholas replied, tapping on the control pad to activate the spines.

"Are you sure you want to do that, Captain?" Frank asked. "We are still inside the hangar and there are organic life forms on the hull. Activating the shields will kill them."

"That's the idea," Nicholas said. "Confirm activation. Charge the spines."

He noticed a glow around the blackness of the camera feeds. The view cleared immediately afterwards, the dead trife tumbling from the ship to the hangar deck.

Nicholas activated the ship's internal comms. "I hope everyone is strapped in back there. We're out of here in five. Four. Three."

"Colonel Shepherd!" Jennifer said.

He noticed the trife queen in the side-facing feed, racing toward the ship. He didn't have time to finish the countdown. He slid the thrusters open, the heat of the plasma spewing from the rear of the craft forcing the queen to back away.

Pressed back in his seat from the heavy acceleration, Nicholas scanned the feeds, searching for a sign of Grimmel. He didn't see the man anywhere, unable to confirm if he had died or survived. Returning his attention to the display, he quickly targeted the blast doors in front of them and fired a volley from the spines. The ion blasts sizzled against the metal, instantly vaporizing it.

Foresight shot through the hole and out of the hangar, headed for orbit.

Chapter 18

Nicholas guided Foresight into a gentle ascent, gaining speed as he climbed. His heart pounded, his body ached, and his soul burned with a mix of fury and despair.

Luke.

He couldn't believe what had happened. He couldn't believe he had seen it unfold as it happened. Already, he knew he would never shake the chilling memory.

Nothing would ever be the same again.

He stared at the forward display, eyes fixed on the cloud-spotted horizon, hands suddenly beginning to shake from the trauma and residual adrenaline. He didn't think it was possible, but they had made it on board the ship and gotten away from the base.

Grimmel had said they could fix this. All he had to do was escape. He had escaped.

Now what?

He brought the ship around, banking slowly to avoid jostling his passengers too much as he made a one-eighty and tapped the control to recharge the spines.

"Captain Shepherd?" Jennifer said, observing the

change of direction from the co-pilot seat. "What are you doing?"

"The trife are in the hangar," Nicholas said. "The USSF doesn't need the hangar anymore."

The spines gathered excess energy from the ship's power supply. The individual needles began to glow. Nicholas focused on the slagged outer door into the hangar, lining up the shot. The blast would burn Luke's body to ash. His son deserved better than that, but it was still better than being dragged out into the open by the trife and picked apart by vultures.

And Luke would want him to deliver one last blow against the trife. In his name. For his sake.

"Nick, don't," Yasmin said, appearing at the back of the flight deck, holding fast to the bulkhead. Her floral dress was torn and dirty, her makeup and hair in shambles, her eyes red and teary. She looked as though she had just crawled out of the rubble he intended to create. "The system only has so much energy, and you don't know how much we'll need."

"I don't care." Nicholas replied, still in a daze while his wife seemed to have already recovered. Why didn't she want to punish the trife for Luke's death? "I want them to pay."

"I do too," she hissed back at him. "But avenging Luke isn't the mission, Nick. You heard what Grimmel said. This wasn't supposed to happen. If we interfere this way, it might negate whatever we can do to bring Luke back."

His opportunity to fire on the hangar threatened to pass. "What Grimmel said doesn't make any sense."

"No, it doesn't. But it's the only thing we have to hold onto. The only thing that will keep me sane right now. Please, Nick. The base is lost. We need to think about the future, not hold tight to the past."

Nick split his attention between Yasmin and the hangar. Cursing under his breath, he tapped the control to disarm the spines, returning their energy to the power supply. "Okay," he said. "But only because you're his mother and you asked. You should go strap yourself in. We'll talk once we're in orbit."

"Thank you," Yasmin said, retreating from the edge of the flight deck.

Nicholas sighed heavily, readjusting Foresight's course. He ascended over the mountainside, looking down on the trife lining the slope. Only a hundred or so were gathered near the escape hatch. Few enough that the remaining MPs and Marines should be able to fight their way out and lead the survivors to...where? Back into the wilds, where humankind wasn't the apex predator anymore. At least until the USSF could send transports to pick them up.

The aliens seemed to be in a state of shock, barely moving as Foresight passed overhead. It was a positive sign, suggesting their queen had died in the fighting. Leaving them rudderless until they either created a new one or were absorbed by another nest.

He followed the tell-tale signs of their trek to the mountainside, expecting the lines of damaged earth, crushed vegetation, and other debris and destruction to flow directly south to the position. Instead, he altered Foresight's path again to follow the tracks as they curved a short distance past the base, cutting west for nearly ten miles before breaking south.

Nicholas' face wrinkled in confusion. He had never seen a slick move like that before. Trife were never afraid to attack humans head-on, but this group had intentionally circled to the rear of the compound to take them by surprise.

It was unheard of.

He decided to trace the path of the slick back to its source, staying low over the landscape in an eager search for answers. At the speed Foresight flew, it didn't take long.

When Nicholas realized where the trife had originated, he nearly choked on the knot of agony that stuck in his throat. Following the trail of destruction into the distance, his gaze came to rest on the remains of the Invenergy solar array, still smoldering from the ruin he had made of it hours earlier.

"No," he hissed out through gritted teeth, unwilling to believe what he knew to be true. He had fired on the array on a whim, thinking he was delivering one final blow to the trife before leaving Earth behind. Instead, he had destroyed their source of energy, disturbed the nest and queen, and brought the aliens down on their heads.

Luke was dead, and it was all his fault.

"No," he said again, as if denying the outcome could somehow change it. It couldn't be possible. The base was over a hundred miles away, and it had been four hours since he hit the array. He knew the trife could cover a lot of ground in a day, but he had never heard of them moving that fast.

But it was more than that. The trife had circled the compound, attacking from the rear. The queen wasn't just looking for a new place to nest. The action was retaliatory. Malicious.

Payback.

Luke was dead, because of what he'd done.

His heart pounded. He felt nauseous. Dizzy. He could barely breathe.

"Frank," he said softly. "I'm passing you the stick. Take us into orbit, following prior mission parameters."

"Confirmed, Captain," Frank replied. "I have the stick."

"And take it easy," Nicholas added. "We have vulnerable passengers with no G-suits."

"Confirmed. Adjusting G threshold to its lowest setting."

Foresight's ascent became increasingly steep as the neural network guided the craft toward space. Nicholas tapped the control to manually release the safety system, freeing himself from the seat. He reached up and removed his helmet, dropping it onto the floor of the flight deck, the incline causing it to roll to the back of the compartment.

Nicholas lowered his head into his hands and cried.

Chapter 19

"Captain Shepherd," Jennifer said a few minutes later, her voice soft, hesitant. When he didn't answer, she tried again, a little louder. "Captain Shepherd?"

Nicholas swallowed hard, squeezing his eyes shut to extract the last of his tears before wiping them away with the sleeve of his jacket. He opened his eyes, looking at the display in front of him. Frank had successfully navigated them into orbit a second time and cut acceleration. Considering he hadn't floated out of his seat, he knew the AI had also sensed the additional crew and activated the inner gravity control to keep them comfortable.

"What is it, Jennifer?" he asked, turning his head toward her. Her eyes were red too. Her cheeks moist.

"I don't know how to get out of this seat," she replied. "And I'd really like to not be sitting here with you and feeling alone."

Nicholas nodded. "I know what you mean," he said, getting up and positioning himself in front of the co-pilot seat. He leaned over the control pad beneath her left hand and tapped on the touchscreen to release the safety system.

Jennifer slumped forward and rubbed at her face with her hands, drying off her cheeks before looking at him again. "We're in space?"

"Yes," Nicholas confirmed.

"I wish I could enjoy it."

"Me too."

"Captain Shepherd, I—"

Nicholas cut her off a second time. "I know. Let's head back and check on the others. We can regroup together." She nodded, and he helped her to her feet. "You did a brave thing back there, Jen. All of you did."

"It doesn't mean anything to me right now, Captain Shepherd. My mother..." She trailed off, leaning into him, a fresh round of tears wetting the collar of his jacket. He wrapped his arm around her and held her for a minute, wanting to tell her that her mother would be fine. That the trife on the mountainside had looked as though they had lost their queen, which would render them less aggressive for a period of time. Instead, he told her he was sorry and did his best to comfort her despite his own pain.

She finally pulled away, wiping again at her tears. "I'll be okay," she said. "I have to hope. They were evacuating civilians. Maybe she got out."

"Maybe. It's certainly possible." But right now, he couldn't be sure of anything. "Are you ready to check on the others?" he asked.

Jennifer nodded and Nicholas led her off the flight deck and through the short passageway to the center compartment where their five passengers sat. They all turned their tired eyes in his direction. Yasmin's eyes remained puffy and moist, her body trembling from exhaustion and shock. He wished he could tell her everything would be okay, but he didn't know what to think right now. In the span of a few minutes, everything had changed. Maybe forever if Grimmel couldn't pull a rabbit out of the proverbial hat and do what he said he could do. Change everything and bring Luke back. He had to hang onto that one hope despite how crazy it sounded. He wasn't sure if he could remain sane if he didn't.

"Captain Shepherd," Gills said. "Nice flying, sir. Thanks for getting us out of there."

"Thank *you*," Nicholas replied. "Your efforts got us to the ship."

Gills smiled. "Nah, it wasn't us, sir. It was the bot that saved our hides." He looked around the space. "Anybody seen the little guy?" Everyone shook their heads in the negative.

Nicholas agreed with Gills. The bot *had* saved their lives, and he too wondered where it had gone. Regardless, he supposed it didn't matter right now.

"Where are we, Captain Shepherd?" Briar asked.

"In orbit," Nicholas replied. He paused, doing his best to collect his thoughts. He wanted to scream, to rage against the trife, against fate, and against God for taking his son. But none of that would help the people on board.

None of that would bring Luke back.

"I had Frank bring us up here to give us a chance to take a breather and think this out. We have some choices to make," he continued. "I'm sure everyone here was close to someone who died today, and we all need a minute beyond the fog of war to gather ourselves."

"Grimmel said we can fix this," Yasmin said, the

desperation clear in her tone. "That's the situation, Nick."

"I know he did," Nicholas replied. "One of the things we need to do is figure out what that means. Unless you know of some technology Grimmel Corp developed to bring the dead back to life?"

"No. But you heard what he said. Luke wasn't supposed to die. He's supposed to be here with us now," she said, lowering her face and sobbing into her hand.

"I want to believe we can get Luke back too. And not just Luke. Everybody," Nicholas said. "I want to believe that more than anything. But there's so much about this I don't understand. So much that doesn't make sense." He stepped over to her, putting one hand on the arm of her seat as he squatted down to her eye level. He gently pulled her hand away from her face. "If there's any chance in the universe, I'll do whatever it takes. I promise."

Yasmin nodded, leaning forward to press her fore-head against his. "Me too."

Nicholas stared into her eyes. He wanted to tell her about the trife from the array, and how he had caused the attack that had led to Luke's death. What good would it do? She would blame him as much as he blamed himself, if not more, and he didn't know if he could take that. Besides, this wasn't the time or the place.

Or was it?

If he held back now, the wound that had already opened inside him would fester. It would change him, and when he finally did tell her she would be even more angry and upset because he hadn't come clean sooner. So maybe...

He swallowed hard. "Yazz, I need to tell you some-thing. All of you." He paused, looking around at everyone. They deserved to know too. He dropped his eyes, choking up at the thought of spitting out the truth. His action had affected all of them. Cost all of them. "I followed the trail of the second slick from the air on our way up here. The one led by the queen." He looked up, locking eyes again with Yasmin. "Damn it, Yazz." He stopped to blink away his tears. "They came from the array. The Invenergy array. They came because I blew the shit out of them with the weapons test. It's my fault the queen attacked the base. My fault Luke is dead. My fault so many people are dead."

He forced himself to hold Yasmin's gaze, both to accept her fury and to avoid looking at anyone else. His body trembled from the admission, along with the fading adrenaline and the pure exhaustion overtaking it.

"I never thought…" He trailed off, shaking his head. "I'm sorry. To you especially, but to everyone else here too. I'm sorry."

Yasmin didn't look away. Her eyes stayed with his. A thousand emotions flashed behind them in an instant. Anger. Blame. Sadness. Resolve. Like a game of roulette, even she probably didn't know where she would settle.

The ship remained silent. Nicholas stayed with her, patiently waiting for her reaction. The rest of the assembly waited with him.

"Nick," she said at last. "I...I can't handle all of this right now. It's just too much." She reacted suddenly, hitting the safety release on the side of the seat and jumping to her feet. "I need time to process…" She trailed off again as she pushed past him, hurrying to the ladder that led up to the bunks.

Nicholas watched her leave, his heart in pieces. He knew when she said she wanted time alone she meant it, but it didn't make it any easier. She needed time. So did he, but that wasn't a luxury he could afford at the moment. He could only hope as the hours passed that they would come together in the aftermath of Luke's death, not fall apart.

"Well, we're in space," Gills said, breaking the silence. "That's pretty cool." He paused. "Always thought I'd enjoy riding in this baby more." He went quiet again, succumbing to the mood.

Nicholas exhaled sharply and turned to the others. "First things first. I'm going to return us to Earth, to the Pilgrim launch site. Scott, Briar, Jennifer, you can disembark there and go on with your lives as best you can. Tell the officer in charge what happened. Tell him about Grimmel, especially. They'll likely send a search and rescue team out to look for survivors. Hopefully they'll find your loved ones alive."

"I don't have any loved ones still alive," Scott said. "Excluding the people already on this ship. If it's all the same to you, Captain Shepherd, I'd rather stay with you."

"Scott, you're not even seventeen yet," Nicholas replied. "And a civilian."

"So you're saying that you plan to ask permission to remain in charge of this ship once you return to Earth?"

Nicholas stared at him, recalling his conversation with Grimmel from before the trife attacked. The tycoon had broached a plan to make a unit of Marines disappear so they could load up Foresight and go scout the universe. Grimmel had known USSF Command would either reject his plan or center everything around it, neither of which was a net positive for humankind. In the same way, Nicholas knew he couldn't turn the starship back over to the USSF. Not if he wanted any control over his promise to Yasmin.

Not if he wanted any chance, no matter how slim, to see Luke alive again.

"You still aren't old enough to make that decision," Nicholas said, the words sounding foolish as they escaped his lips. He corrected himself before Scott had the chance. "Said the old pilot to the kid who survived alone in the wilds for nearly a year."

"Now you're starting to get me, sir," Scott said.

"I'm out of arguments," Nicholas admitted.

"I'm staying too," Jennifer said. "Whatever's going to happen, you'll need help. I'm not much, but I'm better than nothing."

"What about your mother?" Nicholas asked.

"If she's alive, she can take care of herself. I've spent the last two years living in fear of the trife, Captain Shepherd. The last nine months holed up in the compound not able to do a damn thing to help. But this is a chance for me to do something good. Something important. Whatever Mister Grimmel meant, I don't think he said it just because Luke died. There has to be more to it than that."

Nicholas realized she was probably right. Grimmel said family was important to him, but there had to be something else he knew that he hadn't said. Some reason Luke was supposed to survive.

"Okay, Jennifer," he said. He looked at Briar. "What about you?"

Briar bit her lower lip. "My parents are going to be worried about me. If they're still alive. But..." She looked over at Jennifer and Scott. "My friends are here, and if they die because they don't have someone to watch their back, well that's a problem for me. Besides, not to sound trite or anything, but going on a space adventure has to be better than spending the rest of my life in a city inside a starship. Maybe I can become a Jedi or something."

"That's not a real thing, B," Scott said.

"You don't know that," she replied. "Anyway, I'm less useful than Jennifer, but I'm also better than nothing. And I'm eager to learn."

Of all Luke's friends, Nicholas had the most concern about Briar. She didn't have the same fortitude Scott and Jennifer displayed. But it would make things a lot easier if he didn't need to go back to the launch site.

"You're sure?" he asked.

"Positive," she replied.

Gills coughed to get Nicholas' attention. "Captain. Hi. No offense, sir, but I noticed you haven't asked me or Toast whether we or not we want to leave."

Nicholas looked over at him. "You're right, I haven't. You're still enlisted Marines."

"Yes, but everyone in our chain of command is dead and we're supposed to transfer to the Pilgrim on completion of our orders."

"What are your orders?"

"To protect the lab rats until the completion of Project Foresight."

"This is Project Foresight," Nicholas said. "And my wife is one of the lab rats. She might be the only one still alive. Which means your orders are still valid. And I'm part of your chain of command." Gills made a face before opening his mouth to argue the validity of Nicholas' statements. "Besides," he continued. "Do you want to be shown up by a group of civilian kids?"

Toast laughed as Gills' face flushed. "No, sir," Gills replied, clearly unhappy with the situation. "But if you aren't planning to follow your orders and bring this birdie home to roost, then why should I follow mine?"

"I don't want to hold you here against your will, Corporal...?"

"Hess. But everyone calls me Gills."

"I don't want to hold you here against your will, Gills. But while I do need to return to Earth to scrounge supplies, if I'm not dropping off civilians then I don't intend to go anywhere near any of the arkship launch sites. If you're out, you'll need to walk from wherever I land."

Toast laughed harder. "Enjoy the stroll, Gillie."

"Does that mean you're in?" Nicholas asked Toast.

"Yes, sir. I'd rather be anywhere than crammed inside a huge sardine can with a bunch of civvies who think they're better than me."

"Man, why can't you be on my side for once?" Gills asked him.

"Because your side is the wrong side, idiot," Toast replied. "Or did you miss what just happened back there? We owe it to Auntie and the others to keep fighting."

"You heard the Captain," Gills said. "This whole thing was his fault. He attacked the trife and pissed off the queen. And you still want to help him?"

"Don't be stupid," Scott said. "Trife are like organic machines, programmed to do one thing and do it really, really well. They aren't spiteful. They aren't vindictive. They hit the base because they were always going to hit the base."

"I appreciate that, Scott," Nicholas said. "But I don't need you to come to my defense. What happened, happened, and I'm responsible for it." He returned his attention to Gills. "But that has nothing to do with it. You aren't helping me. You're following your orders to protect my wife. It's your choice,

Corporal Hess. Like I said, I'm not going to make you stay."

Gills shrugged. "I'll think about it on the way to wherever it is we're going."

"Have it your way," Nicholas said. "I'm going downstairs to see if we have anything useful in storage, and then I'm going to check in on Yasmin. The rest of you, just do whatever you want until I get back, as long as you don't disturb my wife or break anything. We're safe out here."

"Yes, sir," Scott said for the group.

Nicholas crossed the room to the ladder leading to the lower deck. His emotions had settled somewhat, but he knew that if he didn't stay busy he would lose his focus to anger, guilt, and grief.

Besides, if they were going to travel across the universe they needed to be prepared.

Chapter 20

Nicholas stepped off the ladder, into Foresight's small hold. He flinched as his eyes shifted to the larger entry hatch at the front of the compartment where the decapitated head of a trife rested on the deck, dark blue blood pooled around it. The head reminded him how close they had come to not making it onto the ship. No matter what, he refused to turn the craft back over to the USSF. Grimmel wanted him to pilot the ship...somewhere. As far as he was concerned, Grimmel had put him in charge of its future.

And the future of so many others. Including Luke.

Leaning back against one of the storage lockers, Nicholas rubbed his face with his hands again, fighting to keep his focus while recalling exactly what Grimmel had said to him in those last few fateful moments.

This isn't supposed to happen. Something's changed.

He dwelled on those two statements. What had Scott just said? The trife from the Invenergy array hadn't attacked the base because of him, but because something else had motivated them. He had fought the trife long enough to know Scott wasn't completely wrong. The trife had never exhibited vindictive qualities before. They had a method to their madness, along with a certain morality. They didn't kill prepubescent children or women who couldn't bear children. They didn't kill anything that wasn't human. Luke's friend was right. They were like organic machines. Programmed. He had never thought about it that way until now.

But if they were programmed, who had written the code?

The thought sent a chill down Nicholas' spine. Scott's statement wasn't the first time he had heard the theory. Some scientists on the base had always claimed the trife were too perfect to be random. That the meteor shower they had rode in on wasn't bad luck, but an offensive strike against humankind. The sickness had weakened their defenses. The trife had finished things off.

This isn't supposed to happen. Something's changed.

The statements suggested that Aaron Grimmel knew what was supposed to happen, as if he had access to a crystal ball to foretell the future. The thing about Grimmel was that Nicholas couldn't completely rule out the idea that the man did have access to some kind of advanced technology serving that purpose. The man had helped guide humanity forward in leaps and bounds. To hear Yasmin tell it, Grimmel's strength wasn't even in the science of his company's designs. It was in his ability to open other people's minds to the *potential* of the science. To act as a circuit-breaker around impossibility. He had convinced the world's greatest minds that anti-gravity was possible. That nuclear fusion could be miniaturized and made viable. That the laws of physics were pliable.

So why couldn't he invent something to let him see

into the future? And if he had, what had he mean by *the present not aligning itself with the future?*

How could it go wrong?

We can fix this.

The four words echoed in Nicholas' mind. The future hadn't occurred the way Grimmel had seen it in the past. Was the flaw in his crystal ball technology or in the timeline itself?

Nicholas shook his head. Those kinds of questions were better posed to Yasmin. To him, *we can fix this* was the shot of hopium he needed to keep pushing forward. Something had affected the future Grimmel had seen, but he believed that future could be changed.

No, that was wrong. Grimmel believed the past could be changed.

Was Foresight a time machine?

Find your way back here before it's too late.

Nicholas didn't get the impression Grimmel had meant for him to return to the compound some time in the future, but before some unknown event occurred in the past. He believed Grimmel meant to the same point in time before Luke died. Which certainly suggested a time machine. But he hadn't said anything about traveling through time during their dinner with Colonel Haines. He had only talked about his slip drive technology that would somehow let them travel faster than light.

To cross the universe in hours instead of centuries.

Had that been another misdirection? Or had he suggested the true purpose of the starship?

Nicholas couldn't get his mind around the idea of Foresight as a timeship. He didn't believe time travel was possible. Then again, he didn't believe seeing into the future was possible either. Knowing it might be his only way to see Luke alive again, he wanted to keep an open mind. Only the more he opened himself to the idea, the more it frightened him.

Find your way back here before it's too late.

It couldn't be a timeship though, could it? If Grimmel had conquered time travel, why would he stress the need for Nicholas to return to the place and time of Luke's death, instead of suggesting he go back two years or more to warn Earth's governments about what was coming?

Because, he realized, they wouldn't believe him.

But how could they not when he showed up in a starship? He even had the trife head to prove the existence of the aliens.

It wasn't as simple as he wanted to make it. That much was certain. The only way he would learn the true meaning of Grimmel's words was to stop questioning and follow them. As an experienced Marine, he was good at that.

We can fix this.

Those were the most important words Grimmel had spoken. Those were the words Nicholas repeated like a mantra as he turned around and opened the storage compartment behind him.

Empty.

It didn't surprise him. He hadn't expected to find anything stowed down here. In truth, he had just needed an excuse to get away from the others and take a few minutes for himself to think without showing any sign of weakness or indecision. He knew his unintended crew looked to him to provide strength and stability. Especially Luke's friends. Especially now.

He continued along the bulkhead, checking each of the compartments and still coming up empty. Checking the storage on the other side resulted in the same outcome. The rearmost compartments were smaller than the others and sloped inwards to follow the shape of the craft toward the reactors and thrusters. A series of small compartments arranged in three stacked rows of six, they weren't big enough to store much of anything.

At least, that's what he thought as he approached them, unwilling to bypass any of the compartments without confirming their lack of contents.

Before he could reach the compartments, the door on one swung open, and a drawer slid out to reveal a black cube. As he watched, it unfolded, quickly transforming into the small robot that had helped fend off the trife.

"Well, hello," Nicholas said, uncertain why the robot had revealed itself now or why it had been in the drawer in the first place.

The robot didn't respond, though it did jump down to land gracefully on the deck. It took two steps forward to close within a few feet of him before tilting its head back as if it were looking up at him. It didn't speak, but it clearly knew he was there.

"Do you need something?" Nicholas asked. The bot didn't reply. He crouched down in front of it to look more closely, finding the Grimmel Corporation logo stamped to its chest above a designation. DAG-1. "Dag. Is that your name?"

The bot didn't react, and Nicholas suddenly felt awkward trying to speak to it. The USSF didn't use voice activated robots. It was too easy for commands to be drowned out or distorted in the heat of battle. Still, the machine had emerged from storage on its own to save their lives earlier and had done so again now at his approach. It obviously had more intelligence than a Butcher. And it *had* come from Grimmel's labs.

The robot's head swiveled to follow him as he rose to full height. "I don't know if you understand me or not," he said. "But if there's something you need to do, feel free to do it. I have more important things to deal with than trying to decipher your purpose."

The robot still didn't move, so Nicholas returned to the ladder, climbing back to the main deck. The others were still where he had left them, sitting in shocked silence. Except for Gills, who had fallen asleep.

"Did you find any supplies, Captain?" Briar asked.

"No," Nicholas replied. "The cupboards are bare. No surprise there. We'll have to touch down somewhere and see if we can supply ourselves before we do anything else."

He stepped onto the deck, crossing toward the ladder leading to berthing.

"Looks like you found something, Cap," Gills said. Nicholas looked over his shoulder. The robot had followed him up the ladder, trailing close behind. "Aww, isn't he cute? He's following you like a puppy."

"Weren't you sleeping?" Nicholas replied.

"Maybe," Gills said. "Maybe not."

"He wasn't sleeping," Toast said. "Knowing Gills, he was probably daydreaming about your co-pilot."

"Come on, man," Gills snapped. "She's just a kid."

"When has that stopped you before?"

"I'm traumatized from what just happened at the base. The last thing I'm thinking about right now is a girl."

"Then why were you smiling?" Toast pushed.

"I wasn't smiling."

"Yes, you were."

"Fine. Maybe I was daydreaming about a girl. But it wasn't the co-pilot."

"It better not have been my wife," Nicholas said.

"What? N...no, sir. Just a random figment of my imagination, I swear." Gills looked at the robot. "Uh... Captain. Can you call him off or something?"

Nicholas' eyebrows rose in surprise at the small robot advancing on Gills, the same small blades that had torn through the trife extended from the back of its hands.

"Dag, what are you doing?" Nicholas said. "Stop."

The bot stopped moving, proving it understood verbal cues.

"That little guy was about to go all Chucky on me," Gills said. "Where did he come from?"

Nicholas exhaled, realizing the banter between the two Marines about Jennifer had angered him. Had the robot reacted to that?

"He has a small storage compartment in the hold," Nicholas replied. "One of a dozen or so. There may be more robots down there. I haven't checked them all yet."

"I'll go take a look," Gills volunteered.

"How's your ordnance, Corporal?" Nicholas asked, switching gears.

"Huh? Oh, my guns? Out of ammo, sir. Permanently, I guess."

"Mine too, Captain," Toast said.

Nicholas turned to Scott. "How about you?"

"I think we're all out, Captain," he replied.

Nicholas nodded. "We'll have to be a little more careful about where we source our supplies since we can't really defend ourselves at the moment."

"Are you kidding?" Gills said. "You've got him."

Nicholas looked at Dag again. The blades had retracted back into the robot's wrists, and it turned around to face him. Gills was probably right. The bot would come in handy. But if the future they were in didn't match the future Grimmel had seen, what had it originally been intended to protect him from?

He hoped he would never need to find out, but he had a feeling that was wishful thinking.

"Give me a few more minutes to check in on Yasmin, and then we'll get this show on the road."

Chapter 21

Nicholas paused at the base of the ladder leading up to berthing to look back over his shoulder at Dag, trailing along behind him. "Stay here."

"It's so cool you have your own droid, Captain Shepherd," Briar said.

"That remains to be seen," he replied before climbing. Thankfully, Dag didn't follow, remaining at the base of the ladder and turning around as though it had been posted there to guard him.

He exited the small space that separated the ladder from the rest of the area, turning right to bypass the latrine and shower and enter the common area, the ship's tiny kitchen at his back. In front of him, a pyramid of bunks sat on either side stacked two on the bottom, one on top, each with a thin privacy screen on the outside of each. He found Yasmin in the top rack on the left. She was on her side, her back to him. She hadn't bothered to close the screen.

"Yazz," he said softly, walking over to her and gently resting his hand on her shoulder. "Honey?"

"Go away, Nick," she replied.

This time, her tone of voice told him she didn't really want him to go away.

"Do you mind if I join you?" he asked.

"This rack isn't big enough for both of us."

"I know you're upset. I—"

She turned onto her back, looking at him with puffy, still-wet eyes. "Upset? I can't even begin to understand how I feel right now, let alone describe it. But I'm pretty sure *upset* isn't anywhere close to how I feel."

"Is angry one of them?"

She surprised him by shaking her head. "I feel like I should be. But how can I blame you? You requested permission, Colonel Haines granted it. And I know you wanted to show Foresight off to Grimmel as much as I did, and probably for my sake. I wanted you to do it. After two years, we thought we knew our enemy." The tears sprang to her eyes again. "We were wrong."

Nicholas didn't ask again. He climbed into the bunk and laid down beside her, silently taking her in his arms. As she sobbed into his shoulder, he allowed himself a few more tears too, but only a few.

"Damn it, Nick," she said a few minutes later, after she calmed some. "So many people have lost their children. I was so sure we had gotten lucky. That Luke would make it through this nightmare alive. We were so close to finishing up. So close to heading to the Pilgrim. How many different decisions might we have made to change the outcome? How many things had to go wrong for this to happen? Luke shouldn't have even been in the hangar, but I understand why you did it. I want to find fault in everything. To blame someone or something. But we both know how dangerous the world is. We both know these things happen." She looked up at him. "Do you think Grimmel was right? Do you think we can fix this?"

"I need to believe it," Nicholas replied. "But it's so strange. Do you know if Grimmel had some means to see into the future? Do you think he built a time machine?"

"What? No. Time travel isn't possible."

"I thought Grimmel taught you not to consider anything impossible."

"Maybe not anything else. You can't change the flow of spacetime. You can warp it. You can fold it. But you can't change its direction."

"Then how would we ever bring Luke back? Grimmel said we could fix it. He said to…" Nicholas gave his best impression of Grimmel. "…*find your way back here before it's too late.*"

"I don't know," Yasmin replied. "Despite my position on the development team, I didn't know him very well at all. He was always someone you saw pass by in the halls or at the front of the auditorium giving a presentation. Every once in a while we passed an email back and forth. And on a rare occasion he spoke to me directly. But he was an enigma to everyone on the team, and everyone else in the company I spoke to. The eccentric wealthy genius trope to the max."

"Do you know if he has any family? No wife, I know. What about siblings? Parents?"

"I heard rumors his mother died when he was a child, and his father died of the trife sickness. But I also heard he was adopted as an infant. Talk about hitting the jackpot. No brothers or sisters that I'm aware of. I don't know. It doesn't seem that important now, does it?"

"It probably isn't," Nicholas agreed. "I'm just trying to make sense of things. I mean, I thought the world had gone crazy when the trife arrived and the war started. But this ship, Grimmel's instructions, Luke's death. I'd go back to flying bombing missions in a second."

"I feel like I want to stay here and cry for the next year or two," Yasmin said. "But that won't do us much good. We got away from the trife. What now?"

"We need supplies and equipment," Nicholas replied. "Food, water, a change of clothes. Guns and ammo if we can find them."

"You don't need to worry too much about water," Yasmin said. "Everything we use is recycled. Even our excrement is broken down and purified. The loss is minimal. What we have on board should last a full crew at least a month, two if we stretch it."

"That'll help. But Grimmel wanted me to bring a contingent of Marines along for this ride. He didn't exactly get his wish, but that's all the more reason we need to supply them properly."

"I don't like the idea of relying on three teenagers."

"Luke's friends are good kids. But I know what you mean. I offered to drop them off near the Pilgrim launch site. They refused."

"You can make them go."

"I could, but what good would that do us? Grimmel wanted six. We still only have five. Anyway, we need to find a place that might have everything we need without the risk of getting waylaid by the military."

Yasmin's face wrinkled in consideration. "Grimmel Corp has a second headquarters in London with a full R and D lab. I have security clearance to get into any of the corporate buildings. I'm sure we can get anything we want from there."

"What about the Royal Space Force?"

"They pulled out of the area over a year ago. The

trife ran rampant through the city, but it's been abandoned so long it should be a ghost town by now. There's no reason for the RSF to keep an eye on it and definitely no reason for them to waste any resources there."

"In that case, it sounds ideal. We don't have to go right away. We can stay up here for a while, take some time—"

"No. I don't need it or want it. We should go as soon as possible."

"The others might need a little bit of a breather."

"You're in charge up here, Nick. How much they breathe is your decision."

"How much energy do they need to walk around a building and grab things?" Nicholas said, smiling. "I'll let the others know. Do you want to stay up here?"

"I told you, Nick. I want to lay here and cry forever. But I want to know what happens next even more, and treading water won't save us from drowning if we never reach dry land."

Nick slid off the rack and offered Yasmin his hand. "In that case, come on. I'll introduce you to Dag."

"Who's Dag?" Yasmin replied.

Chapter 22

As Foresight descended through the broken clouds, bleeding off altitude as comfortably as possible for the passengers, Nicholas kept his eyes glued to what he could see of Europe's mainland. With population centers established so closely together, it looked like a checkerboard of blackened ruins. So much destruction. Despite the attempted evacs, a lot of people had died here, and it was depressing as hell. Hopefully, they'd be able to find what they needed in London.

"ETA, six minutes," he announced through the ship's comms, alerting the others to the approach. Their plan was simple enough. Put Foresight down as close to Grimmel Corp's tower as possible and use Yasmin's biometric security clearance to enter the facility, grab what they could carry, and get the hell out as quickly as possible.

Nicholas had expressed concern that the building might have already been looted or destroyed, but Yasmin insisted that wouldn't be the case. With the sheer volume of trade secrets and advanced prototypes involved,

Grimmel had always kept a high level of security for his facilities. When the shit truly hit the fan with the trife, he had put the buildings into an alert status that made the bottom levels impenetrable. It was possible the trife had scaled the exterior of the building and gotten in either through the windows or the roof, but even if they had, the demons had no need of the food, clothing, and equipment Nicholas was after.

As Yasmin had explained to him and the others, the odds were higher that there were still employees locked inside the tower, living off the same supplies they wanted to take. Nicholas hoped that wouldn't be the case. Scott, however, had verbalized his concerns about people left to fend for themselves against the trife. They often became more like the trife. Their desperation to survive even overrides their morality, removing all barriers to aggression and violence. Murder, rape, slavery, and other forms of mistreatment were growing in prevalence the more society degraded. In the wilds, it was everyone for themselves.

Nicholas kept Foresight's descent angle shallow, banking gently in a wide spiral to keep from stressing his passengers. While he was eager to load up the starship and move forward in their plans, it wouldn't help to make his people sick from a rapid drop. Two more minutes passed before the spacecraft entered the cloud cover completely obscuring visibility above the British Isles..

He didn't need to visually see to fly Foresight. At least, not until they got closer to the ground. Instead, he monitored the readings projected onto the HUD, using them to navigate. Using the still-functional positioning satellites in orbit overhead, Frank had already set a marker on their destination. All he had to do was wind around it until he dipped below the ceiling. At that point he would need to eyeball a landing spot, but he didn't expect much difficulty accomplishing that.

Another minute and Foresight broke through the ceiling, the thick shield of white and gray giving way to less dense clouds and revealing much of the city beneath them. Nicholas remembered traveling to London with Yasmin soon after they were married, one of the few vacations they had managed to squeeze in between her workload and his deployments. There was an outside chance Luke had been conceived in one of the hotels in the city, but they had been so hot for one another back then, still so into intimacy that the exact time and location was impossible to guess. Even so, it was near enough to the time that London had always held a special place in his memories.

Another small piece of him died to see it now.

While no nukes had ever fallen on London, it almost seemed as if they had. So many of the buildings were in ruin across the entire expanse. Some crumbling, some fully collapsed, nearly all of them damaged. The bridges that allowed crossing of the Thames had all been demolished at some point in an effort to keep the trife on one side, but the desolation proved it had been too little, too late. The burned out husks of long-abandoned cars lined the streets, joined there by military vehicles, each one with armor plating, tires, and treads marred by the too-familiar wounds delivered by the trife.

Garbage and dust had settled everywhere. Storefronts showed signs of burning and looting. And not a single living thing made itself apparent anywhere Nicholas looked.

In this case the lack of activity was a good sign. He slowed the starship to a relative crawl, activating the hull's anti-gravity systems to keep the craft aloft as he adjusted course toward the target Frank had painted on the HUD. Grimmel Corp's tower was nearly a mile east along the river, a short distance from the former United States embassy. Unsurprisingly, it had avoided the worst of the destruction. It's nearly one hundred floors of glass remained completely intact while the structures around it had fallen into heaps of rubble.

There was little doubt in Nicholas' mind that Grimmel had specifically requested that the RSF respect his contribution to the war effort, and later their escape, by not destroying the sites where most of his researchers and developers were hard at work.

"I've got a visual on the tower," he said over the comms. "I'm opening access to the feeds." He tapped on the left-hand control pad to activate the individual access stations in the center of the ship, allowing the others to see what he saw through the forward windscreen. "Yazz, can you confirm the target?"

"Confirmed," Yasmin said. "It looks good."

"Almost too good," Nicholas replied. Like a diamond in the mud, the glass tower was a stark contrast to the city's desolate backdrop. "I've got my eye on the railroad tracks as an LZ. That'll put us about three hundred meters from the building."

"What about the rooftop?" Yasmin asked.

Nicholas eyed the top of the building. Most of the crown was rounded, but an area had been left flat to serve as a helipad. "Too small," he replied. Foresight was miniscule compared to the ark ships, but at half the length of a 787, it was much too large to put down on a helipad. "I could use the anti-grav to hover beside it but that would drain a lot of power we might need."

"Understood," Yasmin said. "Three hundred meters is still pretty close."

Nicholas eased the spacecraft toward the railroad tracks, continuing to reduce thruster velocity and increase power to the anti-gravity plates. He scanned the wide view through the windscreen, his gaze stopping on a large, square building surrounded by a quartet of large stacks near the riverfront.

"Yazz, do you know what that is?" he asked, marking the location.

"Battersea power station," she replied. "The stacks are from the original generation plant, but the plant itself was replaced with a quartet of tokamak fission reactors a few years back. In part to help provide enough power for Grimmel's needs."

"That's a lot of juice," Gills said. "What did he need it for?"

"I don't know. I never gave it much thought."

"More importantly," Nicholas said. "After the humans left, did the trife move in? I don't see any outside, but that shell is pretty large."

"If they did, they probably heard us coming," Gills said. "I'm not really in the mood to get into it with those bastards again right now. Especially since I don't have any bullets."

"Agreed," Nicholas said. "I'm going to swing a little further east along the tracks so we can put the tower between us and the power plant."

"Good idea."

Nicholas floated the ship over the tracks at less than a thousand feet, side-slipping Foresight while keeping the bow facing Grimmel's tower. The building rose like a glass monolith in front of them, nearly twice as high as their current altitude.

"Check all the feeds," Nicholas said. "If anyone sees anything moving, call it out."

He couldn't see the central compartment from his seat, but he could imagine each of the crew members at their stations, actively flipping through the feeds on their individual displays. He continued drifting while he waited for any of them to raise an alarm. When no warning came, he cut the thrusters completely and let the ship slowly drop to the tracks, deploying the landing skids and touching down over the rails.

"Jennifer, you're in charge while we're gone," Nicholas said, releasing himself from his seat and removing his helmet as he stood. He turned to face her in the co-pilot's seat. "You remember what I showed you?"

Jennifer nodded. "Yes, sir."

"If anything happens, it's vital for you to get the ship out of danger. If you need to lift off, meet us at the helipad at the top of the tower."

"Yes, sir. I'm not sure how well I can handle the controls, but I'll do my best."

"Frank won't let you screw anything up too badly," Nicholas said. "The neural net won't allow you to crash. Besides, I have faith in you."

"Thank you, Captain Shepherd. Good luck. Be safe."

Nicholas nodded and left the cockpit. Dag waited in the short corridor, and he stepped over the bot on his way to the center of the craft. He didn't need to look to know Dag followed him. The little robot really was indeed like a puppy.

A killer puppy.

The others were all standing when he arrived, waiting expectantly. Nicholas looked each of them over.

They looked exhausted. He doubted he looked any better. "You all know the plan."

"Yes, sir," Gills said. He picked up his rifle despite its lack of ammunition, propping it over his shoulder like a club. "It's better than nothing."

"Come on," Nicholas said, leading them to the ladder to the lower deck. They descended quickly, and Nicholas activated the control panel to open the forward hatch and deploy the ramp. "Dag, take point."

He wasn't sure the robot understood him until it scooted between his legs to the edge of the extending ramp, riding it down to the railroad tracks. A light mist hovered over the ground, the overcast skies adding another level of dreariness to the destroyed and deserted landscape.

Dag stepped off the ramp and advanced about ten feet before turning around, waiting expectantly for Nicholas and the others to follow.

"How does he know where we're going?" Gills asked.

"It might be interfaced with the ship," Yasmin replied. "I'd need more time to review its programming to determine for sure."

"We'll see about that when we get back," Nicholas said. "It looks like we've got a straight, easy shot to the tower. Let's get in and out before we can get in any trouble."

"Copy that," Gills replied.

Chapter 23

It only took a few minutes for Nicholas and the others to reach the tower, stopping in one of the alleys between two of the many damaged residential buildings that surrounded the area. It took a moment for Dag to realize he had stopped, and the small robot spun its head around before walking backward to their position.

"It looks clear," Gills said, joining Nicholas in sizing up the approach. A fair share of abandoned cars, rubble and broken glass lined the street between them and the rear of the Grimmel corporate tower. The windows of the building began about fifteen feet above ground level, with a garage tucked underneath and a ramp leading down into it.

"It does," Nicholas agreed. "I'm also looking for a path through the debris. If we can find a cart inside, it'll be easier to make a single trip."

"A truck would be even better."

"We're not likely to find one," Scott said. "Most survivors made off with the larger, heavier vehicles early on. Easier to push smaller cars out of the way and easier to hide from the trife in the back."

"If they took any trucks from down there, they took them before the fighting," Nicholas said. "Or there would be a path cleared through."

"Some of the debris looks like it might have been blown down from rooftops by a storm," Yasmin said. "It doesn't look as though it's been on the ground for long. I actually stayed in that apartment there." She pointed toward one of the buildings, above where the sloping roof had partially collapsed, having sloughed down onto the street like an avalanche. "I was here for a conference four years ago. It was a nice apartment."

"There may be a better route in and out on the other side," Scott suggested.

"Closer to the power planet?" Briar said. "No, thank you."

"We don't have confirmation that there are trife inside."

"We also don't have any guarantee there's a better way in," Nicholas said. "The density of the surrounding buildings made it hard to spot a clearing from the air. Our best bet is to get into the tower and check the front from there if we can."

"Sounds good to me," Scott said.

"Dag, we're headed for the garage. Pick the easiest route."

Nicholas still wasn't sure of the small bot's capabilities so he didn't expect much of a result from such a generalized instruction to *pick the easiest route*. But Dag didn't disappoint, running out through the debris field and picking its way around the worst of the rubble and garbage. The group trailed behind it, Gills and Toast splitting to the flanks and keeping an eye out for interference, trife or otherwise.

They reached the ramp to the underground parking area without incident. A barrier of thick steel bars blocked their entrance, score marks from trife claws visible as rusted scars across the metal.

"Someone was in here at some point after the gate came down," Scott said, running his finger along one of the deeper gashes. "A slice like this, they had to be just on the other side of the barrier when the slick got cut off."

"It could have been someone already on the run when the trife cornered them," Yasmin said. "They saw the closing gate and ducked inside."

"Makes sense," Scott agreed.

"Can you open it?" Nicholas asked.

Yasmin nodded, crossing to the security panel on the left side of the garage. Unlatching and opening the hardened cover revealed a touchpad and biometric scanner beneath. "Let's hope the building still has power," she said as she touched her thumb to the scanner.

A green light flashed on the panel. Mechanisms that hadn't operated in a while creaked and groaned, and something cracked loudly enough that it echoed across the street, causing Gills and Toast to stare back the way they had come.

"Could we make a little more noise?" Gills said. "That would be perfect."

That gate started rising.

"Dag, I don't suppose you have a light?" Nicholas asked, peering into the garage. The visibility from the dim spill of sunlight only covered the first fifty feet of the space.

A light appeared at the top of the robot's head, quickly intensifying until the beam stretched across the floor of the garage. Dozens of cars were still parked inside, covered in a thick layer of dust and ash that had blown in from outside. Nicholas didn't see any footprints or disruptions to the sediment, confirming no one had passed this way in a long time. While the debris outside was too thick for the smaller vehicles to navigate, maybe they could find a larger truck inside after all.

"Dag, stay close," Nicholas said. The small bot didn't move when the gate rose far enough for it to duck beneath, instead waiting until it was open enough for the rest of them to follow.

They paused again inside the gate as Yasmin used the security panel on the inside to close the barrier again.

A sharp crack from outside caused Nicholas to whip his head around at the same time he took a subconscious step toward Yasmin. A woman in a ratty sweatshirt and torn pants appeared around the corner, her eyes darting to the closing gate, a look of desperation sweeping her face. She tried to change direction, skidding on the wet surface and losing her balance. Falling on her backside, she quickly rolled herself over and onto her knees, aiming a small revolver back the way she had come.

"Shit," Gills said. "Stop the gate." He and Toast ducked beneath it, rushing up the ramp to help the woman.

"Yazz, bring it back up," Nicholas said. "Dag, help Gills and Toast." The bot raced away as the gate came back up, pausing to look back at him. "I'm fine. Go!" Without any more delay, the robot darted after the Marines.

The woman fired her revolver, two more rounds echoing between the buildings. A man came into view, stumbling forward before falling flat on his face. Additional gunshots sounded from nearby, bullets hitting the ground near the woman. She turned her head toward Gills, momentarily fearful.

"Come on!" he shouted, looking in the direction of the gunfire before ducking low. More bullets crackled across the street, fired at the Marine.

The woman jumped to her feet, limping down the ramp where Toast grabbed her. She flinched at the sight of his burn-scarred face but didn't try to pull away, letting him lead her back toward safety. Dag stopped nearby, facing the top of the ramp.

"Hurry up!" Nicholas shouted, waving them toward the garage. He wished he had a firearm to help support their retreat with cover fire.

Dag sprinted forward then, launching itself into the air as another man came into view. The man pointed his rifle at the bot, failing to get a bead on it before it reached him. Blades extending from its wrists, it scored the man's throat before bouncing off his chest, somersaulting in the air and landing cleanly back on the ground. The man dropped his rifle and reached up, pressing his hands against his throat in a futile attempt to stem the blood flow. He dropped to his knees and then fell face down, dead before he hit the cement.

The little bot didn't remain static for long, darting around the fallen attacker and vanishing out of sight. Gunshots rang out, clearly targeting him but missing as he reappeared behind Gills and Toast. They made it back behind the barrier with the woman, Dag running to catch up.

"Yazz, close it," Nicholas said.

"Fall back! Find cover!," Nicholas shouted as Yasmin hit the controls to again close the gate.

Everyone but Dag was able to duck behind parked cars before a group of a dozen men and women in a mix of ragged clothes and military hardware reached the ramp. They fired Royal Space Force rifles at Dag, their aims off the mark as the bot dove head first under the closing gate just before it clanged against the ground.

The attackers came to a stop, staring into the garage as Dag rolled to its feet and circled around the car Nicholas crouched behind, heeling beside him.

"We saw your ship, mate!" one of the attackers said. "All we want is a ride out of here to somewhere safe. I hear there's a bigger ship taking passengers up north. We deserve a chance too."

"If you saw our ship and wanted a ride, why were you shooting at us?" Nicholas shouted back, remaining behind cover.

The man didn't answer right away. "Sorry, mate. Just a habit by now, I suppose."

"Bullshit," the woman they had rescued spat.

"You can come out and let us into your ship, or we can go take it for ourselves."

"Yeah, good luck with that," Scott shouted. "You idiots wouldn't get within fifty feet of it before our co-pilot blasted you to bloody ash."

Nicholas shot a hard look over at Scott. He shrugged. "They're already afraid of us. Might as well make them afraid to get near the ship."

Nicholas couldn't argue the point.

"Yeah, well," the leader said. "You have to come out of there sometime. We'll be waiting for you."

The group retreated from the ramp, vanishing from sight.

"Little do they know we'll be armed when we come back out," Gills said. "Limey bastards. You can't even go for a nice stroll anymore without someone trying to shoot your face off."

"They're just trying to survive, like everyone else," Yasmin said.

"The trife have better morals than that lot," the woman said. "They were planning to ambush you when you came out. That didn't sit right with me, so I told them either we talked to you peacefully or I was going to warn you."

"They obviously decided against parlay," Gills said.

"That they did. They said the RSF promised to send help months ago and none ever came, so they don't trust nobody who ain't a raggie."

"Raggie?" Briar said.

"Ragamuffin. A survivor," the woman replied, looking Briar over. "You look a bit like a raggie now that I look at you."

"We are," she said. "The military installation where we were hiding was attacked. We barely got out alive."

"Same shit, different day, eh? They're convinced there's a big spaceship up north taking on passengers for a trip to another planet. I thought they were crazy until I spotted your ship comin' in. Says to me there's a way outta this nightmare."

"Not for most," Nicholas said. "If the RSF hasn't come for you by now, they aren't coming."

"Figures. What about you lot? You got an extra seat on that ride of yours? I don't suppose it's like Doctor Who. You know, bigger on the inside?"

"No," Scott said before any of the others could answer. "It's a small ship."

"Well, shit," the woman said. "You can't find room for one more?"

"We don't know you," Yasmin said.

The woman laughed. "Aye. I suppose I do need to earn your trust if I want to earn a seat. I'm Macey.

Macey Lane." She raised a hand with a fingerless glove on it and wiggled her fingers. "Hope you keep in mind I did come to warn you."

"That you did," Gills said. "Glad to meet you, Macey. I'm Gills. That there is Toast. And that's Captain Shepherd. We're with the USSF. The rest of our group is civilian. Yasmin, Scott, and Briar." He pointed them each out.

"Thank you for not abandoning me out there," Macey said. "I would have been a goner for sure." Her attention shifted downward as Dag stepped in front of Nicholas. "And who might this be?"

"This here is Dag," Gills replied. "Captain Shepherd's bodyguard."

"Oy! He's a slick little guy. Thanks for saving my life, Dag." The robot didn't respond. "Yeah, well, anyway. Welcome to London."

Chapter 24

Yasmin used her security clearance to call the elevator on the west side of the garage while Gills kept watch over the gate, making sure the group of raggies, as Macey called them, didn't start shooting at them again. Nicholas wasn't all that concerned about the gang harming them, especially once they had resupplied, but the group was a problem because he was trying to move fast and they would only slow him down.

"How come you have access to the doors?" Macey asked. "And the lift?"

"I work here," Yasmin replied. "Well, used to work here. For Grimmel Corporation."

"You worked for the man himself, eh? I think I saw Mister Grimmel once, pulling up to the front of the building in his limo. Tall, skinny chap with a beard, right? Handsome if you don't prefer a little meat or muscle on the bones."

"That's him," Yasmin said. "Did you live around here?"

"Sort of. I worked as an au pair for one of the

mucky-mucks. Roger Baron. Oh, I miss those kiddos. Sarah and Jane. Beautiful little girls. They were like my own."

"What happened to them?" Briar asked.

"Sarah died of the sickness. Jane…" She shook her head. "I don't know. Maybe she's on the ship up north. When things got crazy I went back home to be with my mum. We hid in our basement for months, only came out during the day when the sun was shining and the buggers were all lazy from a night of killing. I scavenged anything I could find to eat. Anything I could find to protect me and mum with."

"I spent time out there alone," Scott said. "I can relate."

Macey looked at him. "Yeah. It only got tougher as time went by. The market nearby got nicked of nearly everything so I had to start searching houses for whatever was still good. Canned goods, mostly. Plus processed shit that could survive anything. That worked for a while, but some of the things I saw in those houses are burned into the backs of my retinas." She shook her head. "One day when I was out, I came back and found someone had chosen my house to scavenge. They happened on Mum and shot her dead so they could take our stash."

"That's horrible," Yasmin said.

"This whole world is horrible, ma'am," Macey replied. "I didn't know what to do, so I headed back this way to see if Jane was okay. A stupid idea, I know. But I wasn't thinking all that straight at the time."

"You managed to stay away from the trife?" Scott asked.

"No," she replied. "Turns out I'm barren. I didn't know until one of them had me cornered down an alley and left without slashing me." Her face darkened. "I didn't find Jane, but the raggies found me. Chapman and his blokes grabbed me coming out of the apartments. I put up a good fight, but it was four against one. They roughed me up a bit and made me do things for them. Scavenging and scouting mostly, with a tracker on my ankle so I would know I couldn't escape. After a while, I figured I was better off with them than on my own so I did my best to become part of the gang and earn their trust. There's got to be a line somewhere though, right? Something that makes us better than the trife? I tried to explain that to Chappie, but being out here fighting for survival made him too hard. Anyway, I'm sure I'm not the only one here that's lost everything they care about."

Nicholas glanced over at Yasmin, who flinched in response to the statement. "No," she agreed. "We all have. Every last human on Earth has."

"That doesn't mean we can't find new people to care about," Briar said. "New families."

"Here's to that," Macey said, giving Briar a thumbs up.

The elevator dinged as the cab arrived, the doors sliding open. Dag took point, entering the elevator ahead of the others, his head swiveling to examine it before he turned to face Nicholas. Despite a lack of features or expression, Nicholas still had the impression the bot waited impatiently.

"Let's go," he said, leading the group into the cab. "Yazz, what floor?"

"If I remember right, there are stock rooms on almost every floor. Cafeterias on two, fifty, and eighty-seven," Yasmin replied. "The guard station is on the ground floor, of course. But there's also Research and Development on Sub-zero."

"Sub-zero?" Gills asked.

"Underground," Yasmin answered. "About fifty meters below the bottom level of parking. Fully automated hazardous containment, just in case there's ever an accident."

"What the hell did Grimmel do down there?" Scott asked.

"Honestly, I don't know. I don't have clearance to that part of this facility."

"So we can't get in," Nicholas said.

"We couldn't get in when it was guarded," Yasmin replied. "Now? We just may need to find a way to open the door."

"That sounds like it may take a while. I don't want to leave Jennifer alone for that long and I definitely don't want to give the raggies more time to set up their ambush."

"Considering Grimmel's last words to us, I think it may be worth the attempt," Yasmin said. "Who knows what kind of goodies we might find."

"What do you think you would need?"

"A little bit of luck and some time with the computer at the guard station. As long as the intranet is up and running I might be able to do something with it. I won't know until I try."

"Okay, then let's hit the guard station first. Ground floor please, love."

Yasmin entered the floor and they began to rise, arriving less than a minute later.

Dag stayed in the lead as the elevator doors opened, moving out into the darkness of a lobby lit only by emergency floor lighting. Moving in behind the robot, Nicholas immediately noticed the thick metal shields that had dropped down over the street level windows and entrance, preventing anyone or anything from entering.

Otherwise the lobby looked as though it was frozen in time.

A large white shag rug occupied the center of the lobby, plush white leather seats placed in a square along its perimeter. A silver coffee table stood in the middle, a handful of old magazines still spread across the top. A row of metal detectors lined a security checkpoint near the sealed entrance. A few bags, laptops, and briefcases had been left behind on the conveyor belts, while large displays lined the walls, all currently dark. A long reception desk nearby on Nicholas' right proved how busy the building had been at its peak, which suddenly seemed like a lifetime ago.

"Access to the guard station is this way," Yasmin said, leading them toward the reception desk. As they neared, Nicholas noticed a door on the right labeled EMPLOYEES ONLY. It sported a biometric access panel.

"I thought you only spent three weeks here," he said. "You seem to know your way around like you were here for months."

"Pete took me on a tour when I first arrived," she replied.

"Pete?"

"The Regional VP. Peter Howser. I'm sure I mentioned him to you before."

Nicholas shrugged. "If you did, I don't remember. So how personal was your tour?" He raised an eyebrow toward her.

"Shut up, Nick," she replied, stopping at the panel and letting it scan her thumb. The door clicked and she pushed it open. Dag maneuvered around her, entering the area first.

A long hallway led them around the elevator banks to a dark steel door marked SECURITY.

"So, I don't get it," Macey said. "You escaped a bad situation in the States in a starship, and the first thing you decided to do was come here?"

"We left in a hurry," Nicholas replied. "No food, no supplies. This place is locked down, so the odds are good it'll still have what we need."

"Why didn't you just talk to your military people? Arrange for a drop-off and passage on one of the ships? Or at least go to them for supplies? That has to be easier than breaking and entering here."

"Is it breaking and entering if we have the keys?" Scott asked.

"Maybe not," Macey replied. "Not really the point, though. I'm sure the US military could have given you everything you need. Unless…" She paused, her expression changing. "You aren't supposed to have the ship, are you? And you don't want your people to know where you are. That's rich."

"Has anyone ever told you that you talk too much?" Yasmin said, opening the door to the guard station.

"My mum," Macey said. "And my exes. Too many people nowadays don't appreciate a good conversationalist."

Dag took point again, and Nicholas followed the bot into the front of the station. It was simply appointed, with six desks arranged in two rows near the back, a door behind them. Another doorway sat on the left, offering access to what looked like a monitoring room for security cameras positioned both inside and outside the building. Another heavy steel door waited on the right, a security panel on the wall beside it. Like the lobby, it appeared the station had been quickly abandoned.

Nicholas assumed the evacuation occurred before the defensive barriers entombed the building.

Why would Grimmel install such heavy-duty defenses in the first place? Had he known the trife would come?

"That should be the armory," Yasmin said, pointing to the metal door.

"What kind of tour did Pete take you on?" Scott asked, laughing until Nicholas cast a sharp eye his way to silence him. He looked away, summarily chastised.

Yasmin tried her thumb on the scanner for the armory, but it didn't work.

"I guess you don't have access to everything," Nicholas said.

"Not yet," she agreed, crossing to one of the desks and sitting. She pushed a moldy, coffee-stained mug to the side to work with the keyboard and mouse for the computer terminal on the desk. The display activated when she tapped on the keys, offering a login screen. "Do me a favor. Search the other desks for anything that looks like it could be a password or other personally identifying information. Check under the keyboards too."

She took care of the desk where she sat, lifting the keyboard and checking beneath it for a written password. Nicholas did the same for the desk next to hers. Entirely clear of anything on the top, he pulled open a drawer to search.

"I've got something," Briar said, holding a keyboard bottom up. A small piece of paper had been taped to it, a series of random letters and numbers written on it.

"Read it off to me," Yasmin said. Briar repeated the series, which Yasmin entered. The computer unlocked, passing her to the desktop. "Too easy."

"Man, I didn't think anyone was still dumb enough to do that," Gills said.

"Yeah, you have your password scribbled on your tighty whities," Toast said.

"Number one, I don't wear tighty whities," Gills replied. "Which I can easily prove." He pulled down the waistband of his pants to show off the waistband of yellow boxers. "Number two, my password is your mom's name, followed by how many times I've——"

"Hey Captain Shepherd," Scott said from the doorway to the monitoring room. "Come look at this."

"Hmm, it looks like I can update my clearance to include the security systems," Yasmin said. "I'm adding my record now."

"What about Sub-zero?" Nicholas asked.

Yasmin shook her head. "There's no access from here. Giving it a little more thought, Grimmel's workstation is a better bet. It's in his office on the top floor."

"Do you know the password?"

"No, but according to the terminal records it isn't locked. Only the door into his office is bolted. Security has an emergency override which I just gave myself permission to use."

Nicholas smiled. "Lucky for us."

Yasmin stood up and approached the door to the armory.

"Captain Shepherd," Scott repeated, more insistently this time. "You really should see this."

Nicholas crossed to the monitoring room. Scott went to one of the two seats and sat down to work the controls.

Yasmin put her finger on the scanner. The locks on the door opened with a thunk. She grabbed the handle and tugged it open.

"Shit," she said, slapping her palm in frustration on the doorframe. "It's empty."

"What?" Nicholas replied, going back to the doorway to look at Jasmine.

"Captain Shepherd," Scott said again. "I know where the guns are."

Nicholas' head whipped back toward Scott, staring at the camera feeds the kid had activated.

A group of men and women were in a hallway, all of them wearing bulletproof vests and helmets with SECU-RITY printed on the front and carrying an assortment of rifles, shotguns, and pistols they had taken from the armory.

"Macey," Nicholas said, calling her over. "Are these people with you?"

"Nope," Macey replied. "I've never seen those wankers before in me life."

"Scott, do you know where that hallway is?"

"Yes, sir. And whoever they are, they're headed our way."

Chapter 25

"Yazz." Nicholas motioned her over to where he stood in the open doorway to the monitoring room. "Do you recognize them?" He pointed to the people in the feed.

Yasmin leaned around the door frame to get a better look before shaking her head. "It's impossible to tell with the helmets they're wearing and the angle." She pointed at one of the men. "That one looks a little familiar. I mean, if I had to guess I would say they're all employees who were trapped here. Look at their clothes."

"Yeah, I noticed," Nicholas replied. "Pants and skirts. Business apparel. Not ragged street clothes like Macey's. No offense."

"None taken," Macey said.

"They've been here since the trife came then," Yasmin said. "The building went on lockdown eighteen months ago."

"That's bad news for us," Scott added. "How much food do you think they have left? And what are the odds they'll share anything with us?" He turned to look at

Nicholas. "They might have been corporate snobs once, Captain Shepherd, but the invasion changed people, and most not for the better. They could be just as dangerous as the crew outside, and they'll be here in less than a minute."

"How did they even know we were coming?" Briar asked.

"This can't be the only place to view the security feeds in a building this big," Nicholas said. "They probably saw us, the same way we're seeing them."

"Then hopefully they noticed the USSF uniforms," Yasmin said. "They'll know we're friendly."

"Uniforms don't mean shit anymore," Macey said. "I can nick a Royal uni off a corpse any day of the week. Big boy here is right, you can't know what their mindset is, except they saw us coming and decided to come on down fully armed and armored."

"She has a point, Cap," Gills said. "Maybe we would have been better off scavenging supplies from the street, or taking whatever the raggies have."

"That's not how we do things," Nicholas replied. "Someone has to maintain a semblance of honor and dignity."

"The way I see it, you can take your honor all the way to the grave," Macey said.

"I didn't say we shouldn't be cautious. I'll go talk to them. The rest of you wait here."

"What?" Yasmin said. "If Scott's right, they're more likely to shoot first and ask questions later. I should go out. If they're former employees, maybe they'll recognize me. If they start shooting, at least you'll have time to prepare for them."

Nicholas shook his head. "I'm not putting you in more danger."

"You can watch me on the cameras. We don't have time to argue this."

"No, I'll go with you."

"And if they shoot you, who would fly Foresight?"

Nicholas didn't want to let her go alone, but she had a point. Whoever these people were, whatever the war might have done to them, they were bound to be less aggressive against someone they knew. "Fine, but Dag's going with you."

"I don't know if that's a good idea," Yasmin said.

"He's one of Grimmel's bots," Nicholas said. "It'll only support your right to be here. Dag, go with Yasmin. Don't let anyone hurt her."

The robot didn't react, leaving Nicholas unsure if it understood the instructions.

"They're almost to the adjoining corridor," Scott said.

Yasmin and Nicholas locked eyes before she hurried out the door of the security station and into the passage. Dag trailed behind her, slipping through the door just before it closed.

"Well, this is intense," Gills said.

"I want you and Toast by the door, ready to back her up if things go sour," Nicholas said.

"Clubs against bullets," Gills replied. "I'm not especially thrilled with the idea."

"That's an order, Corporal Hess."

"Yes, sir," Gills replied, joining Toast near the door as Yasmin stopped halfway down the corridor.

The other group of people rounded the corner ahead of her, their weapons suddenly pointing at her as her presence took them by surprise.

"Scott, do the feeds have audio?" Nicholas asked. Yasmin's lips moved, her hands going up. Dag was nowhere to be seen. He hoped the little bot had found somewhere to hide near his wife.

"I'm looking for it," Scott replied. "Ah, here. I think this is it." He tapped on the keyboard.

"Doctor Shepherd?" someone in the group said. "Is that really you?"

Yasmin's head tilted as she searched for the speaker, who pushed his way through the group to the front.

"Peter?" Yasmin said.

The man laughed. "Yes," he replied. "I can't believe it. Harry, this is Doctor Yasmin Shepherd. One of our top people from the United States. Yasmin, this is Harry Doolittle, head of security."

"A pleasure to meet you, Harry," Yasmin said, putting out her hand.

"You work for Grimmel Corporation?" Harry asked without moving to shake it. Stocky, with a square jaw and deep set eyes, Nicholas wasn't sure if he held mostly muscle or fat beneath his guard uniform.

"For Grimmel Corporation," Yasmin replied. "Before the world went to hell."

"That explains how you got through the parking garage security gate. What are you doing here?"

"They seem friendly enough to me," Briar said, having joined everyone else in the monitoring room.

"Are you kidding, B?" Scott asked. "Harry's posture doesn't look welcoming to me at all, and he sounds more like he's interrogating her."

The security guard stood with his hands on his waist, conspicuously close to a pair of guns hanging low on hips like an old West gunfighter, his expression stone-faced.

"We barely escaped a trife attack," Yasmin said. "We

came into the building hoping to find food, water, and protection."

"I see. Well, I'm sorry to disappoint you. You won't find any of that here."

"Harry, we have——"

Harry shot Peter a look that cut him off immediately. "I'm afraid you're out of luck. You and your people should go."

Nicholas watched Yasmin glance at the other former employees. He could tell by the look on their faces that they didn't necessarily agree with the guard's words or demeanor.

"You don't have anything you can spare?" Yasmin asked. "Nothing at all? The only thing we have is the clothes on our backs."

"Heh. Don't lie to me. I saw two of your people carrying guns."

"As clubs," Yasmin said. "We ran out of bullets during our escape."

Harry seemed pleased by the statement.

Scott groaned. "Why did she just admit we have nothing to fight back with?"

"You've still got two pops in my revolver," Macey said.

"Against nine people wearing bulletproof vests?"

Macey shrugged.

"Relax," Nicholas said. "She knows what she's doing." He had to at least trust her on that.

"We're not looking for much," Yasmin said. "We searched the armory for guns, obviously there weren't any because you already have them all. We were going to head to the cafeterias to check the pantries. Anything you could spare would give us a chance out there." She turned her head, looking directly at Peter. She wasn't trying to convince Harry to help. She hoped to convince the others.

But the others seemed totally cowed by the former head of security.

"I told you, we can't spare anything," Harry growled, showing signs of frustration. "Go call the rest of your people out here, and we'll escort you back to the garage. If you want to stay, you can hide down there as long as you want, but you'll get nothing from us. Not a single can of peas, not a single bottle of water, and definitely not a single bullet."

"Fine," Yasmin said, looking dejected. "Can I ask how you wound up trapped here?"

"We aren't trapped," Harry snapped. "I don't know if you noticed, but there's nowhere else to go. This building is safer than anywhere on the planet. Even during the bombing the Royal Air Force avoided Grimmel's properties."

"There is somewhere else to go," Yasmin said. "There are ships set to leave Earth within the next month. What if I can get you all seats on one of them?"

"Ships?" one of the others said. "I didn't know—"

"She's lying," Harry hissed. "There aren't any ships. There's no way out of here. It's a trick to get our supplies."

"It's not a trick," Yasmin insisted. "I'm scheduled to transfer to one of them. The Pilgrim. If you help us, we can take you there."

It was Nicholas' turn to groan. How were they supposed to make good on that promise? Even if they could squeeze a small group into the ship, they had already decided to avoid military installations.

"So, you *do* have room on board," Macey said, compounding the error.

"We'll talk about it later," Nicholas said.

"Assuming there is a later," Briar replied, earning a sharp eye from him. "Sorry."

"Stop lying," Harry said. "We've had enough empty promises. The only reason these people are here is because Mister Grimmel asked them to stay past the lockdown to handle some of the sensitive information. He swore if the military couldn't get them out then he would."

"Except he never came back," a woman in the group said. "Neither did any rescue team, military or otherwise. The building was meant to support nearly ten thousand employees self-sufficiently, so it has clean, running water, climate control, and plenty of power from the reactors next door. After a few months of waiting, we decided to stick it out and hope the trife would either die off or go dormant when they couldn't find anyone else to kill."

"Did you decide?" Yasmin asked. "Or did he?" She motioned to Harry. "I understand how they were left behind. Why are *you* here?"

The others in the group glanced nervously at one another before looking to Harry for the response. It seemed strange to Nicholas that the security guard had wound up in charge of the survivors. He was eager to hear the answer to Yasmin's question too.

"I don't need to explain anything to you. Enough stalling. I want you all out of here. Now."

"There *is* a ship," Yasmin pressed. "I swear. We have a smaller ship that can transport you there. It's parked on the railroad tracks nearby. It'll be packed, but—"

Harry forced a hard laugh. "Nobody believes your bullshit, Shepherd." His hands dropped threateningly to the handles of his guns. "And I'm tired of listening to it.

You've got one more chance, and then maybe none of you will ever leave."

"I see," Yasmin replied, glancing up at the camera for a split second. Nicholas knew the look. He was too far away to do anything more than cringe. "And who died and left you in charge? I bet you're only here because you were scared shitless to leave."

Harry's face wrinkled and flushed with anger. "Why you little bitch!" he cursed, guns rising from their holsters. "I'm going to kill you and everyone who came with you."

He had barely freed the twin pistols from their moorings when Dag dropped from his hiding place beneath Yasmin's dress and launched itself at Harry. The former guard cried out in shock and confusion as the small bot hit him in the chest, twisting one way to remove his left hand, and then the other to remove his right, moving so quickly he never had a chance to fire. The bot sprang back to the floor, landing between Harry's severed hands, which still held fast to the pistols.

"Kill them!" Harry screamed, blood pumping from the stumps of his hands with every heartbeat. "Kill them all!"

The others looked at him and then at Yasmin.

"There *is* a ship," she repeated again.

"I said shoot her!"

The former Grimmel Corporation employees lowered their guns.

"Why don't *you* do it, Harry?" Peter asked mockingly. "I always said you would get what you deserved one day."

"Go to...hell, Howser," Harry stammered, already beginning to pale and shake from blood loss. "You're a traitor. All of you! Traitors." He fell back into the wall, sliding down it to his ass as he moaned. "My hands. Oh, my hands." He started to sob. "Somebody, help me. P-please."

Yasmin looked at the camera again and smiled before turning her attention to Harry.

"If you can spare a first aid kit, I can fix that up for you."

Chapter 26

With Harry neutralized, Nicholas exited the security station with the others, joining Yasmin in the hallway. Dag retreated from his wife's side to heel beside him, its wrists wet with the former security guard's blood.

"What is that thing?" he heard Peter ask as he approached. He couldn't help noticing the man was handsome, with a strong jaw and piercing light blue eyes. A hint of jealousy tweaked his heart. He knew he should trust his wife more, but they had spent a lot of time apart the last few years, even before the war, and things hadn't always been the best between them. He couldn't say he would be surprised if he ever found out she hadn't been completely faithful.

And he couldn't say he would blame her.

But what did any of that matter now?

"This is Dag," Nicholas replied ahead of Yasmin. "He's one of Grimmel's bots. I think Grimmel programmed it to act as a bodyguard." He reached Yasmin's side and put out his hand. "Captain Nicholas Shepherd, United States Space Force."

Peter smiled, talking his hand and shaking firmly. "Peter Howser," he replied. "Former Grimmel Corporation VP. I always wanted to meet you, Captain. I've only heard good things."

"Really?" Nicholas replied, sincere in his surprise.

"You're a war hero," Peter said. "I know you're in the USSF and not the RSF, but anyone fighting the trife is on the same side. Thank you for all that you've done."

Nicholas smiled, disarmed by the compliment. "Thank you. I really appreciate that."

"I'm sorry we didn't stand up to Harry sooner," Peter said. "When the building locked down and nobody came back for us, we needed someone to take charge. Harry was here. He had security clearance to most of the building and seemed to know how to survive. So we let him take charge." He looked over at Harry, who was staring at the stumps of his wrists. "He wasn't always like this. In the beginning, he was kind and helpful. But he became more arrogant and demanding as time went on, like he was a king and we were his subjects. Then he started getting violent when we didn't do what he wanted."

"He liked having the power," Yasmin said. "He didn't want to give it up." She raised her voice. "And look where that got him."

Harry didn't react. His power lost and a lot of his blood with it, he had fallen into shock and despair.

"I have the first aid kit," one of the other employees said, moving through the others and holding it out to Yasmin. He was around Luke's age, similar in height and build, and a similar mop of brown hair. Yasmin stared at him in tense silence before taking the first aid kit with a trembling hand.

"Yazz, are you okay?" Nicholas asked.

She nodded, exhaling sharply and bringing the kit with her to treat Harry. She knelt in front of him, speaking softly as she opened the kit and lifted out a hand-held laser, a syringe that probably contained a pain killer, a tube of antiseptic ointment, and finally, bandages.

"So, you really do have a ship," Peter said, continuing the conversation with Nicholas.

"Yeah, we do," Nicholas admitted. "Honestly, it isn't meant to hold so many people, but I think we can make it work. We were hoping not to have to go near any of the launch sites. Since Yasmin promised you passage out, we can't avoid that now."

"So you aren't supposed to have the ship?" Peter asked.

"That depends on who you ask. Grimmel was with us in the facility during the attack. He told us to take the ship and fulfill its mission."

"What mission is that?"

"Did you work closely with Aaron?" Nicholas asked.

"I knew him as well as anyone in the company," Peter replied. "We spent time in meetings together, made small talk on occasion."

"How much of his research were you familiar with?"

"I had a hand in funding and logistics. I filled requisitions and monitored accounts payable. So I know what we were spending on a lot of the R&D, at least in this office."

"Did he ever mention something called slip technology?"

"Slip?" Peter paused before shaking his head. "No. Not that I recall."

"What about Project Foresight?"

Peter shook his head again. "No. I'm sorry, Captain. Why do you ask?"

"Because you wanted to know what the mission is. And to be honest, I'm not completely sure. Our side quest was to try to find some answers at the same time we were picking up supplies. I know there's a development lab deep beneath the building. I don't suppose you have access?"

"No," Peter said. "Wait. You said Grimmel was in the facility with you?"

"That's right."

"And it was attacked?"

"Yes."

"What happened to Grimmel?"

"I don't know."

Peter's mouth hinted at a smile which flattened almost as quickly as it arrived. "That's a shame. I hope he made it out."

"Me too."

"Yes, well, I can't help you with your questions or the research lab," Peter said. "But if you're going to take us to a ship then we can help you with supplies. As you can see, we have the guns and armor from the security station. There's more at the ground level cafeteria where we've settled in." He paused, his expression tensing.

"What is it?" Nicholas asked.

"Food might be a concern. It depends on how much you might need. We've already gone through ninety percent of what we found in the lower pantries and the loading docks. I'm certain there's more in the upper level storerooms, but..." He trailed off again.

"But what?"

"You can't get up there," Harry said, as Yasmin

unceremoniously jabbed the syringe through his pants and into his thigh, delivering the medication.

"Why not?" Yasmin asked, noting Harry's wince of pain.

"Why do you think?" he replied, scowling at her. "The trife scaled the building and came in from the rooftop."

"You mean there are trife in here?"

"That's what I said. This whole area is crawling with them. They have a nest inside the Battersea plant right next door."

Nicholas' heart pounded. "I didn't see any trife on my approach. And we weren't exactly quiet getting in here."

"I haven't seen any trife either," Macey said. "And I've been living nearby with a group of raggies for the last three months."

Harry laughed. "Trust me, they're here. I can show you on the feeds. They're mostly dormant though. I think because there are so few people around. They barely move, like they're conserving energy."

He shifted his weight, using the wall to help pull himself to his feet before looking at his stumps again. His demeanor had shifted a third time. "If I help you, will you take me to the starship too?"

"That's not for us to decide," Nicholas said, looking at Peter, who turned to the rest of his group. "What do you all think?"

Harry looked at them too, his expression pleading. "Please. Maybe I did some things wrong, but I was trying to protect us."

"If we leave him here, we're no better than the trife," one of the men said.

"You're a bloody asshole, Harry," a woman said. "But you at least did us right in the beginning."

"We should feed him to the trife," another said. "You almost cost us our ticket out of here."

"Why don't we take a vote?" Peter said. "All in favor of saving Harry's life?" Six hands went up out of the nine. "The ayes have it."

"Thank you," Harry said. "Truly." He looked at Nicholas. "I can show you."

"Gills, make the rest of the introductions," Nicholas said. "Harry, show me the trife on the feeds."

Chapter 27

"You'll have to work the controls for me," Harry said, entering the monitoring room of the security station with Nicholas, Yasmin, and Dag. "If we don't get out of here to someplace with a doctor soon, I'll need someone to hold something else for me too." He laughed awkwardly, his joke falling flat.

"Dag can do it," Yasmin said, still angry at the former guard after Harry had threatened her.

"I'm not so sure I want that little devil around any more of my appendages,"he said, glowering at Dag.

"You can always squat and pee. I do it all the time."

"Yeah, well, you're a bi—"

"Harry, walk me through this or go park your ass somewhere out of my earshot," Nicholas said, interrupting the man's chafing exchange with his wife. While the two of them had been busy exchanging barbs, Nicholas had been making little progress in figuring out the controls for the feeds.

Harry promptly gave him instructions on how to select the floor and the specific cameras he wanted to use to show them the trife. Within no time, the monitor in front of Nicholas displayed a hallway full of the creatures.

"Shit," he said softly. "I was hoping you were lying."

"I don't have any reason to lie," Harry said. "Especially now. But see how they aren't moving."

Nicholas did see. The trife were on their feet but they barely budged, shifting almost imperceptibly as they adjusted their balance back and forth. "How long have they been there like that?"

"Six months," Harry replied. "They ignored the place for a long time so I never thought they would try to come in. Then one day the motion sensors on the rooftop triggered and showed them breaking through the door up there. It was total panic. We came down here, ready to jump into the armory to hide and watch things unfold on the feeds. But they stopped at the eighth floor."

"Why did they stop?" Yasmin asked.

"I don't know," Harry answered. "It confused us too. They milled about for a while and then spent the next week hunting every floor above eight. Tap for the next floor up, Captain." Nicholas did as he asked, flipping through camera feeds that all showed one or two trife. "It's the same all the way up. It's my fault we didn't go and grab the other supplies sooner, but I never expected the trife to come in the building after so much time. I still don't know why they did that. If you want food you have two options. Sneak past the trife to the cafeteria on fifty or talk to the people in charge of the boats off this rock."

"I hate to say it, but the second one isn't an option," Nicholas said. "They'll confiscate our ship and cost us everything. Not intentionally, but they weren't there. They can't understand."

"I still want to get into Grimmel's office," Yasmin said. "His computer is unlocked."

"It is?" Harry said. "How do you know?"

"I pinged it over the network."

"Are you sure? I tried his computer once a while back. It was locked."

"Does that mean you have access to his office?"

"As head of security, I have... had biometric access to his office, yes." He held up his stumps. "Not anymore."

"But your hand still has it," Yasmin said.

"I suppose it does."

"It's one thing to risk waking the trife for necessities," Nicholas said, slightly disturbed at the thought of using Harry's severed hand to open the door to Grimmel's office. "Grimmel's personal computer isn't a necessity."

"That depends on your perspective," Yasmin argued. "If it can give us a more specific idea of what we're supposed to be doing or what to expect, that would be incredibly valuable. If we can enable access to the research lab, that could be valuable too. His office is on floor one hundred. There's a cafeteria on eighty-seven. Lend me Dag again and we can get up there while the others load up food and water."

"It's too risky," Nicholas replied.

"We need to take risks, Nick. There's no way to play any of this safely. And I'll do anything to give us the best chance at success."

"Harry, what happened to the security guard comms?" Nicholas asked.

"The earpieces are back in the cafeteria with the rest of our gear," Harry said.

"You saw we were inside the building. Where were you monitoring the feeds from?"

"A laptop connected to the camera network. That's in the cafeteria too."

"Then I guess that's our next stop," Nicholas said, pushing back his seat and standing to face Yasmin. "I'll feel a lot better about letting you out of my sight once we have comms. But that doesn't mean I like this."

"One foot in front of the other, Nick. That's all we can do."

They left the security station, rejoining the others in the hallway. Gills had finished introducing everyone, and Macey was in the middle of too-loudly recounting how Dag, Gills, and Toast had saved her life. The story reminded Nicholas they would still have the raggies to deal with once they finished up here. Their progress was slow, but at least it was steady.

"Where are Harry's hands?" Nicholas asked, seeing that someone had removed them from where they had landed.

"I put them in the fridge in the break room," one of the women said, "Just in case they can be reattached."

"That's not my concern right now. Can you go get them, please?"

"Certainly." She hurried down the hall, disappearing around the corner and returning in record time with a clear plastic bag. Nicholas made a face when she tried to hand it to him. She'd wrapped the severed hands in gauze to hide their horrific nature, though the bleeding had soaked through, turning the bag's contents more macabre.

"I'll take them," Yasmin said, accepting the bag from the woman. She looked at Nicholas. "I never knew you were so skittish about severed limbs."

"It's a little frightening to me that you aren't," Nicholas replied.

"I worked with cadavers in college. This isn't that much different. It's all just bundles of molecules."

"Let's go," Nicholas said, shrugging off any more comments on the subject.

The ground floor cafeteria was back through the lobby, past the banks of elevators and down a second corridor toward the rear of the building. The survivors had converted the dining area into a shared living space, utilizing the tables and packaging materials to create individual private hovels. They had also barricaded every door with outside access, except the main entrance. Between it and their meager homes, they had erected barriers for cover in the event of an attack. In some ways, the arrangement reminded Nicholas of the defenses at the base.

For all the good it had done them.

"We keep all of the ordnance and comms in my tent," Harry said, pointing to the largest of the makeshift living spaces.

Located in the rear corner near the entrance to the storeroom and the kitchens, Harry's 'tent' was similar in construction to the other hovels—nothing more than a stack of tables lined with layers of cardboard—save for its overall size. Unlike the other structures, his had a solid door with a padlock on it. While anyone could have easily forced their way in through the sides of the enclosure, they wouldn't be able to do so without making their breaking and entering obvious.

"The key is in my pocket," Harry said, looking suggestively at Yasmin. "If you want to dig it out."

Nicholas resisted the urge to punch Harry in the face for the innuendo. Hands or not, the man continued acting like an ass.

"Dag," he said instead. "Can you please retrieve the key from Harry's pants pocket?"

"What?" Harry said, looking over at the bot. "N...no. Wait. Someone else do it. I don't want that thing anywhere near—"

Too late. Dag jumped up and grabbed onto Harry's waistband with one hand, using it to hold on while it shoved its other hand into his pants pocket, removing the key and jumping back down. It held the key up to Nicholas.

"Nice job," Nicholas said, taking the key and using it to remove the padlock.

He pulled the door open, revealing a swaybacked mattress in one corner and a literal pile of munitions in the other. A second mattress sat near the entrance, covered in old comic books, magazines, and a laptop computer. The screen from the laptop was active, showing the feed of the corridor outside the security station.

"You can have whatever you need in there," Harry said.

Nicholas glared at him. He didn't need the man's permission.

Entering the hovel, he immediately crossed to the guns, ammunition, and armor, finding another small box among the ordnance. Inside were nearly a dozen wired earpieces and transmitters.

He stepped back outside the tent. "Gills, Toast, take inventory of the ordnance and organize it for distribution."

"Yes, sir," Gills said.

"Can I help?" Macey asked.

"Go ahead," Nicholas replied.

The trio disappeared into the hovel while Nicholas

picked out the comms one at a time, activating them and passing Scott, Briar, and Yasmin each one.

"Can you stick one in my ear, Captain Shepherd?" Harry said.

"Why do you need one?" Nicholas asked.

"Because I'm coming with you."

"No you aren't."

"I know, you think I can't be of any help like this, but you're wrong. I know this place better than anyone. If you need somewhere to put up a defense, if you need somewhere to hide, if you want to corral some of the trife, I can help you do that."

"You're a walking claw sharpener without hands, Harry," Nicholas said.

"So if I die, then I die," Harry replied. "It's no loss to you."

Nicholas considered the request. "Fine," he said. "It's your life to lose. But I'm not making any special accommodations for you."

"I don't expect you to."

Nicholas shoved one of the comms in Harry's ear before inserting another into his own. "We leave as soon as the Marines are ready."

Chapter 28

"It's okay if you want to wait here," Nicholas said.

"No, thank you, Captain Shepherd," Briar replied. "I didn't come with you to hide when things get dangerous." She shifted her hips, still adjusting to the weight of the G19 handgun holstered there. "I'm in."

"So am I," Peter said, accepting a shotgun from Gills.

"Peter, you don't need to do this either," Yasmin said.

"Yes, I do. If you all die up there, who's going to get us out of here? You need all the help you can get."

Nicholas nodded, picking another comm out of the box and handing it to him. "Let's do a comms check. Nicholas, check."

All eight of his team checked in, beginning with Yasmin and ending with Briar. Dag said nothing but did raise its hand, confirming for Nicholas that it could listen in on the comms.

"All right," Nicholas continued. "The plan is simple. We'll take the elevator directly to eighty-seven. I expect the trife on the floor will become alert as soon as they hear the elevator approaching, so we'll need to make a fast break to the cafeteria when the doors open. Once we're there, we hold the line until we thin the herd. Then Peter, Macey, and Briar will grab a cart and load as much food as we can carry while Yasmin, Harry, Dag, and I make our way to Grimmel's office."

"Nick, you can't—"

"Forget it, Yazz. You can't keep risking your neck and leaving me behind because someone has to carry on for Luke. Either I come with you or we forget about Grimmel's computer."

He could tell she wanted to argue, but she nodded instead, accepting his ultimatum. She still wanted into the underground lab badly enough she was willing to take on additional risk to both of their lives. He couldn't help wondering if there might be something down there she already knew about and wanted to reach.

"We'll meet back at the elevator. If we get access to the underground lab, I'll head down there with Yasmin. Gills, you and your team will head directly to the parking garage. I expect the rest of the supplies to be loaded and waiting for us down there."

"It'll all be ready," Annie said. She was the woman who'd taken possession of Harry's hands and had taken charge of the group after Harry's sudden dismissal.

"What about the raggies?" Briar asked. "They're going to ambush us the second we show our faces outside."

"We don't have a choice. We'll need to punch through them. Lay down cover fire of our own and break for Foresight. Once on board, I'm sure I can scare them off with the spines."

"Okay," Briar said.

"You all know what to do," Nicholas added. "Let's move out."

The group left the cafeteria and returned to the elevators. They piled in, and Yasmin stretched her hand out toward the touchscreen to enter the destination floor. She let her finger linger over the panel for several seconds.

"Are you ready?" she asked, looking at the others.

"We're ready," Nicholas replied.

She entered the eighty-seventh floor. The doors closed and they began the ascent.

"If I die up there, it was nice knowing you all for the last hour," Macey said. "Especially you, muscles."

Scott glanced back at her. "You know I'm only sixteen, right?"

"What?" she said. "You don't look sixteen. Well, you're a handsome lad, anyway, but I guess I'll have to settle for Gillie then."

"That's fine with me," Gills replied, smiling back at her. "But I'm not joining the you on the arkship."

Macey sighed. "You're so into your duty. I respect that."

"Get ready," Nicholas said, watching the floors count up. The elevator rose quickly, each number flashing past. "Weapons hot," he said as he felt the elevator begin slowing. He shouldered his rifle. Gills, Toast, and Scott did the same. The others carried mostly handguns, which would be easier to manage while they took on their additional tasks.

Dag scooted between Nicholas' legs, positioning itself as close to the doors as he could, ready to defend Nicholas. Harry dropped back toward the corner, of no use in a fight.

The elevator cab came to a stop. Nicholas' eyes

narrowed, focusing on the seam between the doors, waiting for them to open.

A toothy mouth greeted them as the doors spread apart, a trife already waiting to charge into the cab. Its hand slashed forward the moment it had enough space between the doors. Nicholas fired, his single round hitting it between the eyes, and it toppled backwards like a felled tree.

"Dag, go!" Nicholas snapped, not that he needed to give the order.

The bot turned sideways to clear the door, charged around the fallen trife, and leaped at the nearest demon. A cacophony of hisses filled the hallway, and Nicholas saw at least a dozen trife between them and the intersection leading to the cafeteria.

He fired again, knocking a second creature down. A third round killed another. Dag caught up to one, leaping at it with blades extended. Another creature hit the small bot in midair, sending it crashing into the wall. It bounced off and landed on its feet, lunging between the trife's legs. One swipe from each blade cut the demon's feet off at its thin ankles. It collapsed forward on its face, struggling to get back up.

Nicholas moved into the hallway, still firing single rounds, causing maximum damage at close range. The others filed out behind him, Gills and Toast on his flanks, Scott and Macey covering the rear once the elevator was no longer behind them.

Shots rang out one after another, the rest of the trife in the immediate area succumbing to the overwhelming firepower until they cleared the corridor.

Dag stayed in the lead, hurrying to the intersection and turning in a full circle before racing off in the direction of the cafeteria. Nicholas heard the hissing before he turned the corner to see Dag tearing into the demons, their vocalizations changing to high-pitched cries as they fell. More trife came down the passageway from the other way. Frenzied, they sprang at Dag, their jaws slathering froth.

"Gills, Toast, take the right," Nicholas said, turning left to follow Dag. The two Marines went the other way, setting off a burst of gunfire that chopped down the incoming trife. Nicholas didn't bother to shoot, conserving ammo and watching Dag as the little bot made short work of the aliens "Scott, Macey, join me on point. Gills, Toast, hold the rear."

"Copy that," Gills said.

Scott and Macey moved past the others, joining Nicholas at the front of the group as they reached the end of the next hallway. The entire floor was a typically open corporate office. Neutral colored walls, grey carpeting, overhead LEDs with individual cubicles. Office doors lined both sidewalls, an occasional framed print breaking up the monotony.

Nicholas turned the corner, finding the rest of the passage to the cafeteria clear, a sudden thumping sounding above them.

"They're on the move upstairs," Gills said, looking ominously at the ceiling.

"Heading our way," Nicholas agreed. "It's going to get ugly in a few minutes. Come on."

They sprinted down the hallway to the cafeteria, pushing open the twin doors into the space. He came to a sudden stop, eyes fixing on the hundreds of trife that filled the room, pressed together so tightly it was hard to tell where one ended and another began. They were all soaking in the limited light that spilled through the floor-to-ceiling windows at the corner of the tower.

"Shit," Nicholas said, putting up his hand to stop the others.

One of the trife turned its head, its squinted eyes opening to full size and latching onto his gaze. The trife's mouth opened in a soft hiss, and more of the creatures began lifting their heads to look at him.

"What's going on?" Yasmin asked before spotting the trife. "Oh my…"

"Back to the lift," Nicholas growled into the comm. "Now!" He fired into the horde of trife in the cafeteria. The density made it impossible to miss, causing some of the demons to cry out as others reacted to the damage, pouncing on their brethren to put them out of their misery. The rest worked to untangle themselves and give chase, racing after the retreating humans.

Scott joined Nicholas in shooting at the trife as they exploded through the cafeteria doors, some springing off powerful legs and bounding off the walls, others flipping over and crawling along the ceiling, LEDs shattering under their clawed feet. The hallway darkened, a slick of angry aliens gaining in a hurry.

Nicholas fired his last round and quickly dropped the spent magazine, grabbing another from his belt, his legs pounding under him as he slapped it in. He resumed shooting, his attack bolstered as Gills at his side and Scott in the rear joined him.

"This was a bad idea, Captain," Gills said.

"No shit," Nicholas replied.

"Maybe we can throw Harry at them."

"It's tempting."

"Incoming!" Toast shouted from the other side of the group, his rifle reports echoing in the hallway. Macey and Peter joined him a split second later, their barrage pausing as they made short work of the trife in their path.

"Pick up the pace!" Nicholas shouted as Scott's rifle went dry. He released the magazine and grabbed another, struggling to get it in place. His hands shook with adrenaline while he cursed, finally slapping the mag home.

A trife leaped toward him, claws slashing at his face. He shoved the barrel of the rifle into its mouth and pushed it to arm's length before pulling the trigger and splattering its brain matter across the demons behind it.

Dag zipped through the alien masses, a tiny power-house of activity. Slicing and dicing, it ricocheted off the walls and tumbled through the air, landing on a trife's head and stabbing it through the skull. Leaping at a demon on the ceiling, It cut the thing open from chest to stomach before stabbing a third one in the eye.

"Dag, fall back!" Nicholas said into the comm. The robot reacted instantly, sprinting away from the trife and reaching the group in retreat.

They turned the corner, the elevator directly ahead, the door to the emergency stairs positioned adjacent to it on the left side.

It slammed open, the first few trife from the upper and lower floors emerging into the hallway to block their escape.

"Now can we throw Harry at them?" Gills asked.

"Dag, we need to get to the elevator," Nicholas said as they gunned down the leading demons. The robot responded by winding its way forward through the legs of the others.

"Keep moving," Nicholas urged. "Don't stop. Scott, can you close that door?"

"It won't stay closed," he replied.

"Anything to slow them."

"Yes, sir."

Nicholas continued shooting at the trife still pouring toward them from the rear. They had killed at least fifty of the creatures already, but there had to be two or three hundred in the cafeteria, with more arriving from other areas on the floor. He was sure the entire mass of aliens in the building had come out of hibernation, awakened to the sound of fighting.

Nicholas' rifle went dry again. Instead of reloading, he let it hang from his shoulder and switched to the pair of Glocks he wore on his hips. Pulling them from their holsters, he aimed and fired, his rounds punching through the delicate skeletons of the trife and killing both his targets and the demons directly behind them. Briar joined him at the rear, and even Yasmin pulled her handgun and started firing. Nicholas found himself suddenly grateful for all the times she had joined him at the range.

Dag plowed into the trife, slashing their legs, leaping up and cutting their throats as Toast and Peter mowed them down. The doorway out of the stairwell served as a strong bottleneck, keeping too many from entering at once and clogging the hallway. Once the gunfire cleared the path ahead, Dag dived into the stairwell, vanishing among the dark alien mass. The effort was enough to relieve the pressure on the door, allowing Scott to throw his weight and strength against it. He held it closed as Dag created bloody havoc on the other side.

"Yazz, get the elevator ready," Nicholas said. "Gills, Toast, Macey—help me cover Scott." He stepped up behind the kid, turning to shoot at the approaching trife. The others joined him while Yasmin hit the control and opened the cab door, stepping in. "Briar, Harry, get in the cab."

Harry was already stepping in just behind Yasmin. Briar moved reluctantly.

"Macey, go!" Nicholas shouted over the gunfire. The trife were gaining on them, and he was running out of bullets. Scott grunted as the door shifted beneath his shoulder, shoved by the trife. Then the point of a claw dug through the door, digging into his arm. He cried out but didn't let go.

"Son of a bitch," Gills said, shooting through the door, the claw pulling back.

"Peter, Toast, get in the cab! Lay down cover fire. We'll stay to the left."

The two men hurried to the elevator, turning back and opening fire from the doorway, Toast dropping to one knee. More trife collapsed, but they were getting too damn close.

"We make a break for it in three," Nicholas yelled. "Yazz, try to time it so the doors close immediately behind us. We'll have to shoot through them to keep the bastards back."

He waited for Yasmin to confirm before he began the count. Scott released the door on three, just as Nick and Gills stopped firing. He turned to make a run for it, and Nicholas grabbed his arm, helping him gain a little extra speed as the door swung open. A claw stretched out to grab the kid, missing him by a hair.

The trife from the cafeteria, sensing their preys' escape, hissed and leaped at the fleeing humans. Gunfire from the elevator cut them down.

"Dag!" Nicholas shouted as the gunfire stopped. He shoved Scott into the elevator, the kid slamming into Harry and pushing him into the back wall.

Gills fell inside as the doors began closing. Nicholas turned sideways to slip through behind him, looking back in search of Dag.

The robot was nowhere to be seen.

His worry for the bot was quickly forgotten as he and Briar fired the last of their rounds through the metal door to push the creatures back.

He expected the cab to descend back to the ground level.

Instead, it went up.

Chapter 29

"Yazz, we're going the wrong way," Nicholas snapped, heart racing from the encounter with the trife.

"No we aren't," she replied. "Grimmel's office is on floor one hundred."

"Are you crazy?" Nicholas hissed, instantly furious. "We just kicked the hornet's nest, and there are a lot more hornets than we have bullets. Dag is already lost. We need to get the hell out of here, not dive deeper."

"I disagree."

"This isn't a democracy, Yazz. It's not up for a vote. I'm the ranking officer. I'm in charge. That's how this works."

"We're not in the military, Nick. If we want to be honest, we're fugitives from every legal angle of military and civilian justice. Foresight doesn't belong to us. We stole it."

"What?" Harry said.

Macey laughed. "Bunch of raggies yourselves."

"So don't get high and mighty with your superior officer shit. I need to see what's on Grimmel's computer. I need to know if there's anything for us in Sub-zero."

"We're going to die, Yazz. All the intel in the world won't stop that. We can't take on hundreds of trife alone, and you just put fifty floors worth of them between us and freedom."

"As long as we can return to the elevator we can get back down. The cab will crush any that try to get up through the shaft."

"Oh, is that all we need to do?" Nicholas mocked. "I wish I had known ahead of time it would be so easy. What the hell are you thinking?"

"Grimmel didn't expect Luke to die," she replied.

"Tell me something we don't already know."

"Think about it, Nick. Grimmel believed he had insight into the future. It doesn't matter right now why or how, only that he did. But he didn't see Luke's death coming. He didn't expect the trife to attack Fort Hood when they did. Why not? How can you change something that hasn't happened yet? And if you did, how much can you change without causing a massive disruption to spacetime?"

"I'm still not following you," Nicholas said, growing impatient as the lift slowed.

"Luke wasn't supposed to die. But that doesn't mean we weren't supposed to take Foresight. Hell, Grimmel was already talking to us about doing that very thing right before the trife attacked. What if his entire plan was to make off with the ship in the middle of the night? Without supplies. Without weapons. Without anything. What if he expected us to come here? Or at the very least, what if he expected you to come here? You and a squad of Marines hand-picked by Colonel Haines." She stared intently into his eyes. "Harry said Grimmel's computer was locked when he checked it. But now it isn't."

Nicholas returned her gaze. One part of him decided she was coming up with a reason that suited her goals. The other wanted to believe in her logic, if only so he wouldn't have to be so angry with her for putting them in greater danger. "You think he left something for us?"

"Yes. Something important. He had to know the trife would be here."

"How? He can't be everywhere at once."

"Then he had to know we would get out of this alive."

"Unless the trife weren't here in the future he saw. Unless this has changed too."

Yasmin's expression shifted to sudden panic. She clearly hadn't considered that possibility. It didn't matter now. They didn't have time to stop the elevator and go back down. The doors slid open, revealing the corridor, and the trife in it.

The demons rushed them straight away, gunfire from Macey and Briar cutting them down before they could get close to the doors. Within moments, they were clear again, at least until more trife showed up.

"We need to make a decision," Yasmin said.

Nicholas nodded, letting his gut instinct guide him. They were up here now, so close to Grimmel's office. If Yasmin was right, searching the computer could mean the difference between success or failure. It could decide whether they ever saw Luke alive again or not. If she was wrong, then they would have risked their lives for nothing.

But at least they would know.

"You four," he said, turning to Toast, Gills, Macey, and Briar. "Split up and hold the elevator. Keep this corridor clear." He pointed to the emergency stairwell door. "Search the closest offices. Find something to barricade that door. Do it quickly. The rest of you are with me."

"Yes, sir," Gills said.

Reloading his rifle and shouldering it, Nicholas sighted down the barrel as he jogged down the hallway ahead of Yasmin, Harry, Scott, and Peter. A trife came around the corner, a bullet to the head taking it out before it even had a chance to look Nicholas in the eye. Scott cut down the next one. Nicholas glanced back in time to see Gills smash open the door to one of the offices. He went in and came back out with a chair, shoving the tall back beneath the handle of the door to the emergency stairs. Given enough time, the trife would be able to slash and claw their way through the blocked door, but every second they could delay the demons counted in their favor.

Nicholas led everyone around the next corner, headlong into a mass of trife charging toward them. He missed Dag already, half-expecting the little bot to rush forward and jump into the fray. He had to settle for bullets instead, single rounds hitting the trife one after another, mowing them down relatively easily. Every bullet they fired now was one less bullet they would have to shoot later, and there was no doubt in his mind they would need them later.

"Captain, we've got trife on our six," Scott said, firing back into the creatures coming from the far end of the hallway.

"We need to make Grimmel's office," Nicholas replied. "Lock them out, deal with them when we're done."

"They'll claw right through the door."

"I doubt Grimmel has a run of the mill office door."

They reached the end of the hallway and turned right. What had to be Grimmel's office was up ahead. It occupied the corner of the building, the doorway double-wide and made of thick, lacquered wood.

A handful of trife occupied the passage between them and the door. An equal handful of bullets cut them down, and Nicholas stepped over their corpses before they could spill their dark blood on the carpet.

The volume of trife behind them tripled as they reached the door, and Yasmin unslung a backpack, reaching into it for Harry's hand. Nicholas turned around and joined Scott and Peter firing into the oncoming demons.

Yasmin made a face as she unwrapped the shriveling hand from the gauze, holding it bare as she touched the thumb to the biometric scanner beside the door. The LED on the scanner turned green, and the door unlocked.

It was the impetus the trife needed to charge them. Not even bothering to aim, Nicholas unleashed a fully automatic spray. Scott followed suit, spewing heavy metal into the creatures and sending them tumbling back like a wave crashing on the shore.

"Nick, let's go," Yasmin said, ducking inside and holding the door open.

"Scott, Peter—go!" Nicholas called, holding his ground until they were inside.

His rifle clicked empty again. Out of magazines. He lifted the strap from his shoulder and threw the weapon at the nearest trife, distracting it just long enough to duck inside the room. Scott threw the door closed behind him, locking the demons out.

"Too close," Nicholas said, exhaling heavily, his body trembling from the adrenaline coursing through it.

He turned back to the door. He could hear the trife's claws against the wood. The thickness would take some time to breach. Looking into the room, he immediately spotted Grimmel's desk. A long, wide aluminum slab, it looked like it was fashioned out of an old airplane wing. A large monitor and keyboard sat on top of the wing. A high-backed leather chair was placed behind it, in front of floor-to-ceiling windows that provided an incredible view of the Thames and North London.

"Yazz, do what you need to do but make it quick," Nicholas said. "We can't keep the others waiting for long."

Yasmin hurried to the desk, dropping into Grimmel's chair and tapping on the keyboard.

"Were you right about it being unlocked?" Harry asked, following her and taking up position behind the chair. He had managed to stay out of the way of the gunfire, and it seemed to Nicholas that the trife had little interest in an unarmed man.

"Yes," Yasmin said, tapping on the keyboard. "I'm removing the password protection and encryption from the local drive. I'll copy everything on Grimmel's network partition over so we can take it with us and take a look at it later."

"How long will that take?" Nicholas asked, eyes fixed on the door.

"Not long. A few minutes. I can get into the security settings in the meantime and grant myself access to the sub-zero lab."

"The sooner the better. Gills, what's your situation?" he asked over the comm.

"Good, all things considered," Gills replied. "The

trife are bashing the barricade from the emergency stairs, but they can't get more than two or three to the door at a time. The bugs already on the floor seem way more interested in you, Cap."

"Copy that. We're in Grimmel's office, working on pulling data. ETA five minutes."

"Copy. We'll hold. You just need to get back here. Holler if you want backup."

"I might take you up on that offer. Standby." Nicholas continued watching the door, which shook and thumped from the aliens' blows. Getting in had been easier than getting out would be. "Scott, Peter—how many rounds do you have left?"

"I've got ten in the current mag, plus another full cartridge," Scott replied. "Plus about sixty rounds total for the Glock."

"I'm down to my last magazine," Peter said. "My handgun is fully-loaded, two extra magazines."

Nicholas checked his twin pistols. He had a similar bullet count. Close to three hundred rounds in aggregate. There were less than three hundred trife on the floor with them. As long as that number held, they still had a chance.

"Yazz, any day now," he said, glancing back at her.

"Almost there," she replied.

"Captain Shepherd," Harry said, his tone drawing Nicholas' attention. The former guard had turned away from the desk and was looking out the window. "I think we have a problem."

"What is it?" Nicholas asked, quickly hurrying over to his position and looking out. The Battersea power plant dominated the view from the west corner of the office. While it had seemed vacant earlier, it was alive with activity now.

Hundreds of trife spilled out of every doorway, moving toward the tower like an army of marching ants. Some had already reached the building, using their light frames and sharp claws to scale the exterior.

They were about to be inundated with unwanted visitors.

Chapter 30

The first trife to scale the outside of the tower to the one hundredth floor poked its head up adjacent to Nicholas' feet. He looked down at the demon as it sank its claws into the thick glass and pulled itself up to his eye level. Separated by several inches of thick ballistic glass, the two enemies stared at one another. One in anger. The other in relative indifference. It didn't surprise Nicholas to find no true malice in the eyes of the trife, but the vacant depths chilled him all the same.

The trife drew one hand back and took its best shot at the window. Nicholas heard the impact of its splayed claws as nothing more than a dull thump. It created only several minor hairline cracks, but not discouraged, the trife attacked the glass again and again. Each blow added a few more tiny fractures, but like the door it would take some time to break through.

A second trife reached the window and started slashing at it. A third joined in. Then more until their numbers covering the windows began to blot out the daylight and darken the room. More creatures on their way to the top of the building climbed over the trife on the windows, dislodging and sending entire sections of them plummeting to their deaths. The outcome had no effect on the others. They held no fear of heights or dying. They possessed only a programmed desire to destroy humankind.

Nicholas turned back to his wife as she pulled a multi-tool from her pocket and slid off the chair, disappearing beneath the desk. "Yazz, what are you doing?"

"Grabbing the hard drive," she replied. "Otherwise, we're all done here."

"Everyone, head for the door," Nicholas said, pointing. As they began to move, he went to the desk and squatted down to watch Yasmin unscrew the case of the computer. "Gills, we're going to be on our way back in just a couple minutes."

"Copy that, Cap," Gills replied.

Behind Nicholas, the trife intensified their assault on the glass, while the trife at the door remained relentless in reaching them, their blows shaking the heavy door.

"Yazz, hurry," Nicholas said, increasingly concerned by the growing mass of trife all around them. He knew hundreds more were heading for the rooftop where they would have access into the building.

"Almost there," she said.

A loud crack made Nicholas whip his head back to the windows. A pane on the west side had started to splinter, a spiderweb of cracks forming all the way across its surface. The substrate seemed to groan, the weight of the creatures dangling from it becoming too much for it to bear in its damaged state.

"Got it," Yasmin said, taking the hand Nicholas stood and offered her as she climbed out from under the desk. A second, final crack, and her head turned to the window as the pane gave way, tumbling into open air and taking dozens of trife with it. The demons beside the open window ceased their assault, hissing as they fought one another to be first into the room. "Oh, shit."

Nicholas shoved Yasmin back under the desk and pulled one of his guns from its holster, firing just in time to drop the first trife to lunge at him.

"Gills, we need that backup. Now!" he shouted into the comm, taking down two more trife, a third one slashing at his chest. Its claws scraped across his bullet-proof vest. The creatures rushed him en masse, as if they were trying to get to Yasmin to take the unencrypted drive.

But that was impossible.

Wasn't it?

The trife were programmed killing machines. They didn't understand or care about anything beyond the humans in front of them. But not a single demon turned toward Scott, Peter, or Harry even though Scott and Peter were decimating them. Even as Nicholas threw himself under the desk with Yasmin, pushing his back against her to shove her all the way back into the corner.

Nicholas shot the creatures as they crowded in front of the desk, trying to reach them under it. He put bullet after bullet through their skulls until they piled up, blocking the way in. Nicholas breathed a sigh of relief, but he knew they would figure out another way in any second.

They didn't prove him wrong.

A claw sank through the top of the desk, forcing him to duck. And then the demons started pulling their dead out of the way.

And then his gun ran out of bullets.

Yasmin whimpered softly in fear.

"Gills!" Nicholas shouted. Dropping the empty gun, he grabbed the other one, shooting another trife.

"We're in the corridor outside the door," Gills replied. "We'll have it clear in a minute."

"We're pinned down," Nicholas replied. "We don't have a minute."

"We're almost there!" Gills announced.

Another pane of glass broke, directly in front of the desk. He saw more trife fall to their doom through gaps in the dead bodies. Scores of them climbed through the new opening, all of them coming for Nicholas and Yasmin.

Gills' *almost there* wasn't good enough.

Nicholas kept firing until the bodies once again piled up in the opening, this time blocking out every pinpoint of light. The demons immediately began pulling the bodies away again, but whenever a glimmer of light appeared, Nicholas put a bullet through it. Another dead body would fall, blocking out the light again.

And then his gun clicked empty, leaving him and Yasmin at their mercy.

Except the demons ran out of time.

Halos began to glow around the bodies, and Nicholas reacted instinctively, whirling around to wrap his arms around Yasmin and push her face into his chest. He hid his own eyes as heat exploded into the room, the intensity of it on his back like multiple heat lamps on high. Even under his vest and shirt, his back burned like a second degree sunburn.

After a few seconds, an almost peaceful silence settled over the office. Warmth still radiated from the desk, but the intensity of the heat had let up enough for Nicholas to chance opening his eyes. There was dim light under the desk now, and the place smelled like sulphur and burnt flesh.

"Yazz, you okay? he asked, still holding her head to his chest.

She nodded, and he let her lift her head. She gasped, looking over his shoulder.

He swiveled his head around and saw what had horrified her. Blackened flesh hung off the bones of the two dead trife closest to them, their mouths frozen wide open in soundless cries of agony. All the rest of the bodies piled into the opening of the desk were nothing but smoking, blackened skeletons, with small piles of ash lying all around them.

"Are *you* all right?"

"I'm fine." He turned to retrieve his guns and then crawled out. The heat had left his back and neck burning, but the desk had saved him from worse damage. "Be careful not to touch the desk," he added, again offering her his hand to help her up.

They stood there, looking around them, amazed at the destruction. The windows closest to the blast hadn't broken so much as melted; those farther away were crystalized. Remarkably, the blackened floor was littered with piles and piles of ash, blackened feet sitting in some of them, all that remained of hundreds and hundreds of trife.

Looking out through the gaping hole in the corner of the tower, he saw Foresight floating there, the spines still active with gathering energy. He raised his hand in a grateful wave, certain Jennifer could see him from her position on the flight deck. Hoping her Marine mother had taught her hand signals, he directed her to target the roof and then return to the landing zone. He smiled when she responded by gently canting the starship's nose up and down, making it look like it was nodding. And then the ship rose straight up.

"How did she learn to fly like that?" Yasmin asked in disbelief.

"I showed her how to work the basic controls," Nicholas replied. "And she had a couple of hours of simulator time before that."

Behind them, a door literally cracked open. Startled, they whirled around to see Scott regaining his balance after crashing through the singed door on the closet by the office doors. Splintered, the door hung from its lower hinge. The entire lockset, its latch having apparently melted into its fitting in the frame, remained there, Scott having torn the entire mechanism out of the door.

Peter and Harry carefully stepped out behind him, all three of them looking a little sunburned. Peter seemed shocked speechless by the death and damage surrounding them.

"We need to go," Nicholas said, just as the main doors flew open and crashed back against the wall. Gills and Toast swept in ahead of Briar and Macey, their guns at the ready.

"Oh my gosh," Briar exclaimed in response to the destruction.

"It looks like we missed the party." Gills said, surveying the room.

"What did this?" Briar asked, her mouth open in amazement.

"Jennifer brought Foresight up and hit them with the spines," Nicholas said. "Gills, are we clear?"

"Yeah, but it won't last," he replied.

"Take point, let's move."

The reunited group reversed course, running back through the hallways to the elevator. The trife were still working on the stairwell door, where additional furniture from the nearby offices had been brought out to bolster the barricade. Alien arms reached through holes in the upper portion of the door in an effort to enlarge the opening or dislodge the furniture, a cacophony of sharp hisses beyond.

"I thought we were dead in there," Harry said as they all boarded the elevator. "You really *do* have a ship."

"Are you kidding?" Scott replied. "You *still* didn't believe us?"

Harry shrugged. The door to the cab closed.

This time, they went down.

Chapter 31

"We still didn't get any food, Cap," Gills said as the elevator descended. "We aren't going to make it very far without food."

"The underground lab has a small cafeteria," Peter replied. "Since no one's been able to get down there since the evacuation, I expect it'll be intact."

"Perfect," the Marine replied. "I'm starving."

"You might have to settle for condiments and candy bars."

"I love ketchup. Mustard's okay. Mayo... mmmmm. Mayo. Oh wait, we're in England. Do you think you have marmite down there?"

"Are you serious?" Macey asked. "We just nearly got killed about a hundred times, and you're thinking about marmite? Have you ever tried it?"

"I had an Aussie girlfriend once. She introduced me to it."

"Are you thinking of vegemite?"

"Is there a difference?"

"I think they'd both survive the apocalypse," Macey said, laughing.

Yasmin leaned back against the wall of the cab, exhausted, her eyes bloodshot. "I was certain we were going to die."

"Me too," Nicholas replied. "We owe Jennifer, big time."

"She could have killed us, right along with the trife."

"Yes, but she didn't."

She smiled. "Yeah."

"Did you notice how the trife went after you, Captain Shepherd?" Scott said. "They ignored us completely. I've never seen that before."

"I did notice," Nicholas replied. "I'm more concerned about getting that hard drive out of here. I think you were right, Yazz. We're supposed to be here, but the trife aren't. It's almost as if they knew what you were doing. Like they wanted the drive, but not until you unencrypted it. And I don't think they're going to stop trying to get it."

"They'll have to pull it out of my cold, dead hands," Yasmin said, clutching the credit-card sized storage drive. "If what you're saying is true, then it means the trife aren't as mindlessly programmed as we thought. It means the people who claimed they were engineered specifically to win a ground war against humankind were right."

"Wait a second," Macey said. "I heard on the telly the trife came from meteors shedding their outer layers during atmospheric entry. That it was just bad luck the asteroid field had the trajectory it did and that it carried alien life."

"You can't believe everything you hear on tv," Gills said. "Everyone knows that."

"You can't believe any of it," Toast added. "It's never a good idea to trust your worldview to anyone looking to make a profit off you."

"Good advice, mate. Maybe a little too late though."

"The point is, it confirms the trife are like marionettes, and something or someone else is pulling the strings," Nicholas said.

"Just like the attack on the base," Scott said. "I told you it wasn't an accident."

"Someone's been trying awfully hard to keep us from this," Yasmin said, waving the hard drive.

"Or from whatever's in the lab," Nicholas countered. "Or both. And however Grimmel planned this, that someone either already knew or somehow guessed his plan."

"Or saw the same future Grimmel did," Yasmin said. "As impossible as that sounds."

"The important thing right now is to get ready to make a run for the ship," Nicholas said. "We'll need extra bodies in the lab to load up supplies. Gills, I want you and Harry to go to the garage and ensure the civilians are in position. The rest of us will continue down."

"Copy that, Cap," Gills said. "I'll whip 'em into shape."

"Captain Shepherd, I should come with *you*," Harry said.

"Why?" Gills replied. "You can't carry anything."

Harry glared at the Marine. "I'm not totally useless. At least I could hold a door open or something. Every little bit helps." He looked at Nicholas, awaiting an answer.

"All right, Harry. Every second we save down there is a second we gain topside."

A thump on the top of the elevator cab caused all of them to look up.

"Trife?" Briar asked.

"That's my guess," Scott replied, pointing his gun at the ceiling. "If they want that hard drive, they won't give up until either they get it or we're gone."

"It'll take them some time to get down here in enough numbers to overwhelm us," Nicholas said. "If we move fast, we should be out of here before that happens.

The elevator slowed to a stop when it reached the parking garage. The doors slid open, revealing the survivors gathered nearby, three carts of supplies sitting there with them. A few of them pointed rifles at the elevator, tense until they saw humans inside.

"You made it," Annie said, separating herself from the group and approaching the elevator.

"Good luck, Cap," Gills said before stepping out of the cab and turning his attention to Annie. He looked from Annie to the rest of them, as the elevator doors began to close behind him. "We've got a bit of a situation. I need all of you to do exactly as I say so we can get everyone and everything safely out of here. First thing, I need a pair of guards to—"

Nicholas didn't hear the rest of what Gills said, the elevator doors closing on the parking garage, and they continued the descent to the underground lab.

"Gills seems very committed to the mission for someone who wanted to abandon ship at the first chance he got," Scott said.

"That's Gillie for you," Toast replied. "He's always been like that. Last to get in the water, but also last to leave."

"Peter, do you know where the kitchen is located relative to the elevator?" Nicholas asked.

"Yes. It's just at the end of the first hallway on the left. I can lead the way."

"Okay. Yasmin and I will go to the lab and see what we can find there. The rest of you load up on as much food as you can grab; light on the condiments please. We'll meet back at the elevator in five minutes. Don't be late."

"Copy that," Scott said.

The elevator came to rest a second time. Scott shifted his handgun toward the doors, ready for anything as they opened.

"Clear," he said, lowering his gun as Nicholas stepped into the small entryway, with a heavy blast door in front of him—the only thing of note in the cramped area.

Yasmin skirted around him to the door and leaned over to put her eye in line with the green laser that shot out to scan her eye. She placed her thumb on a separate sensor, and the door buzzed, thunking as it unlocked.

"We're in," Yasmin said with a smile, a motor slowly swinging the door open.

Nicholas stepped around the door into a second antechamber clad in metal. Vents lined the floor and ceiling. A second heavy door stood on the opposite end.

"What's this?" Briar asked.

"Decontamination," Peter said. "Everything has to come in clean. The process is fully automated."

The outer blast door closed and locked behind them, making Nicholas tense up. A soft hum followed, and then scented air blew up from the floor vents, collected by the ceiling vents. Bright light filled the chamber at the same time.

"This is actually kind of nice," Scott said. "I'm sure I smelled ripe as hell."

"You sure did," Toast confirmed.

The process ended within a few seconds. The door at the far end of the chamber buzzed and clunked, swinging open.

"Let's go," Nicholas said.

They exited the decontamination chamber into a short corridor followed by a four-way junction. All the walls were painted a slightly brighter than drab gray and nothing hung on them. LEDs on the ceiling offered plenty of light.

Peter led them into a four-way junction and stopped to point down the left-hand corridor. "The cafeteria is that way," he said. "The primary lab is through the double doors at the end of the hallway. There's a smaller lab if you follow the hallway to the right, but if you're right and Mister Grimmel left something for you, it's probably in the primary."

"Thank you, Peter," Yasmin said.

"Five minutes," Nicholas repeated. "We'll meet back here so we can go back through decon together."

"Copy that," Scott said.

Peter went with the others, leaving Nicholas and Yasmin to walk down the long hallway to the lab.

"This is all so surreal," Yasmin said.

"It is," Nicholas agreed. "Definitely not how I expected today to go. A part of me can't believe we're still alive."

"I'd trade my life for Luke's in an instant."

"Me too, but we have to believe we're on the right track. One foot in front of the other."

"What do you think is really going on here, Nick?"

"I can't begin to guess. But I have a feeling it's bigger than Luke. A lot bigger."

"I don't think I want to be a part of it."

"I don't think we have a choice."

"I never believed the arrival of the trife was random," Yasmin said as they reached the twin doors. "I'm terrified of what that means for humankind. The trife are basic. Predictable. Or, they were. Now? If there's something smarter out there running the show, how do we know the arkships will save us from them?"

"Maybe they won't," Nicholas replied, a chill running down his spine at the thought. "Maybe that's why we're here."

"But how could Grimmel possibly know about any of this?"

Nicholas pushed one of the doors open, motioning Yasmin through. "Maybe we're about to find out."

Chapter 32

The laboratory was bigger than Nicholas expected. Much bigger.

"This is incredible," he said, his gaze traveling a room stretching at least four hundred feet from the double doors at the entrance to a large silver and gold machine at the far end. And the room was equally as wide. Too large to see everything at once. Too overwhelming to make sense of most of it.

At least for him.

A multitude of cables and connectors dangled from large steel beams supporting a ceiling nearly twenty feet off the floor. They were connected to numerous workstations spread throughout the room, the stations intermingled with a range of shelving and machines. Works in progress and prototypes rested on the desks or were spilled across the floor. Within the first few seconds, Nicholas identified what appeared to be a newer version of a Butcher, a scale model of an arkship, and a squarish, modern-looking rifle.

"This is a mess," Yasmin said, eying the room with

an overwhelming sense of the massive search this room presented them rather than wonder. "Whoever was in charge of the lab should have kept stricter protocols. It'll take hours to search this room. We have minutes."

"Then we can't waste time guessing," Nicholas said.

"At least the trife aren't down here. Maybe we don't need to rush."

"True," Nicholas said, considering the problem. "I'm guessing there should be a clue somewhere. Something to guide us. Grimmel wanted us here. He made sure we were the ones to get into the lab, but I don't think he would've left whatever we were supposed to find out in the open. Then again, he probably wouldn't have hidden it too well either. "Can you tell if he had his own work-station down here?"

Yasmin started down the center of the room, looking over at all of the stations. "I don't know. I'm looking for something recognizable. Something that says *Grimmel*."

"How about an expensive bottle of wine?" Nicholas asked. "Or an Abraham Lincoln bobblehead."

"Nick, this is serious."

"I wasn't joking."

Yasmin smiled despite herself. "Help me look."

Nicholas moved closer to the left sidewall and started down one of the aisles, moving at a jog. He quickly surveyed each of the workstations, taking note of the contents and trying to match them with Grimmel's personality as he had known the man. He stopped for the first time when he came across a half-constructed robot that reminded him of Dag. Enough so that a wave of annoyance passed through him because he had already lost the little guy.

The workstation had a cabinet underneath, and he pulled it open, pushing aside files in search of…what? He didn't really know what they were looking for. Something out of the ordinary, he decided. There was nothing like that here. He closed the cabinet and moved on.

A minute passed quickly, each second leaving Nicholas slightly more desperate. They had risked everything to get to Grimmel's office and gain access to the lab. What if Yasmin was wrong about the tycoon leaving them something here?

"Anything?" he asked through the comms, making sure Yasmin heard him where she was at the far end of the room.

"Not yet," Yasmin replied. "Keep looking."

"Scott, sitrep," Nicholas said, keeping in touch with the other group.

"Captain, we found the pantry," he said. "The crumpets are moldy and everything in the fridge is spoiled, but we did find some marmite, which will make Gills happy. There's also about a hundred packets of ramen, and some cans of soup. And a vending machine stocked with candy bars."

"At least we'll get a sugar high," Nicholas said sarcastically.

"Has anyone seen Harry?" Briar asked. "He was here a minute ago."

"He probably went to hold open the outer door," Peter replied.

"Any luck on your end, sir?" Scott asked.

"Not yet. I—" He stopped talking as his eyes landed on a small object resting on the desk in the corner. "Scott, let me know when you're back at the decontamination chamber. Yazz, I think I found something."

He ran to the desk, glancing over at Yasmin as she ran to meet him. Stopping at the workstation, he looked down at a watermelon-sized replica of Foresight. It sat in the midst of papers scattered across the desk, along with a moldy coffee mug and a candy wrapper.

"If this is Grimmel's desk, he was a slob," he said.

Yasmin looked at the model and then shifted the papers on the desk until she found an electronic tablet underneath. She tapped on the screen, turning it on.

"It needs a password," she said.

"If Grimmel left it for us, it would be something we could guess," Nicholas said. "Something relatively obvious, I would think."

Yasmin considered for a few seconds before typing SHEPHERD into the field. The tablet unlocked.

"First try," Nicholas said. "Impressive."

"Lucky," Yasmin replied. One of the icons said NICHOLAS beneath it. She clicked on it, launching an app that immediately began playing a video.

Grimmel stood at the desk, the angle of the camera suggesting he had propped the tablet against something to record the video.

"Captain Shepherd," he said. "If you're watching this, it means you've accepted the request to pilot Foresight and have followed my instructions to retrieve the energy unit that will free the ship from its existing power constraints." Grimmel smiled. "Haha! Yes, that is what I've ordered you here to pick up, along with some additional weaponry you may find useful during your travels. I'm sorry to make everything so complicated, but desperate times, as they say. Unfortunately, circumstances didn't allow for me to install the energy unit prior to your theft of Foresight from the USSF, as I was certain there would be too many questions asked about both the origins and nature of the unit. Suffice it to say, the device is extraterrestrial. And no, I'm not referring to the trife."

Nicholas glanced at Yasmin. He couldn't believe

what he was hearing. Another alien race? Then again, if there was one, why couldn't there be two, ten, or ten thousand?

"The energy unit is inside the model of Foresight. Take the model with you. Do not expose the unit under any circumstances until you are ready to install it. It is highly volatile when not properly contained, and destabilization could lead to the complete annihilation of Earth. Haha! I'm only joking about that. But you would certainly die. As for the ordnance, you'll find it in the container under the first desk near the entrance. It isn't much. A few functional prototypes that never made it into full production. But if you get into trouble they might help.

"Nicholas, I'm certain the pain of leaving your wife and son behind is still weighing on you. But I want you to know how important this mission is to all of humankind. You are about to embark on the most incredible adventure of your lifetime, and while I hope it will be smooth sailing all the way through, I'm confident that if it isn't you'll find a way to rise to the occasion. I believe it's in your blood. Good luck out there, Captain Shepherd."

Grimmel leaned forward and stopped the recording, leaving Nicholas and Yasmin in silence once more.

"Energy unit?" she said. "It must be magical to remove all of Foresight's power constraints."

"Alien," Nicholas corrected. "That might as well be magical for us. Anyway, let's take it, grab the guns, and get the hell out of here. We can worry about everything else once we're clear of the trife."

Yasmin nodded and picked up the model of Foresight, tucking it in the crook of her arm like a baby. "If there's something inside, it doesn't weigh much."

"Come on," Nicholas said, turning toward the entrance to the lab at the same time the door opened and Harry entered the cavernous room. "Harry? What are you doing here?"

"Captain Shepherd," Harry said. "I uh…I thought you might need help searching. We're supposed to rendezvous with the others in two minutes."

"We found what we were looking for," Nicholas replied, jogging toward Harry with Yasmin right behind him.

"You did?" Harry said, a tinge of excitement in his voice. "What is it?"

"It doesn't matter," Yasmin answered. "We have everything under control here. Peter and the others might need your help, but instead you're wasting time coming to check on us. Every second counts, remember?"

"I remember," Harry replied, his voice hardening. "But you're wrong. The seconds aren't as important as you think they are."

Nicholas pulled to a stop a short distance away from Harry. Yasmin had already recognized something about the man wasn't right and now he sensed it too. "Harry, are you okay?"

"What?" Harry replied. "Yes, I…" He trailed off, turning stone-faced. "I'm fine." His voice flattened, becoming deeper and more distant. "Give it to me."

"What?" Yasmin said.

His eyes narrowed, the bandages on his wrists flexing as thin tendrils of dark, moist flesh broke through. The new appendages continued to grow and multiply, writhing like snakes at the end of Harry's arms as Nicholas and Yasmin backed away.

Nicholas reached for his gun, only to remember he

was out of ammunition. His heart pounded, his mind racing. What the hell was this?

"Give it to me," Harry repeated. "I huunnnnggeerrr."

Loud pops echoed in the laboratory as Yasmin unloaded on Harry. Bullets slammed into his chest and abdomen, spraying bits of clothing and flesh, blood spilling from the multiple wounds. Harry looked down at the damage, growling like an animal in response to the damage but showing no signs of imminent death.

"Shit," Yasmin said.

"Give it to me!" Harry shouted, charging toward her. Nicholas moved in front of her, setting himself to fight whatever the guard had become. The tentacles at the end of Harry's left arm snapped out at him, wrapping around his forearm when he put it up to block. They gripped him tight before hurling him across the adjacent workstation. He landed heavily on the floor, the breath knocked out of him.

Yasmin screamed.

"Yazz!" Nicholas rolled to his hands and knees, fighting to get his feet back under him. He gripped the edge of the workstation and pulled himself up on shaky legs in time to see dozens of Harry's dark tendrils grabbing hold of her. "Scott, Toast, I need backup. Now!"

"Captain Shepherd?" Scott said. "We're on our way."

"Long have I waited," Harry said. "Long have I hungered. You will not stop the desolation. Give it to meeee!"

Yasmin struggled to break free of the tendrils. One of them tore the model out of her hands, the rest throwing her to the floor. Furious, Nicholas vaulted the desk, pausing as Dag blasted through the door, blades flashing.

Harry somehow saw or sensed the bot coming. He whirled on the little machine, tendrils snapping out and slapping Dag hard enough to send it careening into one of the workstations. The bot didn't stay down long, racing back toward Harry, blades whirling at the tendrils stretching out to meet it. Dag removed one of the appendages before another hit it a second time, again sending the little bot bouncing away.

Nicholas swept his hand across the workstation, knocking paperwork and pens aside as he desperately searched through the mess for something he could use as a weapon. His gaze fixed on the strange rifle he had noticed earlier. Since it was laying on the next workstation over and not with the guns Grimmel had saved for him, did that mean it didn't work?

He had no choice but to find out.

He went for it just as Harry wrapped a group of tentacles around Yasmin's neck and easily lifted her off the floor. She gagged and choked, the tentacles squeezing the life from her, her free hand trying without success to pull the tendrils free.

Dag came at Harry again, leaping from one workstation to another until it launched itself through the air, blades whirling. The tentacles on Harry's right arm twisted around, reaching for the bot, the other group of tendrils still draining away Yasmin's life. Dag managed to slice through another before the rest grabbed the little bot, wrapping around all four of its appendages.

"Pathetic," Harry growled, just as Nicholas scooped up the rifle and aimed it at him. He flipped up the switch near his thumb, and the gun hummed to life, drawing Harry's attention.

Nicholas squeezed the trigger.

One moment, Harry's head was there. The next, it vanished in a spray of blood, the round Nicholas had fired cleanly removing his head with such unbelievable force it dug deep into the bedrock behind him.

Unbelievably, Harry's body still didn't fall. It teetered blindly, tentacles releasing both Yasmin and Dag, both of them hitting the deck. Harry's tentacles whirled around in disarray and then stiffened as the door to the lab again swung open. Scott and Toast exploded into the room, rifles already shouldered. They froze at the sight of headless Harry still upright.

"What the everloving hell?" Scott spat.

Dag again sprang into action, leaping onto Harry's back, one of its blades severing his right arm. The tentacles immediately stopped moving as the former guard finally collapsed, Dag riding the corpse all the way to the floor.

"Yasmin!" He dropped the gun, too worried about her to stand in awe of the weapon's firepower, and rushed to where she lay, one arm braced against the floor, the other clutching her throat. He fell to one knee beside her, his hand cupping her shoulder as she leaned back against his inner thigh. "Yazz?" He smoothed one side of her hair back behind her ear. "You okay, sweetheart?

A look of relief washing over her face, she drew in a long breath and nodded. "I'm good." She looked up and locked eyes with him. "This is crazy."

"You can say that again." He looked back at Dag, the bot still standing on Harry's back. A black creature that looked like a cross between a squid and a centipede dangled from the bot's blade. The thing's head and long, thin tendrils extended from what Nicholas assumed was the bug's head, stretched all the way back to the wrist of Harry's severed arm.

The creature suddenly slipped off Dag's blade, splattering on the floor.

"Eww." Scott made a disgusted face as Dag leaned over to wipe the thing's green blood off on Harry's shirt. "What is that thing?"

Having no idea what it was, Nicholas was sure it hadn't originated on Earth. "I don't think we're in Kansas anymore."

"We left Kansas the day the trife arrived," Yasmin said softly. "Help me up."

"What's this?" Toast said, picking up the model of Foresight. "It looks like your ship, Captain."

"That's coming with us," Nicholas replied as he straightened, extending his hand to Yasmin and pulling her to her feet. "Scott, there should be a crate under one of the stations near the door. We want that too."

"On it," Scott said, starting a search as Dag finally hopped off Harry's body and retracted his blades. The little bot went to stand guard at the entry doors.

Yasmin shook her head. "How are we going to get through this, Nick?"

"It'll be okay."

"Will it?"

Nicholas pressed his forehead to hers. "Whatever this is about, we're still here. We can still fight. For Luke."

"For Luke," she agreed.

Chapter 33

The elevator stopped back at the parking garage. Dag exited first, stepping out into the line of fire of the two guards keeping watch on the shaft. The fight against Harry had left the bot with a slight limp, its left leg dented enough to affect the servo at the knee.

"Dag!" Gills nearly shouted, a big smile washing over his face at the sight of the little robot. "You little rascal. I can't believe you made it."

Nicholas had told the Marine they were on their way up, but he hadn't mentioned Dag rejoining them. From the hole in the top of the cab that he had discovered upon returning to the elevator, it had quickly become apparent that the thump they had heard wasn't a trife after all, but his bodyguard.

He stepped out of the cab with Yasmin. Behind him, Scott and Briar pulled one of the supply carts while Macey and Peter handled the other. Toast kept watch over them, rifle across his body but ready to lift in defense if needed.

"We all made it," Yasmin said, intentionally ignoring Harry's demise.

"Everyone who mattered, anyway," Nicholas said, his anger over what the man—no, the alien controlling the man—had done to Yasmin still smoldering inside him. "Harry was...not himself. He attacked Yasmin for the model of Foresight. We killed him."

"You killed him?" Annie asked, joining Gills. "How could he attack someone without hands?"

"He had some kind of alien bug wrapped around his arm," Yasmin said. "It was controlling him like a puppet. More than that. It altered him in horrific ways."

"He had tentacles that grew out of his dismembered wrists," Toast said. "It doesn't seem like it should be possible, but it was."

"I've never seen anything more disgusting," Scott agreed.

"Annie, was there ever a time when Harry disappeared for an extended period?" Nicholas asked. "I'm trying to understand when he may have been compromised."

"What does it matter?" she asked. "Aren't we leaving?"

"Yes, but we need to be certain he isn't the only plant in your group."

She shrugged. "He used to go off on his own all the time. He had a collection of adult comic books he would bring with him, if you know what I mean."

"Wanker wanking," Macey said. "Gross."

"Do you know where he used to go?" Nicholas asked.

"No. Somewhere he could be alone. Captain, I understand your concern, but we've been stuck here a long time. If weird alien bugs wanted to mind-flay us, I'm sure everyone here has been alone long enough at one time or another for them to do it without anyone else knowing."

"In other words, you could all be contaminated," Yasmin said.

"Yes. But you said the alien was attached to his arm?"

"Somewhere here," Nicholas said, running his hand over his armpit and down his arm. "It flattened itself tight enough against his skin we never would have seen it unless his upper body was bare. We'll need to check all of your people."

"I don't know how I feel about that," Annie said.

"It's either that or you can walk to the nearest arkship," Yasmin said. "The trife are still after us. They'll probably be here any minute, so we shouldn't waste time arguing about it."

Annie made a face before reaching up and unbuttoning her blouse. She pulled it down around her waist and lifted her arms, showing she was clean. "Happy?"

"Yes," Nicholas said. "Briar, Peter, help Annie check the others."

"You got it, Captain Shepherd," Briar replied. Annie re-buttoned her shirt and approached the two guards, who removed enough clothing for her to check their arms. Peter and Briar hurried to the other survivors to do the same.

"Let's see what we've got in here," Nicholas said, turning back to one of the carts. The crate Grimmel had directed them to was on top of the boxes of candy bars, bottled water, and soda pop. Taking a moment to examine it for the first time, he noticed it had a numeric keypad lock on the face to prevent just anyone from gaining access to the prototype guns inside. He entered his birthday as the passcode, smiling when the crate clicked open.

Gills, Toast, and Scott crowded around the crate, eager to review the bounty. Nicholas lifted the cover, revealing a stack of relatively ordinary-looking rifles and pistols inside.

"Cap, may I?" Gills asked.

"Go ahead," Nicholas said.

Gills leaned his rifle against the cart and picked up the weapon on the top of the pile, looking it over. It bore a strong resemblance to the MK, except the muzzle was more square and it had a power switch on the side above the trigger guard. The weapon hummed when Gills flipped the switch, a counter appearing above it, currently set to five-hundred.

"Five-hundred what? Rounds?" Gills asked, sighting down it. "It's got great balance, I'll give you that."

"It looks a lot like a P-75 plasma rifle," Yasmin said.

"A what?" Gills said.

"Plasma rifle. They didn't make wide production before the war, so as far as I know the inventory is all going to Marines on the front lines."

"We still have a front line?" Gills said. "That's news to me."

"You know what I mean."

"If that number is how many shots are loaded, that's a good sign," Nicholas said. "You'll find out how it works the first time you need to use it."

Gills smiled. "Fair enough, Cap. Let's hope I won't need to use it any time soon."

"This one looks sleek," Toast said, picking up the second gun in the pile.

It was more of a carbine style, with a snub nose and wide barrel. Two separate magazines hung from the sides of the gun. Toast detached one of them, turning it to look at the ordnance. The rounds reminded Nicholas of nails, though the tip of each resembled a miniaturized warhead.

"I'm calling it a nailgun," Toast said, slipping the magazine back into place. "Nice." He turned the side of the gun toward Nicholas. "It has a counter too. Two hundred rounds."

"I think Grimmel guessed we might have trife problems," Scott said, picking up a second rifle similar to the one Gills had taken. "You grabbed the best one, T."

Only the left side of Toast's face moved when he smiled. "I have good taste."

Nicholas took his turn, reaching into the crate and removing a handgun made of the same metal as Foresight. It had a small blue stone embedded in the top of the body, and no apparent magazine, battery, or other ammunition, much less a firing mechanism.

"That one's pretty sweet," Toast said. "Definitely high-tech."

Nicholas turned it in his hand, and then held it forward in mock aim on the survivors in front of him— something he would normally never do—and watched their eyes go wide in alarm. A projected targeting reticle appeared over the weapon, along with additional red reticles that locked onto the survivors. Red for stop. Shifting his aim to the extinguisher, he lined up the blue and red, turning the primary reticle green. A viable target.

"It is pretty sweet," Nicholas agreed, lowering the weapon. He replaced his empty Glock with the prototype, glancing back into the crate. A few more guns remained inside, along with a strange weapon partially-obscured beneath them, resting at the bottom of the container. It reminded Nicholas of a small spear, a single piece of Grimmel's rare matte black metal with a hammered grip that tapered into a point. A knife of some kind, he supposed, leaving it in the container.

"Everyone's clean, Captain," Briar said, returning to report to Nicholas. She noticed Scott's new rifle. "Do I get a space gun too?"

"You do, actually," Nicholas replied, passing her another plasma-style rifle. He handed a second pistol like his to Yasmin. "Here, love."

"Thank you," she replied.

"No little black buggies hiding in anyone's armpits?" Nicholas asked Briar.

"No," she replied. "We checked them all."

Nicholas closed and locked the crate. "Then it's time to move out. Gills, Toast, Scott, you'll take point. Remember, we have to keep an eye out for both the raggies and the trife. I don't think the aliens have circled the building yet, but they will soon enough."

"Copy that, Cap," Gills said. "We're ready to rock."

"Good. Peter, are your people prepared to move out?"

"Yes, Captain Shepherd."

"Then let's—" He went silent, watching as Dag sprinted ahead, vaulting onto the hood of a car and across the parked vehicles toward the gate. Looking outside, he spotted what had drawn Dag's attention.

The raggies were coming down the ramp, hands raised high in surrender.

Chapter 34

"You gotta let us in. Please!' the leader of the group begged from the other side of the gate. "There are trife out here. Thousands of them are pouring out of the power station."

"No shit, Fuzz," Macey shouted back. "You wankers didn't want to listen to me when I told you not to shake down the blokes with the starship. You can rot out there. I—" She stopped talking and looked chagrined when Nicholas glared over at her. "Sorry, Cap'n."

"How many raggies are there?" he asked her.

"Total?" Macey replied. "Eighteen or so. You aren't thinking of taking them with us, are you? They tried to kill me. Shit, they tried to kill you and yours."

"When it comes to the trife, we're on the same side," Nicholas said. "Always. Besides, we're moving out. Yazz, open the gate. Gills, Toast, take the lead with Dag."

"Copy, Cap," Gills said.

"Here's the deal," Nicholas shouted back at the raggies. "There's no safe haven here. The trife are in the building too. We're heading out for our ship. You help us get there, you're welcome to come along for the ride. No questions asked."

"Really?" Fuzz said, surprised by the deal. "You'll take us out of here?"

"You have my word," Nicholas said "But you have to do what I tell you. If you don't—"

"Trife!" one of the guards shouted as the first of the demons slammed into the locked door to the emergency stairs, rattling it on its hinges. A moment later, a clawed hand ripped into Dag's hole in the top of the elevator cab, enlarging it to trife-size.

"We're out of time," Nicholas said. "Let's move!"

The steel gate began rising. Dag ducked beneath it, running out into the midst of the raggies, who flinched back from the robot before realizing it didn't plan to attack them. Gills and Toast ducked under the barrier next, trailing Dag to the top of the ramp.

"We're clear for now, Captain," Gills announced through the comms. "But I can hear the bastards coming. It isn't going to last."

Nicholas glanced back. Most of the former Grimmel Corporation employees managed the carts of supplies while the remainder covered their escape. Briar, Macey, Scott, and Peter remained close to the carts to guard their flanks. Yasmin rejoined Nicholas, and he took her hand, holding tight as they moved out of the garage.

A loud crack from behind told Nicholas the trife had managed to claw through the locked door. A thump a moment later suggested they had gotten through the shaft as well. Gunfire echoed in the depths of the garage.

"I'm Fuzz," the leader of the raggies told Nicholas as he reached him.

"Captain Shepherd," he replied. "Stick with the group. If you see a trife, shoot it. It's that simple."

"Yes, sir," Fuzz said, turning to the other raggies. "You heard him!"

They rushed back up the ramp, joining Gills, Toast, and Dag.

"Everybody, stick tight!" Nicholas shouted.

He looked over his shoulder. The bottleneck formed by the shaft and stairs prevented too many trife from getting through at once, allowing the defense breathing room to back away while cutting them down as they appeared. The pressure remained minimal, but he knew that could change in a hurry, especially once the trife outside the building added to the chaos.

The group reached the end of the ramp, exiting the tower onto the debris-filled street. Nicholas stayed just in front of the carts with Yasmin at his side. Up ahead, the Marines, Dag, and the raggies walked along the street, rifles up and ready for action.

The trife outside hadn't come into view yet, but Nicholas could hear them. They were close and getting closer, their hisses and the sound of their shuffling feet echoing through the urban canyons.

Did they know what had happened to Harry? Were they aware of the strange alien bug or possibly even controlled by it or similar creatures? It was a revelation to him to accept that the trife arrival on Earth hadn't been an accident. Was the thing Dag had killed one of their masters?

Grimmel had said he had no concept of the universe and its machinations.

He would have preferred to keep it that way. To live a normal life with Yasmin and Luke. Of course, that dream had died two years ago, every new dream snuffed out since. Right now, he just wanted to get these people to Foresight and out of here alive.

One of the raggies was the first to start shooting, pivoting as he reached the mouth of an alley and managing to get a few rounds off before a trife leaped on him from the darkness. A quick slash shredded his throat. He gurgled in pain and clutched at the wound as he went down. The trife tried to target another raggie, meeting its own death instead.

More trife rushed from the alley, splitting up to overwhelm the closest humans. Further down the street, another group of aliens rounded the corner and charged toward them.

Gills opened fire with his prototype rifle, balls of plasma burning right through the trife, sometimes hitting two or three before losing energy. Toast turned his gun on the demons too, each nail-like round exploding when it hit a trife, creating massive wounds. For now the raggies were equally effective with their conventional weaponry.

"Help!" someone behind Nicholas yelled. He spun around to see the rear guard struggling, the trife making it out into the garage more easily as the distance between them and the defense expanded. The aliens closed on the defenders, leaping at them with gnashing teeth and slashing claws.

Nicholas aimed his prototype handgun, lining up the two reticles that appeared and squeezing the trigger. A beam of blue energy matching the energy from Foresight's spines lashed across the distance and exploded into the trife, the impact tearing through its upper-half. Momentum carried the corpse to the feet of the guard it had tried to attack.

With no time to be impressed by the weapon, Nicholas turned it on another trife, and then another, lining up the reticles and firing beam after beam.

Within seconds, every weapon in the group's possession was in use, a heavy barrage of gunfire decimating
the attacking trife as the survivors slowly made their way
north to the railroad tracks. The firepower was enough
to hold the current volume of trife at bay, but the noise
of the slick and the unsettled tension in the air convinced
Nicholas the worst was yet to come. Meanwhile, they still
had to get across the street and around a block of apartments to reach Foresight.

"Five hundred rounds isn't enough!" Gills shouted
over the comm, alluding to his plasma rifle running out
of energy sooner than later. The same likely went for
Toast's nailgun, which he fired judiciously to preserve the
ammo.

"Just keep moving," Nicholas said. "Don't stop for
anything." He whipped his head to the left in response to
a scream, flinching when he saw one of the rear guards
buried beneath a pile of trife.

If he had comms access to the ship he would have
called Jennifer to request backup. Foresight's weapons
system could decimate the thousands of demons chasing
them. In the back of his mind, he hoped she would see
what was happening out here and take the initiative.
Then again, he didn't know if the ship had enough
stored energy to fire the spines again and still get them
where they needed to go.

Seconds passed like hours as the group made it to the
side of the apartment complex between them and Foresight. The ship came into sight, resting ahead of the
tracks, closer than he had left it earlier. The ramp was
up, the spines jutting out from the hull, ready to fire.

Seeing the starship brought the escaping survivors a
second wind. They were so close to escaping they didn't
want to fail now. The gunfire intensified and Nicholas

joined it, his weapon seeming to have no limit to the amount of energy it could produce. It was the only gun without a counter, and didn't seem to carry any ammunition at all. He fired over and over again, Yasmin doing the same beside him, killing trife after trife.

"We're going to make it!" Fuzz shouted from nearby, firing a short burst from his rifle that knocked down a pair of trife. The windows of the apartments above him shattered then, trife leaping out of them and landing on him. He screamed as they dug their claws into his chest and bit down on his neck, killing him only a short distance from Nicholas.

He fired on the trife, cutting them down too late for Fuzz. More demons crashed through the windows on their right, ambushing the group as it neared the ship. Guns swung toward the demons, killing some before they landed while others managed to get to the nearest people, mostly raggies, jumping on them and delivering vicious wounds.

Dag rushed into the fray, a tiny whirlwind through the densest part of the melee. The bot slashed at the trife, cutting their legs out from under them, scaling some and ripping open their throats, stabbing others in the head and neck and back. Its confrontation with Harry had left it damaged, but it showed no sign of running out of battery power or fight.

Another minute passed, bringing them within a hundred feet of Foresight. The spines activated suddenly, individual blasts lashing out to either side of the ship away from the retreating survivors, suggesting the trife were closing in around them. Even though they were so close, to Nicholas it seemed like they were still too far away to make it.

The sound of gunfire diminished as their guns began

to run dry, the ordnance not already loaded into crates on the carts spent. Within seconds, only the prototypes would still be firing.

A loud groan suddenly sounded in the distance, a noise Nicholas had never heard before. It echoed across the battlefield, the enormity of the sound overcoming the hissing and screaming of the trife, quickly silencing human and trife alike. The sound of splashing water followed, loud enough that whatever created it had to be big.

Really big.

The fight ground to an inexplicable halt, the trife freezing to look over their shoulders, the humans matching the response as they all stared to the south.

"What's going on?" Yasmin asked beside Nicholas.

"I don't know," he replied.

The trife hissed as one before breaking from their static positions, scattering away from the fight as quickly as they could in full on retreat. Rather than a sense of elation at the unexpected victory, Nicholas' heart wrenched with an urgent sense of dread.

"Get to the ship!" He shouted. "Run! Get to the ship now!"

The others did as he said, the survivors abandoning the carts in their desperation to get on board.

"The carts!" he said. "We need the carts!"

The fleeing survivors didn't hear him or didn't pay attention. His people did. Scott hurried to the cart laden with food to recover it. Briar did the same for the cart of guns and ammunition. He and Yasmin joined them, pushing the heavy loads as quickly as they could.

"What in the bloody hell?" Macey said nearby, looking back toward the river.

A large black mass appeared at the end of the

street. Dark and moist, with dozens of thick appendages writhing and churning around a huge globe-like mass. A roundish mouth sat in the center of the body mass, rows of teeth shifting and grinding, while hundreds of segmented eyeballs rested over the maw, appearing to Nicholas as if they were looking right at him.

The creature's body was nearly twenty feet around. The dozens of tentacles extending from it had to be six feet thick and another forty feet or more in length, tapering off to points at the ends. Individual smaller globules with their own set of eyes and mouths capped the appendages in horrific miniaturized versions of the thing's center mass.

Another alien that wasn't a trife. In fact, the trife were terrified of it. But in this case, it didn't appear that the enemy of his enemy was a friend.

The huge creature undulated forward, charging down the street toward them on its tentacles with unexpected speed. It powered through small obstacles and debris, and threw wrecked cars aside as if they were children's toys.

"Come on!" Nicholas shouted. "We can make it!"

The first of the survivors were already reaching the ship, waiting outside for the ramp to descend. Nicholas was sure Jennifer knew they were there, but she wasn't giving them the chance to board without him and the others.

Looking over his shoulder, Nicholas shuddered to see the massive tentacled alien had already closed half the gap between it and them, and it continued gaining speed, hissing and groaning. The ship was close, but the alien's lead tentacles were closer.

"Keep going," Toast said. "I've got this." He broke

off from the group, rushing back in the direction of the alien.

"Toast, no!" Gills said, slowing down.

Nicholas' instinct was the same. He didn't want any heroes. He wanted them all to make it to the ship and get away. But Toast had come to the same conclusion he had. Already, the Marine was too far back to either catch up or avoid the alien. He was committed to confronting the creature, opening fire with the nailgun. Rounds slammed into the monster's tentacles, blasting out huge chunks of dark flesh.

The alien screamed, heaving forward and sweeping a tentacle at Toast. He ducked beneath it and fired again, hitting the creature in its central mass.

"Gills, come on," Nicholas said, sprinting to catch up to Yasmin and the others. "Gills!" He stopped again when the Marine didn't move. "Don't make his sacrifice for nothing."

Gills cried out, wailing as he sent a defiant stream of plasma toward the alien and then breaking for Foresight. The exterior hatch opened and the ramp extended, the survivors piling onto the ship as quickly as possible.

A loud, angry groan drew Nicholas' attention to the giant as it slammed a tentacle into the side of the apartment building, sending debris raining down on Toast. He dived and rolled away from the worst of the collapse, and kept on shooting. One of the rounds hit the creature in the mouth, blowing out a number of teeth. Another hit it in the eye, sending a vitreous spray from its head.

Nicholas started running again. He didn't see Yasmin ahead of him, hoping she was already inside. "Move aside," he shouted, running up the ramp. He squeezed past the carts and the survivors huddled around them. "Move!"

The others did their best to part for him, allowing him to reach the ladder and quickly climb to the main deck. He ran forward to the flight deck, passing Yasmin, already in a seat, and only sparing a glance at Jennifer in the co-pilot seat before falling into the primary. He nearly cried out when he looked at the display in time to watch the huge alien grab Toast with one of its tentacles. The monster deposited the Marine in its oversized mouth where rows of teeth devoured him.

Behind him, he heard Jennifer break out in sobs. His grief ran just as deep, but he didn't have time for tears. That didn't mean he was going to fly out of here without exacting revenge on the creature that had taken Toast's life. Especially since retrieving the energy unit had removed the need to conserve Foresight's existing power, and with it any hesitation to use that power.

Nicholas tapped down on the right-hand controls, "For Toast," he whispered, triggering the spines. A heavy blast of energy burned through the appendages the creature threw up in front of its face to block the shot. It hit the massive alien dead-on between its many eyes. The searing energy burned through its central mass, burning a hole all the way through it.

The huge alien groaned one last time and collapsed.

Nicholas sat there in silence, staring at it, a lump of lifeless black goo, as the dust settled around it.

"Captain Shepherd?" Jennifer said weakly behind him, sniffing back her tears.

"What is it, Jennifer?"

"Did we pick up any new clothes? I think I wet myself."

Chapter 35

Nicholas' heart continued racing long after he had lifted off from London, gently gaining speed and altitude to keep the unsecured people crammed into the ship's lower deck safe and comfortable. He set a course for the Pilgrim launch site and handed the stick over to Frank before making his way off the flight deck.

A handful of survivors had already climbed the ladder to the primary deck, along with Gills, Briar, Peter, and Yasmin. They hadn't wasted any time distributing the supplies, and were in the process of passing the boxes of food and clothing from the lower deck to the upper one. Jennifer waited at the top of the upper deck ladder to receive the boxes, no doubt eager for a change of clothes. Nicholas hadn't looked back when she had spoken to him, but the sweet smell of her urine had wafted across the flight deck, confirming that her fear of the alien monster had stolen control of her bladder.

He didn't blame her. He had only managed to stay in control because of his years of combat experience against the trife. Even so, the huge, tentacled alien was the most terrifying thing he had ever witnessed. If he never saw another like it, it would be too soon.

"Captain Shepherd," Briar said as he emerged from the flight deck. Her face remained pale, her hands still shaking from fear. "What was that thing?"

"Another alien of some kind," Nicholas replied. "It's okay. I killed it."

Briar nodded nervously. "You killed one. What if there are more? There was only supposed to be the trife. They suck, but they aren't anywhere near as terrifying as that thing was."

"It doesn't matter. We're safe up here."

"I don't think there are more," Yasmin said. "I have a feeling that one was lying in wait, in case we got out past Harry and the trife."

Nicholas looked over at her. "That's crazy."

"Is it, after everything else they went through to stop us from getting this." She held up the energy unit she'd been cradling in her arms.

"Maybe not," he admitted,

"Captain Shepherd," Peter said, getting his attention. "I...we can't thank you enough for getting us out of there."

"You don't need to thank me," Nicholas replied. "It was never an option to leave you, once I knew you were there. Do me a favor and pass the word to the lower deck that we'll reach the arkship launch site within the hour."

"Of course, Captain," Peter said.

"I need to thank you too, Cap'n," one of the raggies said. A larger man with a thick beard and tattooed arms. He had tears in his eyes. "You didn't need to take us. Not after what we were planning to do. I'm sorry, sir."

Nicholas put his hand on the man's shoulder and looked him in the eye. "This war's made a lot of good people do bad things. That part of your life is over now. Do you understand?"

He nodded. "Yes, sir. Thank you."

Nicholas turned to Gills next. The Marine had slumped into one of the seats. He looked exhausted, his face damp and sweaty, his posture defeated. "Corporal, are you okay?"

Gills looked at him silently. The reaction spoke louder than any words. He had lost his entire unit, all of his brothers and sisters in arms in a matter of hours. The worst part for Nicholas was that the outcome remained unknown.

The vast majority of the time, there were no survivors.

"He died a hero," Nicholas said.

"They all did," Gills replied softly.

"When we reach the launch site, if you want to join the arkship—"

"Screw that, Captain," Gills replied, cutting him off. "I'm in this now for the long haul."

Nicholas nodded, settling his hand on Gills' shoulder and squeezing before turning to Yasmin. She had the scale model of Foresight sitting on her lap, her hand resting on it. "How are you holding up?"

"I don't know yet," she replied. "I reserve the right to have a nervous breakdown later. Right now, I want to get these things where they belong." She motioned to the door at the rear of the compartment that led to engineering.

"Good idea," Nicholas replied. "We're below fifty percent on the supercapacitors." He looked around the room, past the others gathered there. "Has anyone seen Dag?"

The small robot stepped out from beneath Gill's seat.

It was slightly more dented than before, but still operational.

"I feel a little dumb to be so grateful to see you made it," Nicholas said to the bot.

Dag didn't react.

"Gills, keep an eye on things while Yasmin and I make some tweaks to the power supply."

"Copy that, Cap. Just don't blow us up or anything, okay?"

"I'm pretty sure we won't blow up," Yasmin said.

"*Pretty* sure?"

"She's kidding," Nicholas added. "You're kidding, right?"

"Can you take this?" she replied, handing him the model and ignoring the question. She headed for the rear hatch. Nicholas followed her, Dag keeping pace behind him. Nicholas had never been in the rear of the ship before. Goosebumps formed on his arms as he entered, a chill running through him from the cold.

"It's like a meat locker in here," he said.

"The components need to stay cool to operate at peak efficiency," Yasmin replied, pausing at a kiosk computer terminal directly inside. " If anyone had expected to need to come back here in flight, there would have been coats in storage."

Narrow aisles on either side led to banks of hardware connected by clean wiring, flickering lights confirming their activity. Ahead of the terminal, a clear partition and door separated the space from the reactor and other mechanical components that provided life support for the ship. An even smaller hatch sat at the back of that area, allowing an engineer, if needed, to crawl directly through to the inner workings of the primary thrusters.

Jasmin tapped on the terminal's touchscreen, navigating through a handful of menus until she arrived at a schematic. "If you remember from our initial briefings on Foresight, the ship is powered by a series of supercapacitors that occupy the negative space between the hull and the usable interior space. Solid-state and highly stable, they can store enough energy to power the ship's system under nominal loads for up to two weeks, including multiple atmospheric egress and the Spinal Defense System, as you've seen. They're backed up by a fusion reactor Grimmel called the mini-mak, since it's based on the Tokamak design. It provides enough constant output to maintain life support and slowly recharge the supercapacitors. With enough material for a fifty year burn, it's a useful secondary option but obviously rather limited."

"Obviously," Nicholas agreed, enjoying listening to his wife spout technical specs even though he had a vague understanding of what she'd said or cared little about the specifics to begin with. As long as it didn't kill them all, he was satisfied.

Yasmin used her fingers to zoom in and scroll the schematic. "From Grimmel's message, it seems he designed the power supply to have the energy unit inserted at some point. I'm looking for the exact location in the diagram."

Nicholas waited while she scanned the schematic, rotating the three dimensional blueprint as she hunted for the connection. A few minutes of searching left him feeling impatient, and the cold was seeping deeper into him, making him shiver.

"Dag, do you know where to stick this thing?" he asked, figuring it couldn't hurt to ask.

The small bot lifted its arms toward Nicholas, indicating it wanted the model.

Yasmin looked over her shoulder as he handed it to the bot. "You have to be kidding," she said, watching it walk over to the transparency. Its head swiveled back in their direction, suggesting impatience as it waited for her to open the door. Still shaking her head, she tapped the touchscreen to give Dag access.

"Grimmel left him here," Nicholas said. "I figured maybe he programmed him to be able to insert the unit."

"Him?" Yasmin said. "First you give it a name. Then you talk to it like a human, and now you give it a gender."

"Her doesn't feel right."

"What about them?"

"If I had a dog, he would be a good boy. Dag doesn't care, so him it is."

Yasmin smiled. "Luke always wanted a puppy."

"And that puppy would have been a good boy too."

They fell into a saddened shared silence, watching as Dag opened an access panel on the side of the primary power supply. He lowered the model into it before squeezing himself inside and disappearing.

"Did you look beyond human reach on the diagram?" Nicholas asked.

"No," Yasmin replied. "I didn't think to."

"Grimmel didn't expect you to be here," Nicholas said. "He left Dag to help me, and also probably to insert the energy unit once we recovered it."

"That does make sense."

"There may be more maintenance bots in those compartments in the lower hold."

Yasmin manipulated the diagram on the kiosk again, navigating deeper within the structure. Watching over her shoulder, even Nicholas recognized the contact location when she found it. The connector was the same size and shape as the model, meaning the energy unit wasn't intended to be directly exposed.

"How will we know when Dag installs it?" he asked.

The lights in the compartment went out.Only for a second, and when they returned they seemed a little brighter than before.

"We can check the diagnostics," Yasmin replied, navigating out of the schematic. "But I think that was our clue."

Nicholas smiled. "It seems that way."

"Confirmed. Look at this." She pointed at the screen. The lines had all changed to infinity symbols where there should have been percentages.

"Good boy, Dag," Nicholas said as the bot backed himself out of the unit, replacing the panel before rejoining them in the outer compartment.

He didn't react to the praise.

"Let's get out of here," Nicholas said. "I'm freezing."

Chapter 36

A pair of Reapers came out of the cloud cover and fell in behind Foresight when they were still nearly two hundred miles east of the Pilgrim Launch Site and immediately target-locked the starship. Obviously, the pilots back at the base hadn't realized what it was they were threatening.

A quick relay through the comms on the lead drone to its pilot saved them from being shot down and introduced Nicholas to Captain Bradshaw, the former United States Naval officer in charge of the facility who was slated to command the arkship Pilgrim when it launched, He seemed to be a reasonable, steady-handed man when he told Nicholas about the distress signal he'd received from Fort Hood. He'd sent in an entire company of Marines, but instead of the fight they expected, they'd found the trife milling aimlessly about, both inside and outside the compound.

Without a queen they were easy pickings for the Marines, who managed to clear the base from the escape hatch forward to the hangar, only to find both the experimental Foresight and its designer, Aaron Grimmel, missing. Bradshaw's original assumption was that he had escaped in the ship. The fact that he hadn't immediately brought the experimental starship west to the Pilgrim Launch Site had left USSF command scratching their heads.

The news from Bradshaw had left Nicholas scratching his head, too. If Grimmel wasn't with the others at the PLS, then where was he? Where the hell had he gone?

Nicholas quickly filled Bradshaw in on Foresight's whereabouts over the last eight hours, explaining why they had made a trip to the Grimmel Corporation tower in London without including every excruciating detail. He framed it as a request from Grimmel to ensure he kept his promise to help the employees make it to an arkship. As Nicholas told it, Grimmel had always intended to make that request to Colonel Haines, but hadn't found the right moment before the shit hit the fan. With Haines among the deceased, there was no way for Bradshaw to corroborate the story, and he begrudgingly accepted the delay.

"At least you're here now," Bradshaw said. "And saving twenty-one additional souls is nothing to scoff at either. Though I have no idea where Grimmel thought we were going to put them. We'd be bursting at the seams with all the late additions filtering in from every corner of the globe if the attack on Fort Hood hadn't left us with about a hundred and twelve additional openings."

It was a callous way to look at things, but considering Bradshaw's role, Nicholas figured it paid to be pragmatic. The captain's mission was to see the Pilgrim successfully launched before going into hibernation for the century long journey. Once they arrived at the new world, he would be responsible for leading the fledgling colony, essentially a King instead of a Captain.

Nicholas didn't envy him that at all.

"PLS Actual," he said. "I'm on final approach. Touchdown in t-minus ninety seconds."

"Copy that, Captain Shepherd," came the reply. "You're cleared for landing. Try to bring her in as close to the warehouse as possible. We haven't had any problems with the trife since we started digging, but we definitely don't want them to notice anything that suggests we're out here, like a nice warm reactor in a starship."

"Understood, PLS Actual. I'll hug the LZ as tight as I can."

He adjusted the throttle, further reducing the ship's forward velocity while increasing the output to the antigravity plates to keep Foresight in the air. He had made a long, slow descent into the launch site's airspace, flying as gently as he could for his passenger's comfort.

The drab brown of the desert slipped past beneath the hull, vacant of any signs of life, human or otherwise, while up ahead a series of sharp cliffs helped obscure the entrance to the massive subterranean facility. Nicholas had never been inside any of the launch sites, but he had seen pictures of a few of the unbelievably large hangars where the arkships were being assembled. For as much as Foresight was a miracle of technology, as far as he was concerned the immense excavations that were occurring all over the world were equally wondrous.

A dirt path had been pounded into the landscape by hundreds of heavy vehicles and provided the perfect guide to navigate Foresight to the facility's entrance. Marked by a simple, corrugated aluminum warehouse positioned halfway up the slope of the mountain,

Nicholas was unsurprised to find a welcome party already waiting there for his arrival. He eyeballed a landing zone just west of the warehouse, a little further up the slope but still obscured by the hilltops surrounding the area. It wasn't the absolute closest he could get to the facility's entrance, but he didn't want to get too close.

Bradshaw didn't know it, of course, but he didn't plan on staying.

"Gills, I'm t-minus thirty seconds from the LZ," he said, muting the comms to PLS Actual and using the earpiece to speak to the Marine. "Is everything set?"

"Yes, sir," Gills replied. "The rats are in the lower deck, ready to abandon ship."

"Has Briar made up her mind? We're running out of time."

Between the confirmation from Bradshaw that her parents had survived the attack and made it to the Pilgrim unharmed and the trauma of nearly being killed by the huge, tentacled alien, Briar had expressed an understandable desire to reconsider her place on the ship. While she had been excited by the prospect of a space adventure, the desperate fight for survival had stolen some of her original enthusiasm.

"I have, Captain Shepherd," she replied, cutting into the comm. "I'm happy my parents got out of there alive. I know they're going to miss me. But when it comes down to it, I'll spend a lot more time worrying about my friends if I get off than I will about them staying here."

"Are you sure?" Nicholas asked. "You won't get another chance to change your mind."

"I didn't think I would get this chance to change my mind. I appreciate the opportunity to give it more thought. I'm in, Captain, if you'll have me."

"Of course we'll have you," Scott said. "We need someone to make fun of."

"Why, when we already have your homely face?" Briar replied.

"Okay, that's enough," Nicholas said. "Time and place. This isn't it. Jennifer, you know what to do."

"Yes, Captain. I'll be ready for your signal."

"Good." He unmuted the external comms as he closed the throttle, leaving Foresight drifting forward and down toward the landing zone. The other group started up the slope to greet the survivors. "You have the stick," he said, releasing himself from his seat and leaving the flight deck. He hurried to the ladder, pausing when he saw Macey sitting in one of the main deck seats. "You should be down below with the others."

"Nah. I decided I want to stick around."

"You decided? This is my ship."

"I mean, I could go out there and shout out to the millies that you're intending to steal their precious starship if that's what you prefer, Captain. But the way I see it, you've got eight seats total and only six bodies to fill them, and you need all the help you can get. For my part, my mum is dead. My precious little ones are gone. The raggies are assholes. And I like it here."

Nicholas stared at her. "I can't really argue with that logic."

"No, you can't," she agreed. "Besides, Daggo likes me. That ought to count for something, right?"

Nicholas glanced at the bot stationed beneath her seat. "Fine, but don't call him Daggo."

"Yes, sir."

"Nick," Yasmin said, getting his attention. She held out a small thumb drive. "This is Frank's latest source code. It just needs to be copied and installed on the arkships' mainframes. It'll get them to their new homes safely, wherever that turns out to be."

"I'm sure it will," Nicholas replied, accepting the drive. He descended the ladder to the lower deck, making his way past the people lined up to the exit where Gills waited.

"You don't really think they'll try to stop us, do you, Captain?" he asked.

"They'll try," Nicholas replied. "Frank's too valuable for them not to. But they won't succeed."

"Yes, sir. I don't know why you have to go out there."

He held up the thumb drive. "To give them this. And to maintain proper decorum so they don't get suspicious before we unload the civilians."

"I just think it's riskier than hanging back while the civvies unload."

"I disagree. And it's my call."

"Yes, sir."

"Captain Shepherd," Peter said. "Thank you again for getting us out of there in one piece. We've all lost so much. I'm grateful to have some hope again."

"You're welcome, Good luck," Nicholas said, quickly shaking the man's hand before heading for the forward hatch.

"Captain, I'm touching down now," Jennifer said over the comm.

"Copy that."

Nicholas tapped the hatch controls, the door sliding open and the ramp extending. He waited until it had fully deployed before stepping out. The group from the base hadn't finished scaling the slope, but Nicholas identified them by their uniforms. Captain Bradshaw, bearded and slightly overweight, wearing a Navy dress uniform. Another Naval officer, a Lieutenant. Probably his XO. A unit of Marines paced behind them, along with a pair of medics in civilian clothes.

"Captain Bradshaw," Nicholas said, coming to attention and offering a salute as the man approached—a courtesy as the man was in charge of the facility.

"Captain Nicholas Shepherd, it's good to meet you."

"A pleasure to meet you face-to-face," Bradshaw said, extending his hand as he stopped within handshake distance of Nicholas. They shook and Bradshaw smiled. "I've heard only good things about your skill as a pilot, and I'm thankful..." He pointed to Foresight. "...you got her to safety. We saw the mess the queen made inside the hangar. You said none of the survivors needed immediate medical attention, but I brought a pair of nurses with me just in case."

"Thank you, Captain," Nicholas replied.

The survivors disembarked behind him, coming down the ramp and practically falling into the arms of the nurses and Marines, milling around them, introducing themselves, and otherwise acting as a harmless distraction.

Nicholas held up the thumb drive. "This is the final version of the neural network that will handle navigation during your hibernation. Foresight completed its final test before the attack. Pass this on to the rest of the arkships and you should be good to go."

"Thank you," Bradshaw said, his smile broadening as he accepted the drive. "Now that the original testing is completed, I imagine you're eager to be done with this entire war business and be introduced to the comforts of Metro. I admit it's not Earth, but at least it's trife-free."

Nicholas forced a smile. "To be honest, Captain Bradshaw, I don't think the war is done with me just yet."

"What do you mean?"

"I'm a pilot, Captain. I'm nothing without a ship to fly. I'm taking Foresight. I'm going to use it to help us win this war wherever I can."

"What?" Bradshaw grimaced in confusion. "You can't just take the ship. It's USSF property, and so are you. I can't just allow you to fly out of here on a whim."

"I wasn't asking for permission," Nicholas said, glancing toward the camera positioned at the front of the ship and offering Jennifer a wink. Immediately, the light hum of the idling thrusters changed in pitch. "Goodbye, Captain Bradshaw."

He turned away. Bradshaw grabbed his arm. "Captain Shepherd, I can't let you go. Marines, get on board. Seize the ship!"

The survivors around the Marines blocked their paths. Outnumbered three to one, they couldn't break around them.

"Captain, let go of me," Nicholas said.

"You're not going anywhere, Shepherd. You're under—"

Nicholas' fist hit Bradshaw squarely in the jaw, sending him reeling into his XO, the pair of them stumbling backwards. Nicholas broke for the ramp as Foresight lifted into a shallow hover, the Marines shouting for him to stop. Gills appeared on the ramp, leaning over and grabbing his hand as he jumped on and Jennifer lifted off, heading away from the Pilgrim launch site.

"I didn't expect you to crack him one," Gills said as Nicholas hit the controls to retract the ramp and close the hatch.

"He wouldn't let go," Nicholas replied, racing to the ladder.

"That's a court martial for sure, Cap."

"He has to catch us first."

He and Gills quickly scaled the ladder to the main deck. Gills fell into the seat next to Macey while Nicholas ran to the flight deck. "Nice work, Jen. Anything on the sensors?"

"I think the drones are incoming, Captain," she replied, pointing at the projection ahead of the display surround. The system showed a pair of friendly targets closing from a few miles out.

"That was fast," Nicholas said, dropping into the pilot's seat. He tapped the left-hand controls to activate the shields while the safety restraint system locked over him. "Is everyone strapped in back there?" he asked over the comm.

"We're all in, Nick," Yasmin replied.

"Hold on tight and prepare for some high Gs."

Nicholas opened the throttle, pushing everyone back in their seats as Foresight rocketed skyward, gaining speed in a hurry. The drones adjusted their vectors, unable to match the acceleration but already close enough to open fire.

But would they?

Not right away, at least. They set an intercept course, climbing with the starship and doing their best to stay in range. Pushing the Gs a little harder, Nicholas tightened his gut muscles and added to the acceleration and angle of attack, ascending hard and fast. With eyes on the forward display, he kept glancing at the projected grid, tracking the drones.

Foresight shot through the clouds, hitting twenty-thousand feet inside of thirty seconds. The drones dove into the clouds behind them a few seconds later, nearly twenty miles back and fading fast.

A warning tone sounded on the flight deck, a red

wedge suddenly appearing ahead of them on the grid. "What the hell?" Nicholas said, the bogey appearing so quickly Frank didn't have time to give it an estimated size or shape. He watched the wedge cover half the distance separating Foresight from it in a matter of seconds. Frank recorded a burst of energy from the wedge and the two drones vanished from sensors. "Shit."

"Captain Shepherd?" Jennifer questioned.

The wedge changed course again, morphing from its geometric shape as Frank finished processing the sensor data.

Nicholas stared at the revealed craft. It definitely wasn't from Earth.

It also wasn't alone.

Chapter 37

Curved like a boomerang, the alien ship had an aggressive shape to it, sleek and sharp, with no defined fuselage or cockpit. Its surfaces were uneven as though it were made of hewn rock, and the way it accelerated suggested it was either fully automated or whatever controlled it could withstand unbelievable amounts of G and centrifugal forces.

It also gained on them at an impossible rate. Closing the distance from dozens of miles to less than a handful within a matter of seconds, it maneuvered in behind Foresight as Nicholas guided the starship into the mesosphere and toward space beyond.

At least, that had been the planned course.

Until the grid lit up with eight new bogeys.

They matched the first ship, dropping from space on a direct collision course. Nicholas couldn't begin to guess where they had come from—well, he *could* guess, but he didn't want to even imagine the size of the spaceship that had to have spit them out. Beyond that, he was certain there was no way around them.

"What do we do?" Jennifer asked behind him, voice quivering with fear.

"Just sit tight," he replied, wincing as Frank detected an energy burst from the trailing ship. Foresight shuddered slightly as it washed over them, creating physical force against the shields that jostled them in their seats. A quick glance at the HUD showed him the shot hadn't come close to penetrating the web of energy surrounding the ship, but that only offered minor comfort.

They were outnumbered nine to one, and they'd only absorbed one shot from one ship.

"Attention all hands," he said, activating the ship's comms. "Prepare for evasive maneuvers. It's going to get a little dicey."

He only gave them a half-second to prepare before he used the thumbstick and vectoring controls to throw Foresight into a hard left bank, rolling it over like a breaching whale to make a quick change in direction. G-forces tugged at him, and while his experience would let him manage nearly twenty Gs for a short burst, his passengers wouldn't have that capability. Needing to evade the ships would be hard enough. Doing it without causing G-loc on any of the others would take next level skills.

Foresight handled the hard turn gracefully, not even shaking against the resistance as Nicholas guided her in a descent as sharp as his original climb. He pushed the throttle almost all the way open, gaining velocity as both the thrusters and gravity worked to bleed off altitude.

They lost thousands of feet with each second, hitting the clouds in no time. The alien ships ducked into the soup tight on Foresight's tail. Small movements on the thumbstick translated to quick jerks and jinks as he began flattening the descent near twenty-thousand feet.

A quick glance showed him he was about to pass over the Grand Canyon.

He had seen plenty of movies where fleeing aircraft had used the Canyon's tight confines against a less experienced opponent. While Foresight was considerably larger than an F-14, that didn't mean he couldn't do the same thing.

He dove into the clouds, the projected grid displaying blooms of energy around the chasing alien craft. Fiery plasma swept past on the left, obscuring the cameras with white hot light and causing Nicholas to bank hard left, working the exo-atmospheric vectoring thrusters with his pinkie and ring finger for a little extra push. The plasma bolts remained wide to the right while the alien ships tried to adjust. Nicholas slipped Foresight in the opposite direction and tightened the descent, the rounds flashing overhead as they broke through the cloud cover.

"I think I'm going to be sick," Jennifer said behind him.

"Don't puke on the console." Otherwise, Nicholas ignored the statement.

The canyons were fast approaching, beautiful in their scale and appearance. He hoped to turn them deadly as well. Sparing a glance at the grid showed the additional enemy craft were still trailing the first, which remained stuck to him like glue. Good. He needed them to follow him into the canyons to have any chance of losing them.

"Frank, disable oversteer intervention," Nicholas said. The auto-corrective functionality would make navigating the canyons difficult, if not impossible.

"Disabling oversteer intervention is not recommended," the AI replied. "Please confirm override."

"Override confirmed."

"Oversteer intervention disabled."

Nicholas didn't sense any immediate change, but he knew he would shortly. He banked the ship hard left again as he neared the opening to the canyon with all its side gullies and gorges. He avoided another blast of plasma that chewed into the face of the canyon's rocky northern cliff. Slowing slightly and keeping all of his fingers light on the control surface, he descended another hundred feet between the two escarpments, still a good distance apart but narrowing ahead.

"Okay, assholes, let's see how well they teach you to fly on other planets."

Nicholas punched the throttle again, sending Foresight racing forward. The lead alien ship dove in behind him, its next plasma blast coming up short because of Frank's sudden acceleration. The bogey overshot the approach angle just enough for its wide wing to nearly strike the canyon wall before it corrected. It turned sideways to slip through the narrowing channel and stay on Foresight's tail.

"Not bad," Nicholas said, banking hard right at a fork in the cliffs, and then left at another.

The alien ship matched him on the first maneuver but overcorrected on the second, this time smashing the sharp edge of its wingtip through the limestone. Spewing rock debris, it tumbled away, slamming into the other side of the canyon.

"I take that back," Nicholas said, smirking at the victory.

Taking two quick hits from the trailing alien ships, Foresight almost followed the alien in. Shuddering, the ship pitched and yawed wildly out of control. Fighting to regain control, Nicholas refused to panic. He made micro-movements on the stick under his thumb, easing

Foresight back into level flight in the middle of the canyon.

Quickly checking the grid, he saw that four alien ships were still chasing him. The other four had vanished from his sensors. Fairly certain that wasn't a good sign, he didn't have time to worry about it. The alien ships still with him spread out in a wide section of the canyon and fired steady streams of plasma, hitting Foresight more often than not. The shields were holding for now, but he could tell by the increasing severity of pitching and shuddering that they were getting weaker with each strike.

He broke left, flying into another adjoining gorge and dropping low to the river. The thrusters pushed the water up in a rooster tail of vapor behind Foresight, the alien ships punching through the distraction without any indication it affected them at all. Narrowing their formation to adjust for the width of the canyon, they nearly touched wingtips as they flew in unison behind him.

"AI then," Nicholas guessed. How else could they stick so tight to one another in this environment without crashing? With the water screen ineffective, he went for altitude, banking right at the next split.

He barely had time to react as the canyon narrowed. A winding path to the right was the only way through. With the oversteer intervention disabled, the slightest mistake would send them into the canyon wall, and at these speeds the already diminished shields wouldn't hold for long.

As if to emphasize the point, another plasma blast hit the shields, pushing the shaking ship toward the wall. Nicholas gritted his teeth as he nudged the thumbstick and tapped the vectoring controls, Foresight's jets kicking out loose debris as they passed almost close enough to the cliff wall to kiss it.

Slipping back and forth through the winding terrain, Nicholas watched the rear view feed as one of the alien ships got too close to the side, smacking it and careening out of control. It nearly struck a second craft before tumbling into the river.

Two down, seven to go. Nicholas still hated the odds, but at least he had managed to reduce them slightly. He rocketed out into a wider section of canyon, looking ahead for his next maneuver.

"Nick," Yasmin said over the comm, her voice demanding his attention.

"What is it?" he asked.

"Why aren't you shooting back at them?"

Nicholas had forgotten the others could watch the feeds at their individual stations. How much more could they do from back there? "What do you mean? The shields are active."

"So?"

"So we can't use the spines for offense and defense at the same time. That's what you told me."

"No, but with the power levels the way they are, the switch-over will happen fast. We'll only be vulnerable for a few seconds."

"*Now* you tell me?"

"I thought you knew."

If the situation weren't so serious, Nicholas could have laughed. Instead, he tapped the controls to deploy the spines, which spread away from the hull, carrying the web of defensive energy with them. He would need to be careful with his attack. A few seconds without shields was still plenty long enough for a lance of plasma to kill them all.

"Jennifer, mark the bogeys on the Spinal Control

System," he said, unable to handle added workload while navigating the tight confines of the canyon.

"Yes sir," Jennifer replied, still managing to hang onto the meager contents of her stomach. A red ring appeared around each of the alien ships, marking them as targets. The ring around one of the ships turned green when the SCS settled on a firing solution.

Not yet. He wanted all three rings to switch to green before he risked dropping the shields.

The chase continued, with Nicholas managing to stay a few lengths ahead of the alien ships as they tracked him through the canyons. Occasional plasma bursts hit the rocky cliffs on either side, blowing out huge chunks of debris or striking the shields, diminishing them slightly with each hit. The rings around the targets alternated between red and green, the confines and the alien squadron's configuration making it hard to align the solution.

Patience, he reminded himself. Wait for the shot to come to you.

He banked into another narrow chasm, still splitting his attention between the projection and the view ahead, waiting for all greens. The alien ships slowed slightly behind him, navigating the tighter space more carefully and dropping back as a result. Or maybe they were finally giving up?

He broke out of the chasm and banked to the left, into another gorge splitting off from the main canyon.

His heart jumped when his eyes landed on the four alien ships hovering in front of him at the far end of the gorge, positioned as though they had known he would cross their paths the entire time.

"Captain Shepherd!" Jennifer cried out as if he couldn't see the enemy directly ahead of them.

He only had a split-second to make a decision. Blow through and hope the shields could withstand the concentrated fire of the entire alien squadron or trigger the spines and risk being hit in the meantime. Fight or flight.

He chose to fight.

The visual targeting system allowed him to specify the ships ahead in an instant, simply by looking at them. Frank designated the alien ships as targets, their static positions helping the SCS lock quickly onto them. All four rings turned green on the front side of the projection, two of the three doing the same behind Foresight.

Six out of seven. Good enough.

"Hang on!" Nicholas shouted, cutting the thrusters and activating the anti-gravity coils at full power at the same time he triggered the spines.

Energy beams lashed out at the alien ships in both directions. Nicholas didn't know if the aliens had shields of their own until he saw the beams digging into the ships' surfaces, ablating and passing through the rocklike exterior. The alien ships returned fire, a stream of plasma converging on Foresight from both ends of the canyon.

Nicholas engaged the ant-gravity coils, flinging Foresight forcefully upward. Gs shoved him down hard in his seat, Without shields, the enemy plasma bolts scraped the underbelly, singing the hull on their way past.

The alien ships didn't get another shot as the beams from the spines did their job. Three of the ships immediately tumbled from the air, crashing into the water. The others suffered catastrophic damage that sent them reeling off course. One of them smashed into the lone undamaged target, both of them ending up as two plumes of smoke and falling debris after slamming into the canyon wall. The remaining pair attempted to continue the chase, only to lose power. One plummeted to the water, catching a wing to cartwheel into the rocky end of the gorge, the other skidding to a stop atop the northern mesa.

"Woooo-hoooo! Take that assholes!" Gills shouted from the main deck, so loud Nicholas could hear it on the flight deck.

Nicholas only allowed himself a final satisfied smirk as he reengaged the thrusters and cut the anti-gravity, sending Foresight into a new ascent toward the stars.

Chapter 38

"I always knew you were a good pilot, Nick," Yasmin said over the comms as they climbed. "I never really understood how good. I've never seen anything like that."

"I got lucky," Nicholas replied. "That's all." He kept his gaze glued on the threat projection. "I wish I could say we're home free, but those smaller ships had to come from somewhere. Is everyone okay back there?"

"I changed my mind," Macey said. "I want to go with the arkship."

"No refunds," Scott replied. "That was better than any roller coaster."

"I still think I'm going to puke," Jennifer added.

"Captain, you think there's a *bigger* ship waiting for us out there?" Briar asked. "Like a mothership?"

"I don't know," Nicholas replied. "I hope not, but it wouldn't surprise me."

"No big deal," Gills said. "We'll just blast that one too. We're unstoppable."

"I appreciate the attitude, but let's not get too cocky,"

Nicholas said. "I never imagined there were aliens other than the trife on Earth, and I definitely never guessed they would have starships of their own. Grimmel said we have no idea of what's out here, and he was right. We can't assume anything."

Nicholas' attitude quieted the group. He hated to play the pragmatic downer, but he couldn't afford to let any of them, himself included, be lulled into a false sense of security or superiority. While he was pleased with his ability to maneuver Foresight within the canyons, he wasn't sure how impressed he should be for winning the battle against the alien squadron. They hadn't proven to be anything more than average with regard to their skill, and the spines had made short work of most of the unshielded ships.

More concerning to him was the fact that they had managed to get in front of him without registering on Foresight's sensors until it was almost too late. He didn't know how they had done it, but he guessed it had something to do with the uneven surface of the ships and the fact they weren't moving. Either way, it seemed almost as if the alien ships had been made to defeat Foresight's advanced sensor technology before that technology even existed. He wondered what Yasmin would think about *that*.

"SO WHAT ARE we supposed to do now, Captain Shepherd?" Jennifer asked.

"That depends on what the enemy does," Nicholas replied. "We have the data from Grimmel's computer. Ideally, I'd like to give Yasmin some time to review it. I'm not sure the other side will give us that time."

"We have the energy unit and the slip drive," Yasmin

said. "We don't need to linger near Earth. We can go pretty much anywhere, as long as it isn't here."

"We may have the slip drive, but we don't know how to use it."

"That isn't entirely true," Yasmin countered. "The last patch we uploaded included a slip test, remember? We never had a chance to upload a new patch, so it's still in Frank's data storage. All we have to do is execute the aborted test parameters. As an added benefit, Frank has to sling us around the moon before the slip can happen. If there is an alien mothership or something out there waiting for us, it'll have to keep up."

"You saw how those other ships accelerated. I have a feeling anything they have can pace us."

"In atmosphere, maybe. Those ships were aerodynamic as hell. Foresight is more like a flying almond. It has no right staying airborne against air friction and gravity. But it does. That's our play, Nick. Run the test; let Frank handle the slip drive. Get somewhere safe where we can regroup and figure out our next steps."

"What if we end up stuck in the middle of nowhere? Space is really, really big."

"It's a risk we need to take. These aliens went through a lot of trouble to keep us from getting away from Earth. That tells me that whatever they're up to, we have the potential to stop it. Please. Trust me."

Nicholas closed his eyes. The last time she had asked him to trust her he hadn't gone far enough with his faith. If he had taken the risk to complete the original test parameters then, Luke might still be alive now.

Or not. There was no way to know that for sure. The trife were already on their way from the Invenergy array by then. Would they have evacuated the base in time if the mission had been a success?

He couldn't simply go back to change his decision, but Grimmel had suggested that somehow he *could* go back. All he had to do was discover how.

All he had to do was put his complete trust in his wife. Why was that so hard?

It wasn't.

"Okay," he said, opening his eyes. "Let's do this. Frank, reinitialize mission upload sixty-three delta for retest."

"Yes, Captain," the AI replied. "Mission upload sixty-three delta reinitialized."

Nicholas paused again. "Yazz, I do trust you. But last time Frank wanted to make some pretty hard maneuvers."

"You made some hard maneuvers yourself down in the canyon," she countered.

"Only for a few seconds at a time. This could lead to sustained high-G maneuvers. It might be dangerous."

"No pain, no gain, Cap," Gills said.

"Let's do this, Captain," Briar added. "For Luke."

"Yeah, for Luke," Scott agreed.

"I've got my barf bag ready, Captain," Jennifer said. "For Luke."

Nicholas couldn't hold back his smile. "All right then. Frank, execute."

Chapter 39

With the neural network handling Foresight's climb through the troposphere for a second time and into orbit, Nicholas quickly briefed the rest of the passengers on proper technique for handling lengthy high-G maneuvers. He couldn't be certain Frank would set a course that would make the training necessary until it actually created the navigational dataset, but it was definitely better to be prepared.

Watching Earth shrink in the rear camera feeds, Macey couldn't quite wait for Nicholas to finish his instructions before launching into a whirlwind of animated chatter. "Blimey!" she howled. "Look at that, will ya? We're in space, mates! Oh..." Her excitement faded into a frown when she identified the damage they had done to their own planet in the futile effort to destroy the trife, but her somber mood didn't last long. "Brilliant!" she shouted, "We're bonafide space cadets!"

Scott burst out laughing, and Nicholas closed his mouth, one corner twitching in amusement despite his best effort to dredge up a good chastisement to quiet her.

"Space cadets?" Gills gave her a sour look. "Do you looney Limeys know what that means?"

"I ain't looney," Macey argued.

"You are if you're a space cadet."

"I don't think it means the same to her as it does to us," Briar offered.

"Outlaws," Scott said. "We're outlaws. But good outlaws. Like the A-team."

"Who?" Briar asked.

"The A-team. It's an old television show. I caught it on Netflix Classics." Scott deepened his voice. "In 1972, a crack commando unit was sent to prison by a military court for a crime they didn't commit. These men promptly escaped from a maximum security stockade to the Los Angeles underground. Today, still wanted by the government, they survive as soldiers of fortune. If you have a problem, if no one else can help, and if you can find them....maybe you can hire The A-Team."

Nicholas finally grinned and shook his head, letting his makeshift crew have their banter. After all they had been through, they needed a chance to detox a little while Frank achieved orbit and shifted to the next phase of the test run.

"I don't think we're like the A-team," Gills said. "I'm the only crack commando among you."

"You're the only one with a swelled head among us," Macey quipped, laughing at her slight.

"Maybe we're more like the Dukes of Hazzard." Gills offered, and he started singing... "Just some good old boys. Didn't mean any harm."

"We aren't all boys," Briar said.

"Neither were the Dukes of Hazzard. There was Daisy Duke."

"Try again."

"We aren't outlaws," Jennifer said. "We're more like rebels."

"Rebels without a clue," Scott said, smirking.

"Just don't make this into a Star Wars thing," Briar told him.

"Okay, then maybe we're cowboys."

"Cow...*boys*? More than half of us are female," Briar pointed out again.

"Cowfolk? Cowpeeps? Spacecows?" Scott laughed. "Whatever."

They continued their joking while Nicholas returned his gaze to the sensor projection. They had cleared the thermosphere, and the AI had cut the thrusters, the ship coasting into position. For the moment, they were alone, but his instincts insisted that wasn't going to last. The alien ships that had carried out the running battle with him in the Grand Canyon had dropped in from orbit. They hadn't just come out of thin air; they had originated somewhere. And Yasmin was right. The enemy clearly didn't want them to escape.

"Exo-atmospheric launch complete," Frank said.

"Attention all hands," Nicholas said, using the ship's loudspeakers instead of the personal comms to capture the attention of the others. "Attention all hands. We've completed exo-atmospheric launch. Frank will execute sequence two on my order. So far, the threat projection is clean."

"Ready for sequence two, Nick," Yasmin confirmed.

"As ready as we'll ever be, anyway," Briar mumbled into her comm.

"Copy that," Nicholas replied. "All of you, remember what I taught you. Frank, initiate mission sequence two and display the pattern on the HUD."

"Confirmed. Initiating sequence two. Setting coordinates and executing burn."

Nicholas tensed his jaw while he waited for Frank to create the course settings. Like before, Foresight rotated to reposition itself. The AI's proposed pathway appeared next to the threat display, showing an initial hard burn that would ease off before a second, more prolonged burn to slow the approach. It was a much less physically demanding course than the one Frank had chosen the last time.

"All right, tighten up those gut muscles, kiddies. We're about to be shot at the moon," Nicholas announced, just before the burn commenced. He tightened his own stomach as Foresight blasted forward, pushing four Gs of initial acceleration.

The initial burn continued for nearly five minutes before easing from four Gs down to two, maintaining that pace as the velocity compounded, sending them hurtling through space. Of course, the vast distances made it seem as though they were moving in slow motion, while at the same time the rising circumnavigation of Earth's orbit toward the Moon brought the natural satellite into view within half an hour. By then, even Nicholas felt drained by the strain of the force of acceleration against his body. He could only imagine how the others felt.

"We're heading into the second hard burn," he announced. "A few more minutes and it'll be over."

"Thank goodness," Briar said breathlessly. "I'm getting tired of sucking my gut in."

Nicholas' eyes remained fixed on the sensor projection, which had added the Moon to the display as it had come within range. It drifted ever closer to the fixed center of the projection where Foresight resided, on a marching-ant line showing their predicted path.

The rotation to flip Foresight so that the thrusters faced the Moon was nearly imperceptible inside the ship, save for a few seconds while the G-forces shifted around them before settling. The deceleration pushed Nicholas back in his seat, their approach to the Moon likewise slowing in the projection.

Staring at their trajectory, Nicholas noticed the shape of the Moon changing, a protrusion expanding from the side. He redirected his view to the aft feed, watching as a long, thin asteroid emerged from behind the satellite.

Believing the asteroid to be a threat, he made sure the shields were up and the spines charged. But as the seconds ticked by, he realized he had overreacted. The rock was large, but the sensors weren't picking up any sign of energy or heat, and it moved in a logical orbit around the Moon. It sent a shiver down his spine to think this was one of the asteroids the trife had arrived on. A purpose-sent projectile that had somehow gotten caught in the wrong gravitational field.

Foresight continued to slow, the intensity of the burn increasing suddenly as the projected path changed to avoid a collision with the asteroid. Nicholas tightened his stomach in response to the increased G-force, hoping his passengers remembered to do the same.

For the first handful of seconds, Nicholas believed the opposing paths a freak accident, unexpected but easily avoided. But then the large rock seemed to unnaturally decelerate, altering its velocity to maintain the collision course with Foresight. Yet there was still no reading of energy output or thruster burn. How was that possible?

A tingle of fear ran down his spine. "Frank, we need to get around that asteroid."

"Confirmed. Adjusting course to evade," Frank replied, the AI firing thrusters to vector them toward a higher orbit.

The asteroid again altered course to match, confirming his fear.

"Frank, change course."

"Would you like to abort the mission?" Frank asked.

"No. Mark phase two as a success and move to phase three."

"Mission parameters call for circling the Moon successfully before phase three can be initialized."

Nicholas grimaced. He had hoped to get away with bypassing phase completion. "Yazz, love," he said. "We have a problem."

"What's wrong?" she replied, her voice strained from contending with the G-forces.

"Do you have a visual of that asteroid?"

"What asteroid?"

"Check the rear-view."

"What about it?"

"It isn't an asteroid. It's matching every change I make in our heading, trying to force a collision. We're at five minutes to impact, and I can't force it to the next phase. You wrote the AI. Can you make it skip ahead?"

"I'm not sure. The code deployed on the ship's mainframe is locked. That's why we upload special patches. I don't think there's enough time."

"You need to try, or I'll have to abort the mission. I don't think we want to get stuck here with that thing on an ever-changing collision course." He had just finished the sentence when he spotted small flashes of light near the back of the asteroid. A moment later, twelve new targets were added to the threat projection. "Scratch that. We definitely don't want to get stuck with that thing. It just deployed additional ships."

"What? Damn it, I'm on it, Nick. But I can't make any promises."

"Just do your best. I'll keep them honest." He wasn't sure how since he couldn't retake control from Frank without aborting the mission, but he didn't want her to panic.

The alien starships blasted toward Foresight, their opposing approaches allowing them to quickly cover the distance between them. Nicholas marked each of the targets, not waiting for them to fire before taking the first shot.

The shields went offline an instant before spinal beam energy lashed into the oncoming alien ships and then returned as the beam sheared through them before they had a chance to react. Nicholas watched the alien mothership, waiting to see what they would do next.

He didn't have to wait long.

Another squadron of small ships launched, this time followed by a second group and then a third. The groups were spread well apart from one another as they approached. Meanwhile, the mothership continued adjusting to Frank's course corrections, maneuvering to block their escape.

"Yazz, anything?" Nicholas asked.

"It hasn't even been a minute," she replied. She must have looked at the projection on the holotable and seen the new targets as Frank painted them, because she followed the statement up with a breathless "Oh, shit."

"We can't take them on, and we can't get around this ship," Nicholas said. "If there's anything you can do…" He trailed off as Frank changed tactics, rotating and opening the throttle. The sudden force pushed the wind out of him and shoved him back in his seat.

Jennifer moaned behind him, the intense force having the same effect on her.

"Can't...work...like this," Yasmin strained to say.

The burn ended. Frank had updated their vector to take a much closer line along the Moon's surface. Too close for the mothership to follow comfortably. That didn't prevent it from altering direction again, moving to retain the collision course. Would it rather crash into the Moon than let them escape? It seemed so.

A warning tone sounded on the flight deck as the three squadrons of alien ships opened fire, sending dozens of bolts of plasma across the breadth at Foresight. Frank made a few limited evasive maneuvers, but too many of the shots hit the shields, knocking the ship around and diminishing the overall strength of its shields.

"I really can't work like this," Yasmin repeated in response to the shaking.

'We're running out of time," Nicholas replied. "Can you force Frank to phase three?" He only gave her a half-second of hesitation. "I need an answer now."

"No," she replied. "But I—"

Nicholas didn't wait for the rest of the sentence. "Frank, mission abort. I'm taking the stick. Confirm."

"Mission aborted," Frank replied.

Nicholas regained control and immediately flipped the ship in the other direction, pointing the nose back at the alien mothership. Opening the throttle, he launched the ship at the enemy, confusing the squadrons of ships and circumventing their attack. Dozens of bolts flashed through space behind Foresight as it rushed ahead.

He limited the burn to spare his passengers while he

used the vectoring nozzles to send the ship into a corkscrew that made it harder for the enemy to hit them.

"Captain Shepherd, what are you doing?" Jennifer asked.

It relieved him to hear she hadn't suffered G-loc during the last hard burn, though he wasn't convinced she was better off awake. "I can't get around it. I can't outrun it. There are too many other ships out here to evade them all forever. There's only one option left."

Jennifer gasped audibly. "You're going through it?"

"I'm going to try," he replied.

"I don't think the shields can hold up to that."

"Maybe not. There's no other way."

He continued making evasive maneuvers, an occasional plasma bolt hitting the shields and shaking them up a little. "Frank, how long can we sustain the ion beams from the spines?"

"The estimated time to spinal overload is eight seconds," Frank replied.

Nicholas wasn't sure that would be enough time to blow a hole in the alien ship and pass through it, assuming the beams could clear a path for them. The whole idea was undoubtedly insane, and the fact that it remained their best option proved how desperate things had become.

He pushed the throttle forward more, eyes narrowing as the alien mothership loomed large in the surround. A collision warning sounded, a harsh tone blasting across the flight deck. If he had reinstated the avoidance override, Frank would have already taken over to force a course change.

But there was nowhere else to go. No course they could set that would get them free of the mothership or its squadrons of attack vessels. No way to escape without doing something drastic.

Without doing something crazy.

"Yazz, if we don't survive this, I love you," he said over the comm.

She didn't reply.

Five seconds. Four. Three. Two.

Nicholas' finger rested on the fire control, ready to trigger the spines. The mothership was so close he could make out the individual ridges, depressions, cliffs, and craters in its rocky hull. They would either cut straight through it or slam hard into it.

One...

Nicholas pressed the fire control button.

Foresight's power went out, suddenly leaving them in pitch black and shutting off the forward surround view just before the impact.

The final second passed. Another followed. Then a third. A fourth. A fifth. The universe remained silent, and for a moment Nicholas wondered if this was all there was to death.

Behind him, Jennifer coughed.

He exhaled. Not dead. Then what?

The power returned. The emergency lighting flashed on first, quickly followed by the HUD, the threat projection, and then the surround's forward view. Nicholas stared at the feed, amazed by what he saw.

A planet hung in the black ahead of them. Green and blue and white, his initial thought was that he had succeeded in passing through the alien mothership and Foresight had wound up pointing at Earth.

Except the projection remained empty. No moon. No mothership. No squadrons of smaller alien ships.

"Slip test, stage one complete," Frank said.

Chapter 40

"What the hell just happened?" Nicholas said, confused by Frank's announcement.

"Nick, tell Frank to pause the mission," Yasmin said. "Before it reverses the slip."

"Frank, hold test mission at phase two success. Confirm."

"Hold confirmed," Frank replied.

Nicholas leaned back in his seat and exhaled again, trying to settle his racing heart and spinning mind. "Yazz, what's going on?"

"I couldn't force Frank to bypass phase two of the test parameters and skip ahead to phase three," she explained. "So I triggered phase three myself."

"You could do that?"

"I tried to tell you, but you didn't wait for me to finish."

"I didn't have time to wait. Shit, I nearly sent us through the alien mothership."

"I know. That wouldn't have ended well. We were a

half-second away from being splattered on their hull like a mosquito on a windshield."

"Were you waiting to make saving us more dramatic?"

"No. We really came that close."

"I'm suddenly nauseous."

"Welcome to the club," Jennifer said.

"I already hurled," Briar added. "Right into my lap. If we're going to not accelerate for a little bit, I'd like to change my clothes."

"Just hang tight for a minute, Briar," Nicholas said. "Let's be sure we don't need to escape anything else before you leave your seat."

"Yes, sir."

"You're telling me that's not Earth?" Gills said.

"I don't see any of the nuke damage," Nicholas replied. "And there's no moon."

"I assume we're near a planet one of the arkships is destined for," Yasmin said.

"It looks beautiful," Briar said.

"Should we go down there?" Macey asked. "Check it out? That would be fun."

"We didn't come here for fun," Nicholas said. "Let's all just sit and take a moment to settle. I'll keep an eye on the sensors, and if nothing else shows up to kill us in the next five minutes we can stand down."

"Copy that, Cap," Gills said.

Nicholas returned his attention to the empty threat display before pulling up additional sensor data on the HUD. According to Frank, the planet was the same general size and shape as Earth, with a near-matching atmosphere. If Yasmin was right and this was one of the planets an arkship would depart for, then they were in luck.

Grimmel had claimed that five to seven of the ships would wind up stranded, sent to a system that couldn't support life. The idea of so many thousands stuck in deep space or orbiting a dead planet struck him a lot harder looking at this seemingly perfect world.

The five minutes passed uneventfully, leaving Nicholas grateful for the respite. Ever since the trife attacked Fort Hood, there hadn't been a single moment to lower his heart-rate, take stock of the situation, and really plan their next steps. There hadn't been time to do anything more than react and hope for the best.

But they had escaped from Earth. They had made it...but to where? Across the universe? Hundreds of light years from home in a matter of seconds? The idea of it sent his mind reeling again. How was it even possible? What did the slip drive actually do?

He realized it didn't matter how it worked, only that it did. Five minutes ago, they were a split-second away from death. Now they were here.

Now they were safe.

"Okay," he said as his given timeframe elapsed and the sensors remained clear. "You're free to move about the cabin."

"Thank goodness," Briar said.

"I'm not sure I can stand," Jennifer said. "My legs feel like jello."

"Anybody else want a candy bar?" Macey asked.

"Pass on the candy, but if we've got some of that marmite I'm game," Gills said.

"Frank, set an alert. If anything appears on the sensors—good, bad, or ugly—I want to know immediately," Nicholas said, standing up.

"Alert confirmed, Captain Shepherd," Frank replied flatly.

Nicholas paused at Jennifer's seat, offering his hand. She took it, and he helped her gain her space legs, walking with her to the main compartment. Briar, Macey, Scott, and Gills had already left for the upper deck. Yasmin remained at her station, leaning over to plug in the datacard she had taken from Grimmel's computer. He didn't see Dag anywhere.

"I'm going to go lie down for a few minutes," Jennifer said, seeming to sense that Nicholas wanted a minute alone with his wife. "Thank you for getting us out of there alive, Captain. Doctor Shepherd."

"You're welcome," Yasmin said, straightening up.

Jennifer scaled the ladder to the upper deck. Nicholas stood over Yasmin's shoulder. "I didn't know these stations had the right interface."

"The stations were designed so the ship's systems could either be partitioned to crew members or concentrated away from the flight deck, in the unfortunate event the flight deck was destroyed. You can't fly Foresight with the same precision from back here, but you'd be able to limp back home."

"I don't think we'll be limping home any time soon."

"That depends. I don't know how to access the slip drive directly just yet, and even once I do, it'll take some time for me to understand how it works in order to use it. In the meantime, we can resume the test mission at any time, which will trigger the return trip."

"I don't think we want to go back to where we came from."

"We don't want to go back to *when* we came from," Yasmin corrected. "Grimmel said we could fix things. He said we could save Luke."

"We will," Nicholas agreed. "I have no intention of resuming the test parameters. Do you think Grimmel left anything on his computer that may be useful to us? It didn't seem that he planned for you to be here with me."

"He planned for you to have access," Yasmin said. "Or he wouldn't have left it unlocked. Not only do I think he left information he thought you would need, I don't think it'll be very hard to find."

"Are you making fun of my computer aptitude?"

Yasmin smiled. "Not at all. There was just no reason for him to hide anything. I don't think he planned for Harry to be under the control of a space prawn."

"I thought it looked more like a dung beetle crossed with an octopus. But if he wasn't worried about Harry, then why was the computer locked in the first place? Why was his office locked?"

"I didn't check the security access list. I went right to my name and added permissions. It's possible you were already there. We just didn't know it."

"Okay. I'd pull up a chair, but they're all bolted in." He leaned over her shoulder instead. "Let's see what we've got."

Yasmin used the control pad attached to her seat to navigate to the drive, opening the list of files and folders on the station's display. She scrolled through the list, bypassing hundreds of lines as she scanned it for something meaningful, stopping a moment later on a folder marked *Project Foresight*.

"This looks like the one," she said. "I told you it wouldn't be hard to find."

"Yeah, I could have figured this one out," Nicholas agreed.

Yasmin opened the folder. A second list of files and folders appeared. The first file was titled *Introduction*.

"I'm so tempted to skip that one," Yasmin said.

"Yeah, I think we had our introduction already. But let's open it anyway."

Yasmin selected the file. It opened to what appeared to be a recording of Grimmel sitting at his office desk.

"Captain Shepherd," Grimmel said. "Well, I hope it's you watching this, or something has gone horribly wrong. Haha! Let's hope not. I'm sure by now I gave you a high-level overview of what Project Foresight is. I told you all about the arkships and the slip drive, and how you could save thousands of lives by pre-visiting the selected destination systems to ensure they were habitable before the ships all launch." Grimmel paused, glancing around the room as though he were afraid someone might be listening in. "The thing is this, Nicholas." He paused again, leaning closer to the camera. "I lied."

"What?" Nicholas hissed, suddenly as confused as he had ever been.

Grimmel laughed, leaning back in his seat. "I can picture your expression hearing me say that. Haha! I'm sorry to do this to you, Captain. You don't deserve this treatment. But there's more at stake than you realize. More at stake than you'll immediately understand. The additional files and videos I've included in the Project Foresight folder will help explain, but the only way to truly learn and know is by experience. I won't lie and tell you it will be an easy road you've chosen. But I know you're the right person for this. I know you have an exceptional pedigree." He paused again, glancing around the room. "I'm sure you want a straightforward answer to a straightforward question right now."

"What is Project Foresight?" Nicholas and Grimmel said at the same time.

"The full answer is extremely complicated,"

Grimmel continued. "The simple answer is that you're bait. A dab of peanut butter on a mousetrap. A worm at the end of a hook. Now, I know hearing that is going to make you angry. But you have no idea how important this is. No idea at all. We're fighting a war against the closest thing the universe has to a god, and the only way to win is to know the moves before they're made. *Foresight.* The trouble is, the other side is making moves too. This isn't a battle for our time. This is a fight for every time. For every space. I don't know how or where or when it ends. I'm not even sure where it began. But you need to see this through, Captain Shepherd. The fate of the universe—the fate of all universes—depends on it."

Grimmel stared intensely into the camera, freezing there when the recording ended. Nicholas stared back.

"Is he serious?" he said, trembling from the scope of what Grimmel had just said. "He can't be serious, can he?"

"I don't know, Nick," Yasmin answered, her voice as shaky as he felt. "This is just the introduction. There has to be more information in here. Besides, maybe the mission changed. He didn't expect Luke to die, and that seemed to be really important to him. And he said we could fix it."

"I know. I just don't understand any of this. Who the hell is Aaron Grimmel anyway? The fate of all universes depends on us? It all sounds ridiculous. I just want my damn son back!" He shouted at the top of his lungs, the stress of everything catching up to him. Raising his hands to his face, he couldn't stop himself from sobbing in sadness, anger and frustration.

Yasmin's arms wrapped around him, her voice soft and trembling. "Me too, Nick. We aren't slaves to Aaron

Grimmel. He doesn't get to make all of the rules. The more we know, the better we'll be able to meet our goals. If they align with his, all the better. If they don't..."

"Yazz, how can Luke be more important than whatever it is Grimmel's warning us about?"

She looked up at him, fresh fire in her eyes. "How could he not?" she hissed back.

Nicholas lowered his head against the top of Yasmin's head, leaning on her for strength. "This is all so crazy."

"I know. I agree. It is crazy. I—"

"Captain Shepherd," Frank said, interrupting. "Sensors have captured a radio burst from the planet's surface."

Nicholas lifted his head. "Is it trying to contact us or is it a random broadcast?"

"It has not attempted a direct hail, but it is broadcasting on a USSF channel, Captain," Frank said.

"Let's hear it."

A new voice echoed through the loudspeakers in the main compartment, warm and rich and somewhat familiar.

"Cooperation. Facilitation. I require assistance. Hahahaha. Hahaha. Haha."

Nicholas looked at Yasmin, who stared back at him with a shocked expression, her next words sending a shiver down his spine.

"That sounds like Grimmel."

Chapter 41

Koth the Unspeakable sat alone in his throne room, head bowed and turned so it rested in his open palm. Long, gnarled fingers cradled his cheek, tips pressing lightly against a withered yellow eye.

His mind wasn't with his body. Instead, it occupied the simple brains of the Gulths he had unleashed in pursuit of the enemy, certain that he had learned from his earlier misjudgment.

The ship would not escape.

The Quantum Dimensional Modulator would be his.

Shub'Nigu would be pleased.

Very pleased. Enough to allow him to return home and reward him with the well-earned fruits of his labor. A position within the upper echelon of the Relyeh Ancients. A seat at the most glorious table. A feast worthy of his stature as the greatest and most powerful destroyer of all the Relyeh.

His hunger was great. His victory, imminent.

He watched the human starship prepare itself for a collision against his dreadnought knowing that even if it succeeded in penetrating the outer hull it would fail to breach all the way through, damaging his ship but leaving the target of his desire closer than ever before. He changed the Gulth attack formation to herd the ship toward him, long dormant emotions building as all of his work promised to pay off in one fateful moment. He had altered the course of reality already. Stopping them would ensure there would be no further complications.

Koth's fingers twitched against his face as his excitement grew, the human ship drawing ever nearer the dreadnought, committed to the act of self-annihilation. The tips of the hundreds of alloy spines that formed the ship's offensive capabilities glowed ever brighter, preparing to unleash a level of energy only possible with the help of the QDM.

"Yessss," Koth hissed, mouth barely moving. "I hunngeerrrr."

The starship reached the side of the dreadnought. Nothing could stop his victory now.

"Yessss!" he growled in jubilation.

The human starship disappeared.

Koth's hand clenched, fingertips digging painfully into his eye as his attention snapped back to his body. He pulled his hand away before he tore out the yellow orb. "Nooooo!" he yelled, the raspy shout echoing in the large, empty room. Clenching his hands into fists, he rose from his seat and fumed.

It couldn't be possible. No human could begin to understand how to execute a slip. No human could replicate slip technology.

But that was why the Anomaly had come, wasn't it? To insert itself into their midst and give the humans a chance they didn't deserve. To disrupt the inevitable expansion of the Relyeh in a futile effort to change the prescribed outcome.

Koth breathed out, letting the anger go with the exhale. He sat down on his black stone throne once more, his faded yellow robes spreading around him as his state of mind returned to normalcy. Cold. Calculating. Patient.

It was better this way, he decided. The true pleasure was in the hunt, and having this victory snatched away so suddenly would only make his final success that much more rewarding.

His eyes shifted to the tall door at the end of the throne room as it rotated open, parting at the center to allow General Shurg entry. The large Norg stormed into the room on elephantine legs, his bare feet slapping the floor with each step. The tentacles that hung below his jaw like a living beard writhed and undulated in response to his annoyance. His long, narrow nostrils flared, and small black eyes locked on Koth.

"Master Koth," Shurg said, falling to one knee in front of the throne. "The humans have escaped."

"Yes," Koth replied. "Stand up and tell me something useful, Shurg. Where did they go?"

General Shurg returned to his feet. "The Scry is searching for them, Master."

"They should never have escaped in the first place. It took nearly forty insertions to track the Anomaly to the origin. The humans clearly have a slip-capable starship in their possession. No doubt the Anomaly arranged for the alteration. Do you understand what that means?"

"The Echoes can't be undone. Our victories are assured."

"Idiot," Koth hissed. "The Echoes require amplification to spread. We have set the course, but there is a chance they can be silenced too soon. Shub'Nigu will not be pleased when he hears of my failure." His eyes narrowed, digging into Shurg. "*Your* failure."

"Both the Source and the Anomaly are eradicated, Master," Shurg replied. "You cannot discount the success."

"You display the intellect of a human with that statement. Have you learned nothing?"

"Forgive my simplicity, Master."

Koth shifted in his seat, mind working. Shurg wasn't completely wrong. The death of the Source would be very pleasing to Shub'Nigu. Perhaps even enough for him to escape punishment for the humans' escape. But not if they silenced the Echoes and stopped the amplification. Not if they minimized what he had accomplished here. Complete understanding of the relationship between stacked dimensions was challenging for the most intelligent of the Relyeh, save for himself of course. That's why he had been honored with this assignment. Even with the Anomaly's tutoring, the humans could never possibly comprehend the science behind it all.

The Anomaly should never have been able to understand it either, nevermind reverse engineer the process. But it wasn't like the rest of its kind. Not just because it held a greater intellect. No, there was something else there. Something Koth had yet to figure out.

Why had the Anomaly made this alteration? What purpose would granting a human control over a slip drive serve? Unless…

Koth began to laugh. It had been a long time, but the moment had drawn his reserved emotions outward.

"Master?" Shurg questioned, having never heard the guttural hissing before.

"Unless this Anomaly wasn't an anomaly at all.

Unless the true Anomaly waits on the other end of the slip," Koth said out loud. "Unless the humans were a means to an end and not the end itself."

That was the challenge with the Anomaly. Like him, it remained unique within the stack. Also like him, it had a penchant for using humans as tools. If it were true that the Anomaly had inserted itself in the stack earlier than he had guessed, finishing this business would be more challenging than he had originally thought.

But also more rewarding. How greatly Shub'Nigu would honor him for ending the threat.

"Another Anomaly?" Shurg questioned. "How can there be more than one?"

Koth sighed. Shurg was one of the finest Norg warriors among the Relyeh, but he too was incapable of easily understanding, and Koth didn't have the need or the desire to explain. "It doesn't matter."

He reached out to Shurg's mind through the connection all Relyeh shared, though some controlled it better than others and he controlled it best of all. Seizing the Norg's bodily functions hardly took any effort at all.

"Master?" Shurg said, knowing Koth had taken him and there was nothing he could do about it.

"You were responsible for seeing that the Quantum Dimensional Modulator was recovered. You were responsible for retrieving the Anomaly's full plans. You were responsible for preventing the humans from reaching orbit. You failed on every count. Shub'Nigu will require that I make an example of you."

Shurg reached to the folds of the rich blue robes he wore, cinched at the waist by a thick belt. A blaster hung from the belt, and Koth made him lift it from its holster.

"Master, I destroyed the Source and the Anomaly.

One Anomaly, at least. Should I not be spared for my successes?"

Koth hesitated. Shurg's arm remained static while he considered the request. His General's plan *had* resulted in two important victories. In fact, they were arguably more important than the energy unit or the humans' escape.

Except that escape could cost them everything.

"Master, please," Shurg said, hearing Koth's thoughts in his mind.

"You're a warrior, Shurg," Koth said. "Accept your fate with honor."

The tentacles around Shurg's mouth quieted as the General resolved himself. "Then release me from your thrall, Master, and I will fulfill my obligation."

Koth retreated from Shurg's mind. Shurg didn't hesitate to raise the blaster to the side of his head, placing the muzzle against his temple.

"For the honor and glory of Koth the Unspeakable, Shub'Nigu the All-seeing, and all of the Relyeh."

He fired the weapon, the plasma blasting through his soft skull and burning a hole in his brain. He collapsed on the floor in front of Koth.

Koth lowered his head into his hand, regaining his earlier posture. Reaching out to his subordinates through the Collective, he informed Shurg's second-in-command, Gurlat, of his promotion and ordered his guards to enter the throne room to collect Shurg's body.

There was no need to contact Shub'Nigu to inform him of the outcome. The All-seeing was just that, and he had no doubt the Ancient had already apprised himself of the situation.

For now, there was nothing to do but wait for the Scry to track the humans through the slip.

Once they were located, he wouldn't fail a second time.

He never had before.

THANK you so much for reading Foresight, the first book in the Forgotten Space series. Looking for the next-in-series? Please head over to mrforbes.com/forgottenspace2 for more information.

Thank you again!

Thank you you for reading Foresight, the first book in the Forgotten Space series.

I really hope you've enjoyed the book, and that you'll be back for Formation, book two in the series.

If you weren't aware, while Forgotten Space can be read as a standalone experience, it's also one of a series-of-series set within the Forgotten Universe, a growing collection of interconnected stories in the vein of the Marvel Cinematic Universe. If you'd like to learn more about those books, you can browse the entire catalog of titles at mrforbes.com/forgottenuniverse

If you're all caught up in the Forgotten Universe… WOW! Thank you so much!

Cheers,
    Michael.

Other Books By M.R Forbes

Want more M.R. Forbes? Of course you do!
View my complete catalog here
mrforbes.com/books
Or on Amazon:
mrforbes.com/amazon

Forgotten (The Forgotten)
mrforbes.com/theforgotten
Complete series box set:
mrforbes.com/theforgottentrilogy

Some things are better off FORGOTTEN.

Sheriff Hayden Duke was born on the Pilgrim, and he expects to die on the Pilgrim, like his father, and his father before him.

That's the way things are on a generation starship centuries from home. He's never questioned it. Never thought about it. And why bother? Access points to the ship's controls are sealed, the systems that guide her automated and out of reach. It isn't perfect, but he has all he needs to be content.

Until a malfunction forces his wife to the edge of the habitable zone to inspect the damage.

Until she contacts him, breathless and terrified, to tell him she found a body, and it doesn't belong to anyone on board.

Until he arrives at the scene and discovers both his wife and the body are gone.

The only clue? A bloody handprint beneath a hatch that hasn't opened in hundreds of years.

Until now.

Earth Unknown (Forgotten Earth)
mrforbes.com/earthunknown

Centurion Space Force pilot Nathan Stacker didn't expect to return home to find his wife dead. He didn't expect the murderer to look just like him, and he definitely didn't expect to be the one to take the blame.

But his wife had control of a powerful secret. A secret that stretches across the light years between two worlds and could lead to the end of both.

Now that secret is in Nathan's hands, and he's about to make the most desperate evasive maneuver of his life -- stealing a starship and setting a course for Earth.

He thinks he'll be safe there.

He's wrong. Very wrong.

Earth is nothing like what he expected. Not even close. What he doesn't know is not only likely to kill him, it's eager to kill him, and even if it doesn't?

The Sheriff will.

Deliverance (Forgotten Colony)

mrforbes.com/deliverance
Complete series box set:

The war is over. Earth is lost. Running is the only option.

It may already be too late.

Caleb is a former Marine Raider and commander of the Vultures, a search and rescue team that's spent the last two years pulling high-value targets out of alien-ravaged cities and shipping them off-world.

When his new orders call for him to join forty-thousand survivors aboard the last starship out, he thinks his days of fighting are over. The Deliverance represents a fresh start and a chance to leave the war behind for good.

Except the war won't be as easy to escape as he thought.

And the colony will need a man like Caleb more than he ever imagined...

Starship Eternal (War Eternal)
mrforbes.com/starshipeternal
Complete series box set:
mrforbes.com/wareternalcomplete

A lost starship...

A dire warning from futures past...

A desperate search for salvation…

Captain Mitchell "Ares" Williams is a Space Marine and the hero of the Battle for Liberty, whose Shot Heard 'Round the Universe saved the planet from a nearly unstoppable war machine. He's handsome, charismatic, and the perfect poster boy to help the military drive enlistment. Pulled from the war and thrown into the spotlight, he's as efficient at charming the media and bedding beautiful celebrities as he was at shooting down enemy starfighters.

After an assassination attempt leaves Mitchell critically wounded, he begins to suffer from strange hallucinations that carry a chilling and oddly familiar warning:

They are coming. Find the Goliath or humankind will be destroyed.

Convinced that the visions are a side-effect of his injuries, he tries to ignore them, only to learn that he may not be as crazy as he thinks. The enemy is real and closer than he imagined, and they'll do whatever it takes to prevent him from rediscovering the centuries lost starship.

Narrowly escaping capture, out of time and out of air, Mitchell lands at the mercy of the Riggers - a ragtag crew of former commandos who patrol the lawless outer reaches of the galaxy. Guided by a captain with a reputation for cold-blooded murder, they're dangerous, immoral, and possibly insane.

They may also be humanity's last hope for survival in a war that has raged beyond eternity.

Man of War (Rebellion)
mrforbes.com/manofwar
Complete series box set:
mrforbes.com/rebellion-web

In the year 2280, an alien fleet attacked the Earth.

Their weapons were unstoppable, their defenses unbreakable.

Our technology was inferior, our militaries overwhelmed.

Only one starship escaped before civilization fell.

Earth was lost.

It was never forgotten.

Fifty-two years have passed.

A message from home has been received.

The time to fight for what is ours has come.

Welcome to the rebellion.

Hell's Rejects (Chaos of the Covenant)
mrforbes.com/hellsrejects

The most powerful starships ever constructed are gone. Thousands are dead. A fleet is in ruins. The attackers are unknown. The orders are clear: *Recover the ships. Bury the bastards who stole them.*

Lieutenant Abigail Cage never expected to find herself in Hell. As a Highly Specialized Operational Combatant, she was one of the most respected Marines in the military. Now she's doing hard labor on the most miserable planet in the universe.

Not for long.

The Earth Republic is looking for the most dangerous individuals it can control. The best of the worst, and Abbey happens to be one of them. The deal is simple: *Bring back the starships, earn your freedom. Try to run, you die.* It's a suicide mission, but she has nothing to lose.

The only problem? There's a new threat in the galaxy. One with a power unlike anything anyone has ever seen. One that's been waiting for this moment for a very, very, long time. And they want Abbey, too.

Be careful what you wish for.

They say Hell hath no fury like a woman scorned. They have no idea.

About the Author

M.R. Forbes is the mind behind a growing number of Amazon best-selling science fiction series. He currently resides with his family and friends on the west cost of the United States, including a cat who thinks she's a dog and a dog who thinks she's a cat.

He maintains a true appreciation for his readers and is always happy to hear from them.

To learn more about M.R. Forbes or just say hello:

Visit my website:
mrforbes.com

Send me an e-mail:
michael@mrforbes.com

Check out my Facebook page:
facebook.com/mrforbes.author

Join my Facebook fan group:
facebook.com/groups/mrforbes

Follow me on Instagram:
instagram.com/mrforbes_author

Find me on Goodreads:
goodreads.com/mrforbes

Follow me on Bookbub:
bookbub.com/authors/m-r-forbes

Printed in Great Britain
by Amazon